IN MIND OF THE VAMPIRE

JOHN VANCE

BLACK ROSE
writing

ISBN: 978-1-61296-755-4
PUBLISHED BY BLACK ROSE WRITING
www.blackrosewriting.com

Printed in the United States of America
Suggested retail price $16.95

In Mind of the Vampire is printed in Minion Pro

ACKNOWLEDGEMENTS

Special thanks to all at Black Rose Writing; to Victoria Lea for her early enthusiasm; to my children Hope and Jimmy for their support; to my wife Susan for her enthusiasm and critical eye; and to Erin, Julie, Steve, Andy, and Tina for our early foray into the darkness.

AUTHOR'S NOTE

Bram Stoker's immortal *Dracula* (1897) provides context for this book, several bits of direct wording, and two of the main characters—Lucy Westenra and Mina Murray. Others from Stoker's novel such as Jonathan Harker, Abraham Van Helsing, and Renfield do not appear; nor are they assumed to exist. Julian Hemmings has *no* sense of vampire lore but instead believes that all fear and superstition may be eradicated by a more sophisticated understanding of the mind.

IN MIND OF

THE VAMPIRE

"Everywhere I go I find that a poet
has been there before me."
—Sigmund Freud

CHAPTER 1

London
Autumn of 1897
A time when rational men thought little of matters
unexplained by history and science

He appeared devastated and more desperate than any man I had ever seen. I addressed him as gently as I could.

"It's quite all right, Mr. Styles. I am here to listen. You can tell me everything. Start by repeating what you shared with me at our first meeting."

Without raising his head from his hands, he struggled to push his words past a commencement of sobs. "Please, Dr. Hemmings, call me Joseph. I want to be called Joseph. I must know that is still who I am."

"Very well, Joseph. Please talk freely." I stood from my chair and walked to the sofa where he sat and gently touched his shoulder. More than a gesture of comfort, my touch was needed to assure myself that this poor man wasn't about to dissolve in his evident misery.

He began to speak before I could return to my seat and secure my notebook.

"When I awoke, I found blood on my clothing. I had no memory of how it got there."

"Were you in your own bed?" I was pleased that I asked the question calmly, in manner befitting my new profession.

"No, Dr. Hemmings. I was leaning against a tall but narrow wooden fence in Buck's Row."

"In the Whitechapel area, then?" Yes, in Whitechapel—where the infamous and unsolved "Ripper" crimes occurred almost a decade earlier.

Styles could barely articulate a response. The sudden pain in his stomach had forced him to lift both legs several inches from the floor and press both forearms against his midsection. "Yes, once again in Whitechapel. Each time it has been in Whitechapel."

Each time? I would of course recommend him to a physician friend who could provide relief for his stomach pains—that is, if they were caused by an actual medical condition. But my new profession as a physician of the mind led me to suspect that his pains were caused by the memory of something he had done, perhaps as far back as his childhood—an event that led him to punish himself with the fiction that he had committed horrible deeds to rival those of the notorious Ripper fellow.

"Joseph, you say that you only come to a memory of what happened when you dream of it."

"Yes. Yes. When I dream. Only when I dream."

"Did your recent dream inform you of what you did with the body?"

"No. I dream only of the killing. I awaken before I learn where I have taken the body."

"Joseph, after our first meeting, I checked with the police and they assured me that there have been no young women murdered in that area in the past month."

My assistant Charles Yates stepped into the room. Styles failed to notice his arrival and continued on as before.

"Can't you see that I have hidden the bodies well, Dr. Hemmings? I want to remember where I put them, but I cannot dream that. I want to dream that. I have no greater wish than to dream that. But after knowing where they are, I want to dream no more. Can you do that, Dr. Hemmings? Can you help me locate the bodies and make my dreams stop?"

I cannot lie. The question he asked and the dialogue we engaged in raised my spirits and filled me with a sense of purpose I had never felt, even during my first years as a practicing surgeon.

My assistant Yates interrupted, "London's police are very good at discovering such things, Styles. Almost as good as the New York police, as a matter of fact. Perhaps it is time you began to accept the fact that—"

"Charles, you wanted something?" We were friends. We had long been friends, but Yates had not reconciled himself to my new work. He missed the previous word we had inhabited—the world of hands-on examination of wounds and malignant growths, the removal of unwanted tissue, and the reconstruction of damaged limbs and, in the rarest of cases, the repair of human organs. The human mind provided him nothing to place his hands on or to help remove. The reconstruction I strove to accomplish was bloodless, he complained, and he deeply missed the intimacy with the human form. He couldn't yet see that the mind was the most fascinating part of man. I had already begun to despair that he ever would.

"Julian, the young woman you agreed to meet with has arrived."

I checked the time. She was twenty minutes early for her appointment. "Charles, I'm not yet through here. Please ask her to wait or to come back at 4:30."

"Very well. I shall offer her tea."

As he left, Yates turned over his shoulder and shook his head, suggesting that I had been completely wasting my time with Joseph Styles. Charles would no doubt inform me that Styles was a just one of the hundreds of lunatics scattered about London who deserved a damp cell and a metal eating dish rather than the valuable time of a "medical expatriate" as he had already labeled me.

I began to apologize to Styles for the interruption, but he cut me off.

"He doesn't believe me."

I thought a dash of humor might be appropriate at this moment. "He is an American, Joseph. You know how they are. Generally more skeptical by temperament."

"No, he is just a man who will dismiss what his reason will not permit him to understand."

I was struck by the maturity of his observation. For a moment, his voice took on the tenor of an educated man. "Joseph, you have said that you began to have these dreams only several days ago."

"Yes, and I don't know why I have only now committed these horrible crimes."

He seemed genuinely perplexed. I sensed no conscious effort to embellish anything he told me. "Joseph, have you ever begun to visualize in your dreams a place other than the location where you say you woke up with blood on your clothing or where your dreams tell you that you have killed the woman?"

"Only once. I remember standing in front of a church—one I thought I recognized—but not one I know in London. I thought it might have been . . ."

"Go on. It might have been . . .?"

"I then turned and saw a bridge across a stream, and on the other side I thought I saw the place where I was already standing." He halted and

9

appeared puzzled, as though the thought had been planted in his mind without his permission.

"And where was that, Joseph? Close or far from London?"

He spoke without conviction. "Perhaps in Grimsby, where I was born."

"Ah, yes, lovely up there." I couldn't believe I had uttered such a banality. "Joseph, how long did you remain in Grimsby before you came to London?"

"I can't remember now." He grew agitated. "I don't want to talk about me. I want to talk about my dreams and what I have done. And why I was called upon to do it."

I had seen him but once previously, and had failed to ask where he resided. "Joseph, will you tell me where you live now?"

"How far is Grimsby from here, Dr. Hemmings?"

"Some 150 miles, I would imagine."

"Then I couldn't have taken any of the bodies there."

"No, you couldn't have." I had made my point to him about the distance, but I realized that I had again taken refuge in small talk. I was troubled by my having strayed from the more troubling aspects of his dreams.

"I have butchered several women, Dr. Hemmings. Where could I have taken them?"

"Joseph, tell me more about the dreams." My lack of experience as an analyst left me unsure. I knew not what else to say at present.

Styles ran both hands through his long unkempt hair. "Yet I feel as though these women are only preparing me for one more murder. I feel as though . . ."

"Please, Joseph. Go one."

"Dr. Hemmings, do you really want to hear more? I don't wish to upset you. You have been so very kind to me." All traces of his agitation had evaporated.

"I am here to help you, Joseph. I want you to tell me everything." I steeled myself for what he might say. I confess that when I first committed myself to studying the mind and hearing the painful experiences and imaginings of my patients, I didn't anticipate anyone like Joseph Styles. "Have there been others in your dreams, Joseph?"

"No. Merely two in each dream—myself and the woman."

The moment he made that pronouncement his face contorted in agony. He didn't grab for his stomach but rather lifted his open hands to each side of his neck. He took in two deep breaths as if he were at the same time being strangled.

"Forgive me, I beg you!"

I was startled. His cry seemed to be addressed to someone else. But I regained as much of my equilibrium as quickly as I could. "Joseph, there is nothing to forgive. Haven't I told you that you may trust me with anything you say? That our meetings can do you little good if you are not completely open and honest with me?"

"I am sorry, Dr. Hemmings. How can I show you that I am sincere?"

"By telling me the . . . By telling me who else appeared in your dream." The truth would be more difficult to elicit from him. Yet, in spite of his confessions, I refused to believe this wretched man had ever harmed anyone.

Styles closed his eyes as if he were preparing for the executioner's axe. "There is always someone else. But the face is hooded. I cannot see the features. But I know that it knows me."

"It?"

"It is hooded—it has no face. Whether a man or woman, I don't know. Its voice sounds like a man and a woman speaking the same words at once. Sometimes I think it is one—other times the other. I don't know what to do. I cannot say no to what it asks me to do." Styles suddenly smiled in a painfully pathetic manner. "Can you show me how I might say no and finally be left alone? I want no more dreams, Dr. Hemmings. No more dreams."

I knew I couldn't abandon the man. There was so much more I wished to learn about him. His clothes weren't impressive, but neither were they shabby. Even though his voice and manner took on several manifestations during our time together, I couldn't believe that he was devoid of education—at least in some respects. Was he married? If so, did he have children? Was he a man of about thirty, as I believed, or could he be younger than that? Yes, I would have to see him again and continue seeing him.

I took a pencil and wrote on one of my cards. "Joseph, we will meet again at this time."

He was reluctant to take my card. "But what if it happens again before our next meeting? I have great fear of it."

"I understand your concern, Joseph. If you again have that dream, I will permit you to come to my rooms and awaken me—and we will talk." I jotted down my address on the card.

He leaned forward and whispered, "Dr. Hemmings, it's not really the dream I have a fear of. It is the fear of killing again."

IN MIND OF THE VAMPIRE

I heard Charles's speaking to the woman waiting in the parlor. "Dr. Hemmings should be finishing his session soon. You are to be admired for your patience." As was his habit in such situations, he raised his voice enough for me to hear through the closed door.

"Joseph, here—take the card. I will show you out the back way." The rear door of my inner office served me well. I didn't wish the young woman to see this tortured soul.

Styles stepped through the door and pulled me by the coat sleeve. He was only inches from my face when he spoke. "I fear so much, but most of all I fear that you will soon forsake me." In his watery eyes I saw the reflection of my own. "I cannot even take refuge in my own history, for it is fast disappearing from my memory, Dr. Hemmings."

CHAPTER 2

History. As for my own, I was born when the year 1863 was in its last throes, my birth being recorded at 11:51 p.m. on December 31st—nine minutes before all thoughts turned to the New Year. As one of the year's remnants, I always believed I would grow up to live in shadows. And two years later, my mother was lost to me on that very night. I was told it was just a dreadful coincidence and that it wasn't rational to fear a life of misfortune—and yet I did fear it.

But I was blessed with skills very few possessed. Ever since I could remember, I had sketched. The precision and minute detail of my drawings amazed even those long skilled in the art. I was but six when my talents were revealed. One morning my father discovered under my bed several sheets of white paper covered with what he called "startling depictions" of each room in our spacious house. My father was an editor of periodical pieces, as well as a writer of sermons for sundry clergymen. Accordingly, he was always well supplied with paper and therefore had never missed the sheets I took from the bottom drawer of his immense desk. One can only imagine the expression on my face when the sheets were discovered—an expression of a child anticipating a severe reprimand for having pilfered his father's belongings. My father's sudden and joyful embrace of his only child made me shout as if I were getting the jump on the pain I thought was about to experience. I will never forget the feel of my father's arms around me and the tears forming in his eyes, as well as the four kisses he gave, two on each side of my face—the kind of affection I never received previously but would daily for another several years. "My blessed Julian," he repeated as he held me close. Recalling that late winter afternoon of 1870 often enlivened my consciousness during the many subsequent moments of discomfort or emotional distress over my childhood fear of misfortune befalling me.

For the next eight years, I was taken to meet artists in London and Paris for a validation of my talents. And not one of these authorities was indifferent to my gifts. When I passed the age of ten, my father would introduce me and then ask me to sketch something in the immediate surroundings—the inside or outside of whatever house we were visiting. I sought always to please him and immediately complied with all such requests, and in each case he had me present the scene as a gift to our host. I had already placed a number of my sketches in newspapers and magazines, the first appearing when I was seven years of age. By the time I was twelve, there was serious talk of a complete volume of my sketches. And when I reached thirteen I had become the subject of articles—each confessing that no young artist had the power to so accurately display the thing he was drawing.

Still, I wasn't encouraged to put paint to canvas until I was nearly fourteen, when it was suggested to my father by someone in Her Majesty's government that the Queen had said something about wishing to have a portrait done of one of the staircases at Kensington Palace—just the staircase with no one depicted walking up or down on it. She had revealed that as a child she was never permitted to walk down the staircase alone, without having to hold someone's hand. She apparently desired to have that staircase captured free of any chaperone. And she wanted that "blessed boy artist," as she called me, to paint it on canvas.

But my father did not embrace the Queen's request with the enthusiasm anyone would have expected. He wasn't confident my talents would translate from the sheet to the canvas. Previously, he had allowed me to do only the most basic shapes in oils—and never on a full-sized canvas. What if I couldn't duplicate the brilliance of my sketches with paint? But my father's concern was completely unfounded. The Queen marveled at the depiction. It was even more lifelike than the staircase itself, said Her Majesty's Prime Minister, Mr. Disraeli. I basked in the glow of further affection from my father, who although he had ceased kissing my face, still embraced me with the same enthusiasm and admiration as when he had first discovered the sketches under my bed. But within a calendar year, all my father's affections would forever cease—the result of one sudden and horrible moment.

In February 1878, a little more than a month after my fourteenth birthday, I found that I couldn't expel a new and sinful image from my mind, which originated in late January when I was walking down Fieldgate Street accompanying my father. He had just concluded an interview with a man working in the London Hospital, who had written a piece my father was editing. My father also wished to find and speak with a severely troubled man who had bolted from the Hospital, after claiming that God wouldn't want him in such a place and expected him to wash clean this part of London.

This man was well known in the area around the hospital—often speaking out against the Jews as well as all "sinful filth" while standing on the Baker's Row side of the Jewish Cemetery, moving his purgation sermons to Old Montague Street, down Osborn, across Whitechapel to Church Lane, then back toward the hospital until he disappeared into one of the buildings either on Greenfield Street or Plumber's Row. The man, whose name was unknown, had apparently done nothing to warrant an arrest but enough to encourage an examination at London Hospital. Two of the physicians were inclined to send the poor soul to one of their colleagues at the Surrey County Lunatic Asylum for at least further examination if not commitment. One of the hospital workers had been struck in the face by the nameless man, who then fled into the street—ending up where no one could say. In any event, my father thought the story was one worth pursuing for his magazine. I recall being utterly fascinated by the nameless man and why he became a lunatic. Could it be possible I wondered even then, for this man and others like him to be studied for how and why they thought and acted as they did and then ultimately be cured?

When my father and I turned down Greenfield Street very late in the afternoon, I noticed a woman in the gathering darkness—I believed then in her early twenties—bent from the waist with the palms of her hands pressed against a brick wall while a man was taking her carnally from behind. All of her clothing, except for a simple black neck choker, was bunched on the ground on top of her feet; yet she showed no reaction to being so exposed in the January cold. Because my father's attention was directed toward the buildings on the other side of the street, he kept walking, and only I had the view of the young woman's exposed and ample breasts, her fair but sullied skin, and for a brief instant the dark hair between her legs. I didn't halt at the sight but turned my head back as I walked, my eyes captured by the indescribable expression of the woman, who seemed pleased that I had seen her in the middle of sexual intercourse. Her gaze followed me as I walked, a smile of triumph on her face, until I turned my head and ran to catch up with my father.

That night, after I had lain in bed for over an hour without closing my eyes, I lit a small candle, made my way to my small desk, and pulled out a sheet of paper. Within two minutes I had finished the sketch. Nothing I had ever drawn before filled me with as much excitement and terror. It was my initial attempt to draw the human form—specifically, the woman I had seen pressed against the wall. I didn't draw her body, but only her face. Soon, I felt dissatisfied with the sketch, feeling that it was impermanent. I took out a canvas and my paints, taking more time to replicate the sketch, capturing with more vivid detail the look the young woman had given me.

Although it was winter and my room presently unheated, I felt completely warmed by my task—and by my thoughts. And for the first time in my young life I had experienced the destructive emotion my father had demonstrated so often since my mother died in a carriage accident on the night of my second birthday. While moving around a slow-moving cart, the right wheels of the carriage had slid on a patch of ice and then caught a sharply angled embankment, flipping the vehicle and sending my father hurtling above and beyond where my mother ultimately lay—her head having slammed into an imbedded rock alongside the embankment.

Yes, now I understood what my father meant by "suffering from guilt." He had blamed himself because he insisted they travel out when my mother was slightly ill and desired to remain home in bed. Because she had died when I was so young, I had only a cloudy memory of what she looked like. My grieving father had removed the portraits of his deceased wife; he simply couldn't bear to view them. I knew not whether they had been hidden or destroyed. As I looked at the face of the woman I had painted, I trembled at the unexpected realization that the hazy memory of a mother's face was replaced by that of the woman I had seen pressed against the wall on Greenfield Street. I was frightened by the connection I made; and I had remained frightened in the years since—frightened of seemingly everything—the change of seasons and all the other ever-present reminders of mutability. My dread made me want to understand why I felt that way, but there was no one I could talk to—no one.

Immediately after I had drawn and then painted that woman's face, I succumbed to the urge to sketch the female body. For the next several weeks I sketched women in as many different postures as my young mind could imagine. These women were always nude or partially so. I never drew a male figure accompanying the woman. But more telling was that I never drew another woman's face. It was only the female body I sketched. And then, while I was returning to London after a visit to Cambridge, my father came home to edit a fictional tale of domestic discord. Shaken by the story, he needed something to calm him—and he had long found my sketches, rather than alcohol, the most satisfactory remedy for his nerves. As he told me, he went to my room and in a fanciful nod to events eight years earlier, looked under my bed and noticed several sheets of paper, which I had failed to gather and conceal. He reached under the bed and pulled them out.

He had never before struck me as a method of discipline or punishment. He never needed to, for I was as complaisant a child as any parent could wish. The whipping I received was therefore clumsily done—from the cutting of the switch to the poorly aimed blows. My father cried; I did not. I barely heard his lecture on sinful thoughts and the consequences of such preoccupations. All I could think of was checking my secret hiding place to be sure my father had not discovered the sketch and the portrait of that woman's face.

From that evening forward the special bond between us remained severed. For days, my father spoke to me only perfunctorily. Each morning I looked at myself in the mirror. I didn't see the angelic expression my father loved; it was gone. I couldn't reshape it—or bring back my old features. Was it due to my advancing age? I was several months past my fourteenth birthday. On my face were spots of facial hair beginning to push through the skin. How badly I wanted my old visage to return.

I vowed never again to display my passion and emotion in an artistic depiction of the female. I even ripped to shreds the sketch of the woman on Greenfield Street, but nothing could persuade me to destroy the portrait. It then happened that I visited a London surgeon to show him several sketches of the human body that might serve as teaching tools to younger surgeons and physicians. He had commissioned me to draw them after he heard about my prowess with internal and external scenes. He couldn't have known that I had depicted the face of a prostitute and promiscuously sketched the nude female body. With the promise of money and with the unenthusiastic approval of my father, I drew one male and one female, both nude. I stood naked in front of the mirror to provide me with a model of the male, but the female sketch came from my memory of what I had seen on Greenfield Street and what I had afterwards sketched. Each of the drawings my father found under my bed and the others he insisted I give him had been tossed into the flames immediately after he punished me with a beating. I believed that the clinical nature of these drawings for the surgeon did not violate my promise of never again allowing my passion or emotion to influence anything I drew or painted—or even thought. Impressed by what I showed him, the surgeon asked if I would provide sketches of the body and the internal organs in the post-mortem state. I agreed and witnessed several after-death examinations, utterly fascinated with everything relating to the human body in its clinical context.

By the time I reached my fifteenth birthday I had begun assisting the surgeon in the operating theatre. He was also a licensed physician who risked a demotion of his social standing by performing surgical procedures. Cambridge educated, Dr. Henry Ridland spent many months in Paris and Berlin learning new and advanced surgical techniques. He was determined to elevate surgical practice in London, regardless of the prevailing social view of the specialty, which many still thought was limited in essence to quick amputations. Dr. Ridland was trained at a time when one in four died as a result of surgery—a percentage he helped to lessen during his long and distinguished career. He saw to it that I attended Queens' College Cambridge, and upon completion of my studies, I returned to learn from him and become another of what he called the "physician-surgeons." My father had no stated objections to the new path I set upon.

At Cambridge I was respected for my intellect, but I had no close friends, only well-wishers and those writing or visiting from London to commission my work. And I had no romances. The memory of my father's displeasure and subsequent aloofness was still most painful. I had no inclination to engage in social outings or courtships of any kind. I rejected all but a few offers to sketch and paint internal and external scenes—memorializing for many what they were not satisfied simply to gaze at. I was offered considerable sums to do portraits, but always found refuge in affected modesty, proclaiming that my talents didn't run in that direction and that the sitter would be most disappointed in the results. My father provided me financial support after I matriculated at Cambridge—because he had deemed many years earlier that I would become a Cantabrigian—but I made enough from my few drawings and paintings to require very little further financial assistance from my father, who certainly required none from me, as his sermon writing and editing continued to provide him with more than a satisfactory living—and he still had funds from his inheritance to draw upon. But the closeness we had once shared never returned. I didn't need my father to remind me that I had gravely disappointed him by my drawings of the nude female form. I was no longer the "pure artist," he said. He never revealed any concern that his role as father was being assumed by Dr. Ridland. Until his death, during the year I became a practicing physician-surgeon, my father never again mentioned the sketches he had discovered in my bedroom—neither the ones that bonded us in a most special relationship when I was six, nor the ones that rent us asunder eight years later. Yet upon his death he bequeathed me almost all of his money, making my future financially secure.

And then on the first day of August 1895, another woman's face came into my life—one that would alter my course once more. The night I said goodbye to her, I broke my promise never again to paint the female visage and went about the task with unrestrained passion and emotion. When I finished, I put down the last brush I ever intended to hold in my hand. I stepped back and looked. I didn't smell the paint; I only smelled the sweetness from the breath of the woman's face I had painted.

19

CHAPTER 3

When I returned to my office after ushering out Joseph Styles, I beheld the disapproving countenance of my assistant Charles Yates.

"Come now Julian, do you really think you're serving *that* patient well with this new approach of yours?"

I was in no mood for chiding. "Enough, Charles. Please."

He stepped toward me and lowered his voice. "I believe my impertinence may be allowable, given the fact that you didn't have your medical training in this particular method of experimental treatment."

His words brought back our initial meeting four years earlier. Charles Yates had come from New York, where he had served as a surgical assistant. As destiny proclaimed it, he fell in love with a widow from London, then visiting her married sister in Manhattan. Confident he could find work in England, he followed the object of his affections across the Atlantic and proposed marriage. Following the death of the surgeon with whom he had initially found employment, Charles applied for the vacant position of my assistant. Always professional and never too indisposed to perform his duties, he impressed me with his dedication and skill. Older than I by some twelve years, Charles helped steady me by his example and bearing when I suffered from periodic bouts of melancholy. I came to see him as an elder sibling, even though I ranked above him in the medical world we inhabited.

Yet my change of mission, as inspiring and necessary as it was to me, left Charles frustrated and often cantankerous. I knew he was trying to talk sense into me, and I indulged him because I felt that if I could answer his objections then I could be sure I had made the correct decision to study and heal the mind. But I soon realized that he felt emasculated by his new responsibilities—now wielding a pen rather than a surgical instrument.

"Julian, I take no pleasure in reminding you that when we began to work together, you were an accomplished surgeon, dealing more with things far more tangible and curable than what you are dealing with now."

What he asserted was true, and I had no way of countering his argument. But I could challenge his characterization of me as "accomplished."

"Charles, you exaggerate the degree of my success and reputation. There were far too many who died on my table—too many faces that you yourself pulled a sheet over. Or have you forgotten that?"

"But you saved many—including my wife. That memory dominates all others, my friend. No one had given her any chance to survive. It was the first operation I did not assist you with in the four years we had been working together. I couldn't have done so and would have been a liability to you had I even made the attempt. When my wife finally opened her eyes and smiled at me, I vowed I would never fail to assist you again. That I would be at your side regardless of what area of the body you chose to invade. I just didn't know that you would choose to—"

"Invade? An interesting choice of words, Charles. But you couldn't know that I would come to lose my nerve."

"That young woman's death was preordained, Julian. You knew the odds were weighed heavily on the side of mortality. You couldn't have been surprised by the result."

Yes, that young woman's death. Yvette Auger had come to me on the recommendation of another physician. I was immediately struck by her beauty and optimism, even though she was dying of a malignant growth in the area of the stomach. On the day of the surgery, her cheerfulness influenced me and I felt as hopeful as I ever had in the face of a most daunting procedure. Before Charles administered the anesthesia, she asked me to lean my face to hers and lifted her head and kissed me sweetly on the edge of my mouth. Hesitating slightly, I drew back horrified by what I took the kiss to mean. That I did not resist her kiss told her that I would save her life—that I would remove the growth from inside her—that she would recover and, in gratitude, repeat her kiss.

Several long moments passed before I was able to proceed. It took two attempts before I could make the incision into her porcelain flesh. When the delicate soul succumbed to the surgery soon after I located the growth, I was badly shaken. Charles prepared the body for the family to retrieve and suggested that I return to my lodgings. But I was insistent on seeing her one last time—viewing her in death after she had so warmed my heart in the last moments of her life. When I came to where Yvette lay, I wanted to apologize for having failed her. I carefully removed the sheet over her face. What I saw horrified me. How such an alteration could have occurred after death was beyond my power to understand. There was still life in her fair features, but her mouth and eyes, free from any grotesque expression, were not the same. I pulled the sheet further down until I saw the incision I had made less than two hours earlier. The broken fingernail on her left hand was still visible. Her hair was the same length and still a soft yellow. But her eyes and mouth were reminiscent of those I had painted so long ago—on the face of the woman on Greenfield Street.

That night I painted the face of my deceased patient—the way I saw it in life, not in death. When I finished I leaned toward the portrait and believed I felt her sweet breath on my face.

"Julian, even our friends could see from the gallery that you were surprisingly nervous at the commencement of the operation on that girl. Standing with you, I gazed first at your hands, which were steady as ever, but the expression in your eyes and paleness of your skin alarmed me."

"No, Charles. My hands did not shake. They just refused to function as they always had. For the first time, I was not at one with my craft." I recalled that I had forced muscles to exert themselves that a surgeon simply should not force. Artists do not force. They cannot force. Then it is no longer art.
"Charles, the young woman had no chance to survive in my hands."

"Nonsense, it was the nature of the growth within her, not the proficiency of your hands, Julian. You had lost others before her, and you took each loss philosophically. Every surgeon who dares to attack the places on the body almost all others fear to approach loses a good number of patients. These are not common procedures, Julian. Risks must be taken. And it is a masterful surgeon who is unafraid of taking these risks."

Dear Charles. He was still attempting to pull me back into the operating theatre. But after that day, I was unable to take such risks again. The more mundane procedures I limited myself to after the death of Yvette Auger pointed to my cowardice and failure. I couldn't go on as the surgeon I was, not even to practice medicine in the less demanding realms. I continued to see that young woman's face and feel her lips on mine. I dared not look on the portrait I had painted of her, as I had never looked at the one of the woman on Greenfield Street since I had completed it. I needn't have compared them by placing one next to the other. The eyes and mouth were reminiscent of each other, yet how different were both women. The one I lost on the operating table was an angel. And I had kissed her.

"Charles, I needed something new—something daring but not devastating in its consequences. And now I have found it, don't you see?"

"But to devote your talents to coddling perverse and egocentric minds and pure lunatics such as Joseph Styles—or even troubled husbands and wives—casts your reputation in the most unflattering light possible. Styles should be committed to an asylum. The diagnosis is simple. The remedy—if such it may be called—equally as simple."

"You don't believe he has murdered anyone, do you, Charles?"

"God knows there are plenty of homicides in this city, some of which have put New York to shame, but no, I don't think Styles has killed anyone. At most he might have strangled dogs or cats, but women? At any rate, I don't believe that applying any of the so-called novel techniques you have learned from that Austrian fellow may do much to murder your livelihood, let alone your reputation."

My patience with my assistant—at least for today—had expired. "I have given you my blessing should you wish to find employment with another physician or surgeon. Charles, I know you are not happy, and my hopes are always for your contentment."

He stared at me for several seconds before he spoke. "Are you ready to see Miss Murray? She is such a delightful young woman, Julian. Really brightens a room, as they say."

The storm between us had passed. I reached for my watch. "Let me see. There are still four minutes left before my scheduled appointment with her. I'm afraid Joseph Styles' colorful admissions of brutal murder have stimulated my appetite. Let me step out to one of the carts for something quick before I begin with her. Have her complete the usual survey and I will be right back."

"It's been completed."

"All right. Then see if she would like some tea."

"Already done. But I'll see if she'd like another cup."

"Good. And you might as well have her come in and sit on the sofa."

Yates took two steps toward the door before he turned back to me. "Julian, I hope that what I said to you . . . well . . ."

"Charles. No explanation is necessary between two long-time friends— you know that."

I left through the back door. There were far fewer street vendors here in the West End than when I was a boy, but I had grown fond of an elderly seller who set up his weather-beaten cart less than fifty feet from my office.

"What looks good on this rather cold early November afternoon, Bracy?"

"Some hot wine, Doctor Hemmings. But if you're in the mood for something to give your teeth a little exercise, then might I suggest the pickled whelks or your favorite hot eels. I'll even sell you eight pieces of eel for the price of six, just because you've been one my best customers."

"Bracy, you know I never touch the eels and hope to heaven they never touch me. Let me have a Chelsea bun and hot coffee."

It was a ritual we engaged in. Bracy knew I never ordered anything but a Chelsea bun or other such treat and always nothing stronger than coffee or tea. He always offered what he knew I couldn't stomach, although many others in the city seemed to have the constitution for such things.

"Dr. Hemmings?"

"Yes, Bracy?"

"I continue to thank you for doing business with me. A gentleman of your standing ought not to dine from my cart. You might be commented upon for friendly conversation with those lesser than you."

"Bracy, my dear fellow, I take pleasure in speaking with you as well as eating your Chelsea buns. There are none better in London. But I'm no better than any other man."

"Well, I think that's true—you're not better than any other man." I admit his pronouncement startled me. "You're better than almost *all* of them. You're a fine example of a good man, is what you are."

After thanking Bracy for his generous compliment, I took my purchase and headed back to my office for my appointment with the young woman waiting there. I was pleased that she was someone new. I needed more patients to justify my work and the profession I was only recently engaged in.

As I reached the rear steps of my office, I happened to look over my shoulder at the sound of the latest novelty sputtering its way down the street. As the smoke from under the motor car cleared, I noticed in the fading light Joseph Styles staring at me from across the way. He made no attempt to nod or wave; he just stared.

CHAPTER 4

As I walked through the rear entrance, I overheard Charles speaking with Miss Murray. I paused in the narrow passage way and eavesdropped on their conversation, while I took several bites of my Chelsea bun.

"Is your tea satisfactory, Miss Murray?"

"Yes, Mr. Yates, it is. Thank you."

I was immediately taken by the soft lilt in her voice. There was something almost childlike in her speech, yet I sensed as well a determination that belied the soothing answer to Charles's question. I imagined her appearance. Young and very likely pretty with auburn hair and blue eyes, I guessed.

Charles cleared his throat, sounding a bit nervous. "Since I am American, my wife doesn't permit me to make tea, Miss Murray."

I enjoyed her brief but polite laugh. "No, you must believe me, Mr. Yates. The tea is quite good."

"Then you are here to speak to Dr. Hemmings about your inability to speak the truth?"

That rascal Charles—so charming and officious. She must indeed be very pretty, I thought as I made my entrance. She sat on the sofa with her back to me; therefore I was free to shoot a playful scowl at Yates as I began to make my apologies.

"Miss Murray, do forgive me if I am late. I barely had time for a light breakfast and have had nothing since but this." I ran my finger across my mouth and wiped some stray crumbs from my lips. I placed the rest of the Chelsea bun on the back table and poured the coffee into one of the attractive cups Charles's wife insisted I keep in my office.

I moved to a place before her and saw that she had lowered her head as if she wished to give me privacy as I performed my domestic duties. "It is a pleasure to meet you, Miss Murray."

Upon my salutation, she looked up and smiled. She was simply lovely.

25

Her eyes weren't blue as I had imagined; they were green and quite fascinating, reflective of both an intelligent and an adventurous mind. Her cheeks were slightly flushed, surely more by nature than by the application of a cosmetic. I'm certain my smile dropped as I noted her hair color—not auburn but soft black—perfectly bound in a chignon that suggested her meticulous personality and self-confidence. But my breath halted as I beheld her skin, which was exquisite—so like that of the young woman who had kissed me before she died under my care.

"Dr. Hemmings?"

I shook free from my paralyzed state. "Well, I assume that Mr. Yates has been a good host."

She smiled at Charles. "Oh, yes. A most excellent one."

Yates was clearly taken with the young woman. He was all butter and smooth edges. "Dr. Hemmings, here is Miss Murray's survey. Call me if either of you needs anything." He turned sharply in his best valet manner, but after two steps he must have realized that he appeared too stiff because his shoulders and upper thighs relaxed and he left my office using his normal gait, whistling some unrecognizable tune as he did so.

I shook my head at Charles's exit, to which Miss Murray added a soft laugh. I reached for her survey.

"Dr. Hemmings, that won't be necessary. I only filled that out because Mr. Yates was so gracious to explain to me why you needed it. You see, I am not here for myself, but for another."

I couldn't help feeling considerable disappointment at her explanation. Of course, she didn't need my assistance. It was obvious from her manner and bearing that she was plagued by neither disturbing thoughts nor traumatic experiences. But before I set down the survey, I quickly examined her penmanship. Without question, it reflected the hand of an educated woman. There was some inconsistency in the lower-case "r" and "e," but what stood out most were the wide spaces she left between each word. It was almost as if she wished to leave spaces to insert modifiers or qualifications.

"So you are here for another, Miss Murray?"

I noted on the survey her first name "Wilhelmina." I had recently seen a survey of the two hundred most popular names for the female in the past two decades. I'm sure "Wilhelmina" did not appear on the list.

"Yes, you see I have come to speak to you about the problems of my dearest friend. I fear for her mind, Dr. Hemmings. I want you to speak with

26

and then treat her."

Her seeming confidence in my abilities so flattered me that I almost agreed on the spot and forgot to issue the professional caveat I promised to share with anyone serving as an agent for a prospective patient.

"Miss Murray, has your friend been examined by a physician? Perhaps her mind is troubled by medical causes—and therefore remedied by what may be more traditionally prescribed."

She lost her smile, put down her tea, and stood from the sofa. "No, Dr. Hemmings, that kind of physician will not do. I have given a good deal of thought to the matter. I know that you have been studying the mind and applying the techniques of an Austrian doctor, who has found success with his methods. I understand that he has a number of followers and that you are one of them."

I wondered how she came to know about me. From one of my few other patients, perhaps? No, it was more likely from a small advertisement I had begun placing weekly in the papers for the past several months. I didn't wish to inform her that Sigmund Freud had more than his share of antagonists as well as followers—highly agitated enemies, I might add, who believed his theories were the dangerous indulgences of a disturbed mind. "How could a patient in need of help treat another patient in need of help?" was a common refrain among other physicians and their assistants—Charles Yates being among them.

"Miss Murray, I just wish you to understand that my techniques are very unlikely to provide immediate results."

She half-smiled at my admission. "I realize that. But you must understand that I have become desperate for the health of my dear friend— my more than sister, whose name is Lucy Westenra. I have determined that there is little to be lost by putting her in your care." She paused. "And so much to gain."

With my head turned once again by her compliment and her trust, I gestured for her to return to the sofa Charles' wife procured for me when I moved to this office. I sat in a comfortable chair while speaking with my patients, even though Dorothy Yates pointed out that its fabric clashed horribly with the sofa.

I placed a pad of paper on my lap. "I should say at the outset that there will be much that you—or rather your friend Miss Westenra—may not understand. I have been introduced to a new language by my exposure to the ideas of the Austrian Sigmund Freud. But if I stray from the comprehensible and utter any strange sounding clinical terms, I want you to stop me and pull me back to plain English." Once more I spoke as if Miss Murray would be sitting by her friend during these sessions.

"Tell me, Dr. Hemmings, how long have you been a student of this new way of looking at the mind?"

"I began almost two years ago. Not long after . . . I came to the conclusion that I would no longer practice as a physician-surgeon." She looked at me sympathetically as though she knew what I had almost said. Had she indeed heard of Yvette Auger's death and my reaction to it? In any event, it was apparent she wanted to know more about my training.

"I left England for the continent, going first to Paris for six weeks and then to Vienna, where I remained for six months—until the early summer of last year. I then studied on my own here in London and eventually took this office and began my new professional life in early March of this year. I understand if you now think I haven't been at my trade long enough to do Miss Westenra much good, but I can promise that my efforts—"

"So, did Mr. Yates join you in Vienna?" She reached for her tea as though she hadn't heard any of my self-deprecating remark. Immediately I recalled a story told to me while I was at Cambridge about the notorious lover of the Prince of Wales, the now admired actress Lillie Langtry, who at a charity bazaar in the Albert Hall almost twenty years earlier had presided over a refreshment stall. One would pay five shillings to be served a cup of tea by this attractive woman, but for an extra guinea she would grace the service by taking the first sip. I thought how Miss Murray might also encourage men to donate more liberally were she to do likewise.

"So, Dr. Hemmings, did Mr. Yates join you in Vienna?" My hesitation had prompted a repeat of her question.

"No. I had of course invited him, but he was opposed to my leaving London and commencing on my new course of studies and therefore declined the invitation. There was work for him to do here with other surgeons."

"But he waited for you."

"Yes, because he was confident I had only temporarily taken leave of my senses and would return to my surgical work. But as I am sure is evident to you, I have so far failed to do what he expected. I somehow have the feeling that he made a wager about my return to the operating theatre and lost a considerable amount of money."

She laughed fully, though still softly. I couldn't imagine at this moment that she had ever once shouted or screamed. I felt palpably comfortable in her company. What was she? Twenty? Twenty-one or at most twenty-two? Around a dozen years younger than I. At the very beginning of her adult life.

"Miss Murray, when would you like—"

"Excuse my interrupting you, Dr. Hemmings. Did you see from the survey that my Christian name is Wilhelmina?"

I hoped my response would not betray my dislike of the name. "Yes, I did see that. I don't believe I have ever known anyone of that name."

"Nor should you wish to. I suppose it's all right to tell you that I have always—since the time I began to speak—referred to myself and had everyone else address me as Mina."

"Oh, thank God," I silently replied. I nodded approval like some idiot stable boy. "Well, can you tell me more about your friend, Miss Westenra?"

"You must talk with her, Dr. Hemmings. All other suggestions I have received about what to do for her are simply dreadful."

"Does she at least at times seem herself?"

"Oh yes. As loving and mischievous as ever. But then without warning she becomes withdrawn, consumed by thoughts she refuses to share."

My interest in Lucy Westenra's mental state would have been piqued regardless—but hearing her described by the lovely young woman sitting across from me pushed my interest into the suburbs of fascination.

"Are hers always frightful thoughts and imaginings?"

Mina's eyes narrowed as a shadow of sorrow lay over her enchanting face. "No. Sometimes they are . . . they are . . . I'm sorry, this is difficult to articulate."

"I understand. There is no need for you to share them. Perhaps it would be best if she herself explained them to me."

Once more, she continued as though my assurance and suggestion had never been offered. "Her thoughts and imaginings are passionate. Often lustful— beyond what I could ever have imagined would escape from her lips. Lucy has always possessed a playfulness that permitted her to touch and push and pinch whomever she conversed with—from children to grown men— even the ancient caretakers up in Whitby."

"Forgive me. Where did you say?"

"In Whitby—in North Yorkshire. Have you been there, Dr. Hemmings?"

"No, I just know of it." Joseph Styles alluded to his home in Grimsby, located some seventy miles south of Whitby. "But you say that at present your friend Lucy doesn't freely touch those with whom she speaks?"

"She does if she is acting normally. But when she is not, she often folds her arms as might a petulant child and touches only her neck." With an expression of grief, Mina placed the fingertips of her left hand on the left side of her neck. I recalled how Styles earlier placed the palms of both hands on each side of his neck.

"Excuse my question, Miss Murray. I see it has upset you."

She took a quick breath to expel her sadness and once more smiled. "My friends say that I am one of the 'New Women' many are talking about."

"I have heard of them. Some say that in fifteen years the 'New Woman' will free her hair from bondage, receive all voting privileges, matriculate at all the colleges at Cambridge and Oxford, and smoke her cigarettes in the public square and at formal dinner parties." I hoped that she would find some wit rather than any insult in my observation. Her broadening smile soon informed me that she did.

"Well, I am for the first three you mentioned, but I can do without the fourth. In truth, I have only told you that because I wished to know if you might call me Mina. 'Miss Murray' becomes a bit of a bore after you hear it three or four times."

I was immensely pleased by her invitation. "Yes, yes, of course I will be happy to call you Mina. Thank you for allowing me the privilege."

"But only in this office. If we meet in public, you are to look at me as Miss Murray—just one of the 'Old Women'—rigorously devoted to all ancient custom and ritual."

Could I be any more delighted by the company of a female? Once more she spoke as though she would at least accompany her friend Lucy whenever the troubled woman came to see me. Had I even formally agreed to see Lucy Westenra? It didn't matter, for I would treat her and do all I could for her and for her devoted friend.

After we granted several moments to enjoy our diversion into wit, I returned to the more serious subject of our discussion. "So Lucy touches herself here." I lifted my hand to my neck. "Anywhere else?"

"She touches her neck here and sometimes touches a spot below it with the tip of one finger. But never on her right side."

"I see." I began to draw a sketch of the female neck in my notebook, but abandoned it when my hand began to shake.

"And at times she touches . . ."

I met her gaze but then turned my eyes away and stared past her at the rear wall. If Mina was going to identify an intimate area of Lucy's body, I thought it best to spare both of us as much embarrassment as possible.

"When she touches here, she . . . Dr. Hemmings, you may look." I adjusted my eyes and found that Mina had placed her open palm in the area under the heart. "When she touches here," she continued, "she cries out. You will see her very soon, won't you?"

I didn't wish to wait until the following day. "I will, Mina. I will return here after supper—at eight thirty. You may bring her then, if you wish. Can you find an appropriate chaperone or male companion to accompany the both of you here?"

"Yes, that will be no trouble. Thank you, Dr. Hemmings. From the bottom of my heart, I thank you." She had returned her open palm to the place under her heart.

"Wait. Can I send a cab to bring all of you here?"

"No, we will make arrangements."

I escorted her to the other room and saw a rather mature gentleman apparently waiting to accompany her to her lodgings. Her elderly father? Perhaps her grandfather? I nodded to the old man and wished to introduce myself, but he seemed anxious to leave. After Mina and the gentleman left, I stepped back into the inner office. I gave in to fancy and imagined the man, who looked somewhere in his seventies, to be a suitor for Mina's hand. I didn't laugh at the thought, for it seemed impossible for a man at any age not to love Mina Murray.

Yates interrupted my blissful reverie by entering my office. "Then you will see the other young woman?"

"Were you listening to our conversation, Charles?"

"Only a small part of it, when I picked up some loose correspondence that had fallen near the door. The original carpenters failed in their work, Julian. The bottom edge of this door is cut too high, allowing the sound to travel unimpeded into the ears of anyone passing nearby."

"*Leaning* nearby, you mean? But to answer your question—yes, I will treat her. Miss Westenra's symptoms are reminiscent of several cases Freud shared with me. I do believe I can help her."

"There are a number of tried and true procedures that may do likewise, you know."

"Charles, we are on threshold of a new century. One that will witness more advances in technology and medicine than you can possibly fathom, my good friend. Your beloved asylums will soon stand as do the decayed cathedrals and castles—broken apart by time and sophistication."

His expression mocked my grand pronouncement—as did his reply. "Really now?"

"Have I said that you are a most dogged and vicious adversary, Charles?"

He paused and dropped his smile. "May you have no other adversary in your life but me, my dear Doctor."

CHAPTER 5

I set out from my office at a little past six. My rooms were but a fifteen-minute walk away, which took me by congested vehicle and foot traffic and the hurried approach of someone wishing me to buy something for which I had no need.

I lived, as many would have it, as a well-to-do West-End bachelor, although the furnishings in my rooms suggested a more modest characterization. I had taken a good portion of the money my father left me to assist in a project he was involved with during his last years—the founding and construction of several large-scale lodging houses, which while not serving the poorest of the male population did offer decent living conditions for hundreds of men in London. I always remained proud of my father's belief that we are put here on earth to sooth the plight of others, even if I never could do anything to mend our fractured relationship. Perhaps I wished him to feel proud of his son from beyond the grave.

Because this afternoon I had not eaten anything other than Bracy's Chelsea bun, I treated myself to a meal at the Langham Hotel on Regent Street. This grand structure boasted of many fine amenities, including some one hundred water closets, and held the distinction of being the first hotel to install electrical lighting. Dining alone, I finished my meal with my spirits elevated and my appetite satisfied, especially by the roast pork and potatoes and the meal-ending éclair—a food item I had never before tried. I cheerfully anticipated seeing Mina again tonight and meeting her troubled friend Lucy. I had never before felt as convinced as I did a present that I had made the correct change of professions.

As I enjoyed a final cup of coffee, I heard the waiter at the next table ask another member of the service staff, "Are you still having those dreams Edmonds?" I couldn't make out Edmonds' reply, but I could see by his face that the dreams were unpleasant and apparently still plaguing him. If anyone knew the damaging effects of recurring dreams, it was I. The visits to my mind of the woman on Greenfield Street and of Yvette Auger, so frequent during my conscious hours, gave me no respite in my dreams. Whereas I generally had control over how long the women lingered there during the day, when I was asleep I was powerless to restrain their appearance, movements, and words. Yet they never intruded on another recurring dream—one I had experienced since childhood—in which I sat at a piano and made splendid music.

When I was six years of age, I asked my father to purchase a piano so that I might learn to play. He gently refused this and subsequent requests, asserting that God had given me one talent to which I needed to devote all my energies. He read me the Parable of the Talents in the Book of Matthew and made much of the servant who hid his one talent and displeased his master: *Therefore take the talent from him and give it to the one who has ten talents. / For unto every one that hath shall be given, and he shall have abundance: but from him that hath not shall be taken away even that which he hath. / And cast ye the unprofitable servant into outer darkness: there shall be weeping and gnashing of teeth.* It was the first time I seriously pondered the meaning of sin. I believed that if I buried my one talent—my ability to draw—I would weep and forever suffer excruciating hell pains. I little imagined at that age that I would confront sin more directly and personally soon after I turned fourteen.

But in these "piano" dreams, I never experienced weeping or the gnashing of teeth. In truth, as a boy I never dared play a chord on a piano and I have yet to do so—nor have I picked up any other musical instrument. Still, I would dream about sitting at a piano and playing flawlessly pieces by Mozart, Liszt, Chopin, and Schumann, and in every instance I performed in front of a large audience. Until I was fourteen, my father took me to hear all forms of music, from concerto to fully-staged opera. It was his way of informing me that he understood my interest in music without allowing me to practice it. I have long tried to understand the meaning of this recurring dream. Because I had since boyhood believed that a grim fate of some kind awaited me, I hoped to alter such a course through music. Might it have been that music was the one true artistic and passionate love of my life—one that was unrequited—similar to a man who dreams of a love he has lost or in fact never had? And as the years passed, I couldn't help wondering if my joyous and flawless playing of the piano in these dreams was merely a reflection of a passionate relationship with a woman I had never experienced.

My interest in dream analysis fully flowered after I arrived in Vienna. While in Paris, I spent the first several weeks trying to comprehend why I wished neither to return to my drawings nor continue my practice as a physician-surgeon. After that time passed, I concluded that I couldn't go back to the skills that marked my youth and young adulthood. But it wasn't until I engaged in a long discussion with a Parisian physician that I began to see hope for my future. He was a disciple of Freud who thought I might find much to my liking in the Austrian doctor's writings and lectures. Little did I know when my train entered Vienna that I would soon read so much of Freud's work—some even in draft in his own hand—or how often I would hear him speak in public. And what warmed me most in retrospect were the private conversations he and I would have in the six months I resided in the city.

Even though she had died when I was barely able to speak, my mother contributed to my education in Vienna. Her family, who came to London when she was still an infant, was German on both paternal and maternal sides. My maternal grandfather, an exceptional craftsman from Augsburg, remained in England the rest of his life, and following my mother's death, insisted that I become fluent in German. With my father's blessing, my grandfather taught me the language throughout my boyhood and up to his own death when I was in my first year at Cambridge. Much to my surprise my learning to speak and read German did not interfere with my becoming proficient in French, the language my father insisted I master not only because it was expected of an educated gentleman but also because he intended to accompany me often to Paris to show and sell my sketches. Therefore I set forth from the train in Vienna with every expectation of understanding and conversing in both German and French.

I had learned a number of facts about Sigmund Freud before I arrived. He was born in Freiberg, Moravia—some 180 miles north of Vienna—-and his family moved to the Austrian capital when he was a young boy. The son of a Jewish wool merchant, he entered the university at Vienna in 1873 and ended his education there in 1881. I was told that he had just begun seriously analyzing dreams and that he had considerable affection for England, having traveled to Manchester twenty years earlier. In the year I arrived, he published his *Studies on Hysteria* and was planning a book on dream interpretation. I also discovered that he spoke with his patients while they sat or reclined on a sofa, as opposed to a chair, and that he was addicted to smoking cigars. But above all that, I believed he might hold the key to a new life for me—one that I desperately wished to begin. I recalled that my thoughts on the plight of the mentally ill while my father was searching for the escaped patient near London Hospital were the very last I held before the incident on Greenfield Street. It stood to reason that I wished to recapture that more innocent time in some significant way, and devoting my energies to studying and assisting in that field seemed to satisfy the need.

I first saw Freud at one of his public lectures at the university—on the Saturday after Christmas, after I had been in Vienna for ten days. When he was introduced, I observed a much different man than I anticipated, a full fifteen years younger than the man in his mid-fifties I expected to behold. His hair was dark and he wore a lush dark beard. Of average height and weight, Freud still commanded the room when he began to lecture. Without using notes, he spoke for almost two hours with a delivery marked by clarity, steady pacing, and unbounded energy. He was fond of the Socratic Method— pausing in his presentation to ask specific and rhetorical questions. I was captivated by the substance as well as by the style of his words, barely paying attention to the vocal skeptics and cynics sprinkled throughout the audience, because I was fully absorbing every syllable of his remarks.

For the rest of the month and through the New Year, I read what I could of Freud's published work. For me, the spirit of his public talks was generally captured in his prose, and although I had to read passages two or three times to secure his meaning, I never grew frustrated—but only more fascinated with each challenging assertion he made. As 1896 began, I had committed myself to studying the human mind and thinking about it through the lens fashioned by Freud—a lens still blurry and out of focus to someone as untrained as I was, but one with every promise of discerning what few had ever seen and might ever see. My thoughts spun as I thought about the exciting and beneficial work I could do for the rest of my life equipped with such knowledge, which would lead me to think and treat my patients in unprecedented ways.

Yet I knew that simply hearing and reading Freud wouldn't be enough. I had to spend time in his company and devour all I could as directly as possible. On the third of January, I took a walk in the city and thought how I might manage a personal introduction. I glanced at every shop window and peered into every vehicle in the hope of seeing him. As I stepped out in the street to get a better look at a passing carriage, I was nearly run into by a man on a bicycle. I heard him curse me in French and realized that I had heard that voice before. As coincidence would have it, it belonged to the disciple of Freud whom I had met in Paris several weeks earlier. He had then mentioned coming to Vienna at the end of January but obviously moved up his arrival time. After apologies on both our parts—mine for not looking where I was walking and his for calling me a *merde embulante!*—we ordered cake and coffee at the Café Landtmann. My Parisian acquaintance allowed me to finish my first cup before informing me that Freud often stopped by this coffee shop. I never expected my good fortune to hold, and it didn't. Freud made no appearance that morning, because, as my companion added, he was seeing patients from eight to noon. But good fortune did provide one more gift—my Parisian "colleague" promised to arrange a meeting between me and the noted man.

It took another week before I heard from my new friend again. The news was good. Freud had invited me to pay a call at 2:00 p.m.—right after his dinner. I had never anticipated the arrival of a day the way I did January 13, 1896. Arriving promptly at two, I was brought to the consultation room where Freud saw his patients. There it was—the famous sofa I had heard so much about, stacked high with pillows and fabric. Directly against it was the chair he sat in during his analysis sessions. The walls had framed art works and photographs, but what struck me most about the room were the many sculptures resting on almost every surface available. It was evident that Freud had his other diversions and that collecting antiques was one of them.

When he stepped into the room, I saw a cigar wedged between his lips. Seeing me staring at the cigar, he removed it from his mouth and offered an impish smile. "I like to say that smoking is indispensable if one has nothing to kiss." I was totally unprepared for evidence of his wit at our initial meeting. We shook hands and he gestured for me to sit on the sofa. I felt like a schoolboy being asked by the Prince of Wales to climb inside his carriage and take a ride with him through Hyde Park.

Memories of that first meeting with Freud, which lasted some forty minutes, are still fresh in my mind and will always remain so. I was quite taken aback to discover that Freud spoke and read English, although he preferred conversing in German and was delighted that I had such proficiency in his language. Even so, he would shift to English without warning. He asked of my medical experience and why I wished to emulate his work in London. I of course qualified my answer, leaving out the dreadful experience in the operating theatre the previous summer. He likely knew I had left out something significant, but he didn't push the point.

"Do you like to walk, Hemmings?"

"I do, and I find it clears my mind to go out—even during the winter months."

"I agree. I must have my walks. When I was a boy, my father took me walking with him and spoke to me about life and the ways of the world." Freud paused, I suppose to see if I would speak of my father, but I remained silent. "Yet I actually despise Vienna, you know. It has a general hatred of Jews, even though half the physicians here are Jews."

We talked of England. "My dear Hemmings, I love your country and have since my youth. I particularly adore your literature. Quoting from literature is a special delight of mine." When I asked him to give me something from his work to ponder and further examine, he dispensed several concise views for my consumption. "I believe you think this is your one and only chance to pick the brain of the notorious Sigmund Feud, but I think I'd like to meet with you—socially of course—from time to time for as long as you are staying in Vienna—or at least until we leave for holiday in the summer."

I told him I would be honored to be in his company whenever he could spare me a few moments.

"You have a strain of politeness and modesty that disguises something more interesting, Hemmings." He laughed and promised he wouldn't be making any formal analysis of me. "What I do informally, however, is my own business."

I must admit I was charmed, shocked, and most delighted by the inescapable fact that he liked me.

"But you asked me for some bits of wisdom. Take these and give them some thought. We can talk about your impressions when next we meet. First off, I consider myself more of a conquistador—rather than a scientist, experimenter, or observer. Second, you must be your own teacher, Hemmings. You cannot rely on me or anyone else to fully educate you. Next, there can be nothing as important as listening—really listening. Resist the temptation to consider yourself first an evaluator. In addition, you can neither be horrified nor bored by what you hear. You have been a surgeon, and what is often needed in the analyst is the surgeon's coldness of feeling.

And one more thing to chew on: there is more to a sexual life than coitus. There, that should do you for a start."

That night I slept little. I felt as though the door of great possibility was cracked open and the light from the other side was seeping into my darkened room. I understood what he said about being my own teacher, although I couldn't help seeing him as the one from whom I would glean an education far more important than the one I took from my father, grandfather, my Cambridge dons, and Dr. Ridland. I felt so giddy that I made up my mind to grow a beard like Freud's. But the following morning I shaved my entire face as usual. Had Freud seen me with a fresh growth on my face, he would have shaken his head and refused to speak with me again. The only worse thing I could have done was next greet him with a cigar in my mouth.

"Another coffee, sir?" I hadn't heard the waiter at the Langham approach. It was time to return to my office and meet Mina's troubled friend Lucy Westenra.

CHAPTER 6

"I believe I afford all my acquaintances a most curious study, Dr. Hemmings, and I think I will you as well."

In personality, she was exactly as Mina described her. Winsome, flirtatious, and confident in her own abilities to stimulate those in her company. Lucy Westenra was likely the same age as her friend—between twenty and twenty-two. She was also beautiful but in a far different way than was Mina. Lucy's skin was a bit paler, though not at all unhealthy in appearance. She was slightly taller than Mina, with deep black eyes set wider on her face. As I hurried back to my office from the Langham Hotel, I guessed that her hair would be light, leaning toward a reddish hue. But like Mina, her hair was black, yet of a different consistency. Whereas Mina's hair was thick and luxurious, and perfectly set in a chignon, Lucy's was daringly dressed in an apparent attempt to look more natural. Her hair's impressive waves seemed to flow from her head, as though she had surrendered them to the majesty of the wind. Her mouth was slightly narrower, her lips slightly fuller than Mina's—as if she were born to confuse as well as entice. Whereas Mina's mouth easily shaped itself into a smile, Lucy's grins were more calculating and less freely given. When she finished her first remark to me, her mouth formed itself into an attitude of triumph, with her bottom lip dropping down to reveal the front teeth slightly clenched. In this respect, her expression reminded me of the one I saw on Greenfield Street almost twenty years earlier.

"I will soon need to talk with you alone, Miss Westenra, but for now, would you prefer that Mina remain with us?

"Dr. Hemmings, I cannot be content if I am to be called Miss Westenra, while you so comfortably address my dearest confidant as Mina."

Mina frowned at her friend. If there could be charm in the act of scolding, Mina demonstrated how it might sound. "Lucy, please cease troubling yourself over such things."

Lucy sat on the sofa and smiled conspiratorially at me, as if she had intended to prompt Mina's reaction. "Mina, how easy it is to discover that your ambitions are nothing more than to be an assistant schoolmistress. You correct so eagerly. But she has told me on more than one occasion, Dr. Hemmings, that she longs to put aside her tablets and text books and be with her friend Lucy by the sea, where we can talk together freely and build our castles in the sky. Am I not right, Mina?"

Mina quickly diverted her eyes from mine. "Sometimes she embarrasses me, especially in front of gentlemen who are quick to judge."

I recalled Freud's admonition. "I am not here to judge you Mina—or you, Miss Westenra."

"Whom did you say?" Lucy had adjusted her torso in a semi-recumbent position on the sofa.

"I said I am not here to judge you—Lucy."

"Thank you. I now feel like one of the club."

So far, I saw nothing suggesting the disturbing behavior Mina alluded to, but that wasn't unusual. Freud made clear to me that many of his patients began with affected disinterest or disdain, but soon enough revealed their vulnerabilities. And yet Lucy didn't seem to be engaged in any affectation whatsoever.

I decided to allow her no further delay in beginning our first session. "Tell me, what are your feelings now—sitting here before a physician such as I am?"

She pursed her lips and wrinkled her forehead. Again, from someone else I would have thought that an affectation, but Lucy seemed to be giving the matter serious thought.

"As I think now, I feel safe." She quickly sat straight up, which startled me, although I didn't react. "I am so wanting to put my life in your hands." I stood in front of her, while Mina sat in my chair. Lucy gave me a quizzical look. "Dr. Hemmings, are you frightened by what I have told you?"

"Frightened? What indicates to you that I am frightened?"

"Your eyes."

Unable to respond intelligently, I turned and walked to my desk. Picking up a single sheet of blank paper, I could feel Lucy staring at me. Mina did her best to fill the almost painful interlude.

"Lucy, perhaps you should tell Dr. Hemmings what is troubling you."

"Soon Mina, but I must ask him something now."

I took the prompt and turned back toward her. "Certainly. What is it, Lucy?"

"Will you advise that they put me in an asylum?"

"Heavens no. I have no thoughts of advising any such thing. I am confident that we may—together—find the cause of your illness and first control and then finally cure it."

"You call it an illness, Dr. Hemmings." She sounded now like a barrister.

"Forgive me, Lucy." I should have said "troubles" or "problems." But I saw no reason totally to deny my characterization. "If it is an illness, it is treatable, Lucy."

She smiled—not at me but at her friend. "The word 'lunatic' comes from the 'lunar'—the moon, Mina. My grandmother told me there was a full moon at my birth, but later someone else told me—while I pretended to sleep—that I was left as an infant lying under the light of a full moon." Lucy slid her body off the sofa and sat on the floor in front of Mina, closing her eyes and placing the left side of her head in her friend's lap. Mina stroked Lucy's hair and looked to me for assistance.

I didn't like interrupting the gentle scene before me. "Mina, that is an old though rather popular belief—more associated with the colonists in North America than with the English."

Lucy opened her eyes. "No, Dr. Hemmings—in England as well. And in Europe. In parts of Europe no one ever talks about."

Mina's face wore a serious expression. "Doctor Hemmings, please tell me what they did to those they deemed lunatics."

I was confused and troubled by Mina's change of mood. I had already become used to her cheerful disposition. At this moment I felt segregated from the two young women before me.

"The remedies branched into two main channels. One had it that there must be a catharsis of some kind."

Lucy lifted her head and gave Mina a childlike expression. "There, Mina. A word you have not long ago taught me the meaning of."

I continued in clinical terms. "This belief held that the treatment must either catalyze or expel what caused the crisis in the mind."

At that moment, Charles entered the room. I could see he was put off by Lucy's sitting on the floor. Mina nodded, but Lucy ignored him, looking only at me.

"And what was done to the lunatics, Dr. Hemmings?"

"Oh, my dear Lucy, it is too unpleasant to relate."

Charles deemed my reluctance as his invitation to contribute to the discussion. "First they would be *shackled* and then perhaps *submerged* in an ice bath until they lost consciousness. Often they would be *bled*." I could tell that he added emphasis as a way to endorse a courser treatment than the one I had determined to be more humane and effective.

"That will do, Charles. Of course, we have fortunately arrived at a time when transfusion is seen as far more helpful than unnecessary bleeding."

Lucy's sigh sounded like a painful grunt. Returning her head to Mina's lap, she pressed her upper teeth firmly into her bottom lip before replying. "I have read that some asylums have sought to create a more pleasant and domestic environment." She paused. "At this moment I am feeling—" She cut herself off, after which she stood and faced the sofa.

Mina once more filled the void in the conversation. "Yes, I too have seen photographs of asylum rooms that include beds and paintings hanging on the walls. Is this the normal way it is? I have yet to visit an asylum to see for myself." Charles chuckled, which made his sarcasm seem even more inappropriate. Mina gave him a disapproving look—one I had not yet seen from her. Lucy's back remained turned toward us as I answered Mina's question.

"I wish I could say that it was normal. But whereas more enlightened science and the practice of relaxation techniques, and of course hypnosis, pushed the treatment of the mentally ill in the proper direction, the barbaric methods for the most part remain popular forms of treatment, I'm afraid."

Charles callously punctuated my remarks. "And the lack of confinement and refusal to employ shock therapy caused a complete breakdown in discipline."

Mina was more disturbed by his remark than was I. "Shock therapy? How dreadful. Come, Mr. Yates. I should wish to have more of your splendid tea. Dr. Hemmings has asked to be alone with Miss Westenra now."

Charles extended his arm. "In fact, I came in just to ask if you'd like some, Miss Murray."

As she strode past me, she smiled—making evident that she had the ability to alter for the better whatever environment she was in. She seemed to have an excellent sense of timing—that is, how long the conversation could go in one direction before it began to waver off course. I found her intelligence a contributing factor to her beauty. For a brief moment I was envious of Charles as the two of them left the room. But the time had come to listen to Lucy Westenra. I checked to see if the door was secure.

"Lucy, please return to your seat on the sofa." Her back was still turned toward me.

"Why are you staring through the door at Mina, Dr. Hemmings? Does she mean something important to you?"

Once more, Lucy had left my sense of control in disarray. But I had to say something. "She is a wonderful friend to you, Lucy."

"But she is more than that. I fear she may be more than that."

"I should like you to tell me why you think such a thing. That is, where that idea first came upon you."

"In dreams."

"Yes. I should like to talk to you about your dreams." At present, I particularly wished Freud had completed his writing on the subject, but in our last correspondence he thought he was another year or more away from publishing his work. Yet, could Lucy be talking more of waking fantasies than of dreams? Freud had encouraged me to understand the difference. Dreams may be translated as wish fulfillment, he argued—again, a concept I had only begun to comprehend.

"But first, Lucy, I wish to give you a brief physical examination and then ask you a few more questions."

She finally turned and took three rapid steps toward me. "I don't wish to be touched by any instruments. I must not be touched by them. No syringe. I will not permit you to inject me. You cannot do that." She was flushed and breathless.

"No, I promise you. No instruments. No syringe. You must trust me, Lucy."

Her face lost its reddish hue and returned to a more aloof appearance. She took a step back. "You may touch me with your hands."

"Good. Now Lucy, give me your arm. Come." She mechanically lifted her left arm for me to take. I felt her pulse. "Lucy, have you felt your own pulse? Has it lately beaten as rapidly as it is doing now?"

Her answer seemed on the threshold of lifelessness. "Faster than this."

I resisted the temptation to guess what filled her with so much anxiety. "Have you heard anything inside your ears? Or felt a pulsation here?" I demonstrated by touching the spot directly behind my left ear.

"Heard anything?" Her anxiety increased. "Anything? Yes. I have heard and I have sensed . . ."

"Please go on, Lucy."

"I cannot say. I must not say." And then in a softened voice that resembled a haunted whisper, "And I have felt."

I was determined to complete the preliminary examination. "Let me touch your face and forehead, Lucy." She offered no resistance. "How do my hands feel?"

"As if they wish to keep me safe. But they cannot."

It was all I could do to maintain my composure. "No, I mean do my hands feel warm or cold on your face?"

She moved closer to me—less than a full step separating our bodies. "Everything feels warm to me now. Mina says the nights are beginning to require a heavier shawl since it is now November. But I cannot feel the cold. I don't want anything lying across my shoulders."

"I should like to feel you breathe now." I stepped back so that I could touch under her heart with an open palm. As I lifted my left hand, she suddenly grabbed me by the wrist.

"No!"

"Please, Lucy. I have to put my hand here." With my other hand, I demonstrated on myself the exact location. She narrowed her eyes and dropped her lower lip, once more providing the briefest glimpse of her teeth. She released my left wrist and watched my left hand as I placed it below her heart. "Lucy, please take several deep breaths."

"I can no longer breathe deeply, Dr. Hemmings."

"Try to do it—for me, Lucy." She inhaled and exhaled, but I barely felt her torso move. "Please breathe as deeply as you can."

"I have been."

"All right. You may sit on the sofa."

She manifested a different kind of nervousness. "What are you going to do to me?" She began to recline on the sofa with visible reluctance. "I have always hated being examined like this. I don't want to. I don't want to." Her childlike plea further unnerved me.

"No, no. I want you to sit up, Lucy. I must ask a question that is most intimate. You need to remember that I am now your physician. Please don't be upset by what I ask you."

"I have had regular menstruation, Dr. Hemmings. It has been

unvarying."

Could she have read my thought that easily? "And the most recent bleeding was on what date?" She said nothing but altered her eyes just enough to stare right past me. "Lucy, are you willing that I continue?"

She answered almost blandly. "Of course, Dr. Hemmings."

"I wish to touch you on the outside of your dress. I need to feel in several other places. Forgive me if I cause you any discomfort."

As I proceeded with my examination—pushing with my palm on her stomach, back, and sides—Lucy sat placidly without expression. For modesty's sake, I turned my head so I wouldn't look at her. As I continued my examination, I sensed a change in her breathing pattern. She turned her head, and I looked into her face, finding that her demeanor had completely altered. Her expression registered a feeling of arousal. I took away my hands and stepped back from the sofa.

"Lucy, why are you reacting this way?"

She was once more breathless. "The touch. The touch."

"Do you feel I have touched you inappropriately?" I dared not articulate my suspicion that I had stimulated her. Her reply stunned me.

"It is not *your* touch."

CHAPTER 7

I watched Mina, Lucy, and their elderly male chaperone enter the hansom cab, which would take them to their lodgings off Tottenham Court Road near Bedford Square, not far from my office at the intersection of Oxford and Regent Streets. I was relieved that the distance was no hindrance to the planned series of sessions with Lucy, who would always, I now felt confident, be accompanied by Mina.

But having been shaken by Lucy's audacious behavior, I felt uncomfortable remaining at my desk after Charles bid me goodnight. While jotting down my notes, I had looked toward the sofa and imagined Lucy behaving even more outrageously in my presence. Embarrassed by the thought, I quickly grabbed my coat and hat and locked the office door behind me.

I resided in Mayfair not far to the south of Oxford Street and close to Hanover Square. But I was in no condition to retire to my rooms for reading and then much needed sleep. It was now almost ten, and I reasoned that if I walked for a solid hour or more I could purge my unease and miss little sleep. Similar to Freud, I had always been a slave of habit, in all seasons arising every morning at 7:00 and climbing into bed by 11:00 p.m. Yet unlike my Austrian friend, my meals were irregular—catch-as-catch-can. Had I resided at a more formal boarding house or employed a servant, I would have been able to eat regularly and properly, but I wished at this time of my life to be completely alone. I wanted no interruptions from a helpful servant or a loquacious landlady. Besides, I still had so much to learn about my new profession, and it seemed that every time I corresponded with Freud, he gave me something new to consider or assimilate. For example, his last letter, which I received on October 24th, informed me that he was presently engaged in vigorous self-analysis.

My English friend, I must repeat that being analyzed by another is far preferable, but I have begun to burrow deeply in an almost bullying form of self-scrutiny. I am an archeologist of my own past, reconstructing and attempting to connect the fragments of an early life. As I have noted to others here in Vienna, I believe I am in a cocoon, and God only knows what kind of beast will crawl out.

Not surprisingly, I have started the process of my own self-analysis, although I have been much more genteel about it than has been my brilliant friend. I have begun to face up to much about myself and to what I had kept hidden for some twenty years. My habits and preferences, my eccentricities—if such they may be called—and my entrenched habits and predictable reactions. And I have been thinking more deeply on what Freud told me about the subject of sex. I have thought often of the remark he made at the end of our first meeting—"There is more to a sexual life than coitus." In addition, I have had to erase all self-explanations for why I haven't yet married—namely that I am still unsettled in my profession and need several years more of study before I could even consider it. I suppose I saw forty as the age I would enter wedlock and then begin a family. Being close to thirty-four, I would have six more years of study, according to that reasoning.

But tonight I felt loneliness for a woman I cannot remember having experienced—at least since arriving at manhood. I saw Mina's beautiful face in imaginative flashes. My ears still reverberated with her sweet voice, which stimulated my senses as no music had ever done. That I was smitten was impossible to deny. Still, how many others felt about her as I did? How many proposals had she rejected in her young life? I couldn't imagine a more desirable woman with whom to spend one's days and nights.

I headed south on Regent Street toward Piccadilly and turned my thoughts to Mina's friend. The examination of Lucy Westenra still affected me—how she had reacted and what she had said. Was it merely an exercise of power in front of someone she should have acquiesced to in the context of a patient-doctor relationship? Could she be so rebellious by nature that she manufactured her behavior in order to upset or confuse me? Freud insisted that my job was to listen and analyze with an open mind. Therefore, I couldn't begin treating Lucy with suspicions of her motives as they applied to me. I had to concentrate on the unconscious promptings and repressed feelings—and explanations of her actions, especially as they might relate to incidents from her childhood. Yet I found it impossible at this moment to dismiss analysis relating to conscious motives. Had she chosen to distinguish herself from her friend Mina by daring displays and shocking statements? After all, it wasn't unusual for younger siblings to engage in wicked acts and incorrigible behavior so far different from that of their elder brothers and sisters, who are praised by the parent as filial exemplars. Could Lucy resent Mina similarly?

But it was foolish of me to settle on an answer after only a preliminary examination, even if Lucy demonstrated socially offensive behavior. Freud had told me often enough to ignore a patient's logic, word choice, and decorum and just listen. "As an analyst, you cannot be fettered by your own neurosis," he added. I decided to think no more of Lucy Westenra until I next saw her in my office.

I began to feel more like myself the further I walked down Regent Street. The weather had slightly warmed and the expected November fog had begun to make its presence known. Unlike most of London's citizens, I was not at all averse to such conditions. I even enjoyed thunderstorms and driving snow. In my initial attempts at self-analysis, I concluded that I had for the longest time been drawn to concealment. Whether it be closing the curtains or walking in the fog, I took comfort in being hidden from sight. In that state I felt invigorated and safe.

The lumbering mist was only a short distance behind me as I passed Brewer Street. Ahead, a woman approached a gentleman who had apparently come up from Piccadilly. There was no question that she was seeking payment for her sexual favors. I confess that my experience on Greenfield Street when I was fourteen led to a lifelong fascination with women who sell their bodies and perhaps their souls for money. But although I couldn't argue with the more liberal minded in the city, who saw the motivation to prostitute oneself as a need to survive, even if the woman was a deviant, I couldn't help wondering if sexual pleasure and a defiance of moral and parental authority didn't influence the decision as well. Of course, this was a thought I could never reveal to anyone. I believed that my interest in these women had to be associated with the face of the woman I saw and then painted some twenty years ago. Did I hope to see that young woman again? Or did I wish to see someone who looked just like her? If alive, the woman on Greenfield Street was now around forty; therefore, it was most doubtful I would be able to recognize her if she walked right up to me. Still, I wanted to see her, but only as she was then—a stark impossibility. And what would be resolved if I did see a young prostitute who resembled her exactly? Would I speak to her? Ask her if she would look at a fourteen-year-old boy the way the woman on Greenfield Street stared at me?

At times I have given considerable thought to the life of the prostitute, on one occasion even visiting a house in which prostitutes' lodge—that is, those women who refuse to walk the streets or down by the wharfs. I learned then that so many of these women were young, between eighteen and twenty-two years of age, and came to the city from the countryside without prospects of a husband or enough funds to feed themselves or occasionally their illegitimate children. I spoke with several of these young women who assured me they would prostitute themselves for only a few years and then find a husband among the men they serviced. One had even bluntly asked me if I would take her as my wife.

That day, I paid for the opportunity to talk with them and asked if they knew of any girl who matched the description I gave of the street prostitute I long-ago painted. Again, I wasn't seeking to engage in carnal activity with anyone who resembled that particular woman but only to sit in the same room with her. I suppose I thought that doing so might purge from my waking thoughts the memory of that day. The prostitutes I questioned thought I had taken leave of my senses. "Don't you know that some say there are over fifty thousand of us selling our wares in London?" and "May you have good luck, sir, in finding the one you describe" were common retorts. As for my paying for their services as exclusively listeners and talkers, I was most surprised to learn that many men do the same thing—not even attempting to satisfy their sexual longings—either out of some adherence to moral authority or out of fear of sexual dysfunction, which was yet another topic that commanded the interest of Freud.

As I came nearer to the man and woman negotiating a price for the woman's services—hoping to get a glimpse of the woman's face—I heard the sound of footsteps rushing up from behind me. I tuned and saw another young woman—apparently younger than twenty—approaching me. She was devoid of a bonnet and even a shawl, not uncommon for those who walked the streets. Yet her face did not reflect the attitude of one about to offer herself for a price.

"Sir, . . ."

"I'm sorry, young woman. I am not in the market right now." I was always polite in such situations.

"Sir, there is someone on the other side of the street who is walking at your pace but is several steps behind you. I don't like the way he looks. He may be out for your money or worse."

My suspicions were instantly raised. Tales of women and men working various games of criminal exploitation were notorious in the city, and I wasn't about to allow myself to be set up for one.

"Thank you. Now if you will excuse me, I need to move on."

She grabbed my arm. "No, no. This is no trick. I think the man over there is out to do you harm."

I took a quick look behind her for an accomplice. I saw nothing but the fog, which appeared to have halted some forty yards away from where we were standing. I took several steps away from the woman.

"Sir, if you'll only just look over across the street."

I felt safe enough to glance in that direction. I saw him. A man in a dark coat with a heavy scarf pulled up to his nose. The rest of his face was shielded by either a heavy piece of fabric draped from his head or a kind of beret I had never seen worn before. It was hardly cold enough to cover the face and head the way he did.

I took the woman's hand from my arm. "Thank you for pointing him out to me. I will make sure to keep him in my sights." I offered her a coin for her troubles."

"Oh, thank you kindly, sir." She took the coin. "I'll not disturb you anymore. I'll just go back the way I came."

She turned and began walking back up Regent Street toward the stationary fog. I watched the figure across the way stare at me for a moment and then turn and begin walking rapidly until he reached a spot almost level with the young woman. He adjusted his pace to match hers, and soon they were both lost in the fog, which was once more moving toward me. I hesitated for only a few moments, before I too turned and walked rapidly up Regent Street. But when I arrived at the spot where I assumed I would catch up to her, I saw neither of them. The fog was simply too thick.

CHAPTER 8

"Lucy slept well for several hours last night, Dr. Hemmings. Although you spoke only briefly with her last evening, the time she spent with you was most helpful."

"Mina, you are kind to tell me so."

Lucy likely had a more restful night than did I. The encounter with the young woman on Regent Street made it impossible for me to drift off to sleep before 3:00 a.m. I feared for her safety, because assaults of the kind I imagined were not uncommon in London. I had also spoken with her and she had done me the service of warning me of a possible attack or robbery, which made me feel responsible for her—at least for her well being. On the other hand, the fog may have harbored her, allowing her to turn down Beak Street and make her escape from the suspicious man who had turned and followed her. But as I looked at the lovely young woman sitting on my office sofa this morning, I felt nothing but contentment.

"Mina, you seem to imply that Lucy only slept soundly for several hours. Did she awaken in the night?"

"Yes, but I don't know exactly when. It's rather odd. I am a very light sleeper, and I was in the same bed as Lucy. I'm certain I would have heard her or felt her move if she was troubled by any bad thoughts or dreams."

"Then she left the bed?"

"Yes." She lowered her head, seemingly lost in thought.

"Mina?"

She raised her head and my eyes looked into hers. Had I not been a physician, we would never have had this private meeting. That fact only made our discussion more stimulating to me. For once I felt the utter pleasure of being alone with a woman I was enchanted by.

"I looked for her in the other rooms, but couldn't find her. Then I recalled that when we were at Whitby, she would leave the house and walk out toward the edge of the cliffs."

"And why do you believe she did that?" I went to the desk, retrieved my notebook, and sat in my analyst's chair.

"I don't know. It almost appeared as if she were looking out toward the sea—as if she were waiting for something or someone to arrive. When I reached her, she would tremble momentarily and put her head on my shoulder and ask to be taken back to bed."

"I have never lived near the sea, but I imagine that it is common to look for the arrival of a ship of some sort." I smiled. "Much like living at the foot of mountains. One cannot help looking up."

"It was nothing as simple as that Dr. Hemmings."

My smile dropped, and I felt the sting of being mildly admonished by someone for whom I had affection. Mina's face showed disappointment at my comment—or so I took her expression to mean. I wished quickly to redeem myself.

"Where did you find her last night?"

"Outside on the steps. She was looking down toward the street—again as if she were awaiting the arrival of something . . . or someone. When I reached her, she put my head on *her* shoulder and said she would take *me* back to bed."

I was at a loss. "Was she trembling?"

"No. The night air was cool, but her skin was almost burning. I thought that . . . no, nothing."

I risked offending her sensibilities, and I responded as gently as I could. "You forget who I am, Mina. I must insist on your completing your thought."

"I believed I saw a drop of blood on her night gown. But when I said 'Lucy'—with concern in my voice—and began to point to the spot, she groaned in a manner that told me it was improper to ask such a question."

"Mina, this is very important, and I want you to think carefully. Has Lucy been inflicting injury to herself? Has she been cutting or pricking herself? Pulling at her hair or squeezing her flesh to leave bruise marks?"

Mina shook her head. "No. I have not seen anything like that. Then you think it's possible she may harm herself, Dr. Hemmings?"

Her eyes glistened and her face reflected vulnerability and pain I had not witnessed in her. I wished to provide comfort. "I'm sorry Mina, but I must ask these questions. I have to consider all possibilities. Promise me that. . ."

I hesitated—not wishing to violate Mina's notion of proper speech

53

between a man and a woman. "I feel uncomfortable asking you to do this, but promise me you will look at her body—at every part of her body when she prepares for bed and when she bathes. We must know if she is bringing any harm to herself."

"I promise, but I regret to say that she has stopped allowing me to wash and comb her hair. Why I do not know. I feel that such a denial is evidence that our friendship is waning."

Into my mind rushed the image of an Edward Degas pastel I saw in Paris two years earlier. It was of a nude woman combing her voluminous hair, which she had pulled up over her head. The figure sat with her back to the viewer; yet some of her face was visible. She could have been Lucy. But she might also have been Mina, and I am not ashamed to say that the thought warmed me.

Without opening my mouth I clamped my teeth together to force the image from my conscious thoughts. Now was certainly not the time to indulge any such imaginings. "There are understandable reasons for her decision, Mina. Reasons that once determined will explain all of her behavior. You must believe me."

"I do, Dr. Hemmings. I do. Thank you for your kindness and understanding." She seemed chilled. "I wonder if it might be possible to have some warm tea."

It did feel cooler in the office than it should have. It was as if a door had been left open, allowing the brisk morning air into the room. "Mina, Mr. Yates is running an errand for me, so I will have to make the tea."

"Then I can do without."

"Now, I realize that Charles makes fine tea, especially for an American, but I believe that I can make it well enough to warm you."

Mina laughed at my attempt at wit. "I meant only that I didn't wish to trouble you with such a domestic chore. I am very confident you would do a most respectable job of it."

I wondered how this young woman could be any more charming. "Then I will step into the other room and tend to my domestic responsibilities."

Fortunately, Charles had kept the water heated; therefore, I had little to do before returning to enjoy Mina's company. I set the tea to steeping and returned to my office. But I was stunned by the appearance of Joseph Styles standing not three feet from Mina. He addressed his first words to her, keeping his eyes trained on hers.

"Dear lady, I had no dream last night. But I fear that tonight I will dream of you. Forgive me for what I cannot help but do. I have no choice. The mind lacks sufficient armor. I truly wish it weren't so. But it is. I have been told that it is. Why God allowed it to be so, I do not know." Styles placed his fingertips over his eyes, which were wet with tears.

Mina came to my side. As I gently pulled her behind me, I heard Charles enter the outer room. I put out my hand as Styles stepped toward us.

He obeyed my gesture to halt. "I am happy to see you Dr. Hemmings. I had no dream last night. I killed no young woman this time. There was no wall. No blood. What does that mean? Can you tell me?"

Charles brushed past me and pulled Styles by the arm toward the anteroom that lead to the rear door. "It means that you should be committed to an asylum, Styles. Julian, what further evidence do you need?" Charles looked down the short anteroom. "The rear door is wide open. No wonder this room feels chilled. Come, you lunatic, leave the doctor in peace."

"Wait, Charles. Let him stay. Were you hiding back there, Joseph?"

"I wished to surprise you, Dr. Hemmings. But when I came through the rear door, I heard a bird singing to you. There was such beautiful music in her voice. I sat on the floor and listened to all of her songs."

Charles was beside himself with impatience. "You eavesdropped, then. Now you have lost your privilege to be heard by Dr. Hemmings. Come on." As Charles began pulled him more vigorously toward the anteroom, Styles broke free and ran to where Mina and I stood.

"But I only listened to the bird, Dr. Hemmings. I never heard anything you said." Styles looked intensely at Mina. "Will you sing for me again?"

Mina was gentle with her glance. She felt compassion for the poor man and would not chastise him for having frightened her. But I had to be forceful with him.

"Joseph, you must wait until our appointed time. I am happy to hear that you didn't have your dream last night. That might suggest that we are gaining ground on what is really tormenting you. But you must leave now."

"But, Dr. Hemmings, you said I could come whenever I was in need."

He had me. I did indeed encourage him to do so, but then I had not yet met Mina. I reached for several shillings. "Here, Joseph. Eat a wholesome dinner. We are scheduled for later this afternoon. A quarter past four. Come back then—with a full stomach. I was particularly anxious to ask him why he stared at me from across the street when I had returned yesterday to the back door of the office with my Chelsea bun.

Styles took the shillings and held each of them between his two thumbs and forefingers, delicately touching his lips with the coins.

"Oh, I will, sir. Thank you. Thank you ever so much, sir." As he walked to where Charles waited to see him out, he turned and looked at Mina. "I saw you in a dream before. I remember now. The wind was blowing your hair free and over the front of your head. It was the wind that came from the sea." Styles stared at her in a manner that alarmed me. He looked as though he wished to ravish her. But as Charles grabbed his arm, Styles' expression changed to that of a chastised schoolboy. "Dear lady, I hope you will forgive me for all I will do."

Charles shook his head as he returned from the anteroom. "A certifiable madman, Miss Murray. And yet, Dr. Hemmings believes he can talk him out of his illness."

Mina almost whispered the words. "He has killed young women?"

Charles dismissed her concern with a flip of his hand. "Hallucinating nonsense, Miss Murray. It is my view that he sees himself as the reincarnation of the Ripper fellow who killed those women in Whitechapel nine years ago. Styles has killed no one. I am sure of it. But that doesn't mean he shouldn't be in an asylum. There are some dozen or more of those institutions in this city to choose from."

I couldn't let his words stand without comment. "There are now far too many to treat in the asylums, Charles." I should have remained silent, for I only invited him to pontificate further on the subject.

"Miss Murray, it comes down to only two paths we can go. Most—and I am one of them—believe that we must place these lost minds in the asylums, employing methods still effective. Or, one can go the way of so-called 'talk-therapy'—long hours of listening and leading patients in a dozen directions at once."

Mina took on the fight. "But Mr. Yates, I believe that there are special circumstances that traditional methods cannot address. If nothing else, we must try this form of therapy with Lucy."

Charles was enough of a gentleman not to return fire. "And when is she to return here, Miss Murray?"

"We are waiting for her to arrive, Mr. Yates." Mina walked to the sofa. "Mr. Yates, I wonder if you might see to my tea."

"Of course, Miss Murray." When Charles left the room, Mina gestured for me to sit in my chair. She took her place on the sofa.

"She has been more herself this morning, Dr. Hemmings. She wished to purchase a new bonnet and shawl before coming here. I apologize that she is now late."

"That is quite all right, Mina. You need not apologize for anything." I was hoping Lucy would come even later, as it would then give me more time to converse with Mina, but mention of the bonnet and shawl forced me to recall the young woman who came up to me on Regent Street—the young woman who walked the streets without the items Lucy wished today to purchase.

"You are so very kind, Dr. Hemmings."

She offered a smile to punctuate her gentle compliment, but I couldn't return it—for I recalled Styles' parting words to Mina: "I hope you will forgive me for all I *will do.*"

CHAPTER 9

"I beg you to forgive me, Dr. Hemmings. I just couldn't make up my mind between two exquisite shawls. So after many minutes of debate, I took them both." Lucy had arrived only moments after Charles brought Mina's tea. We expected her to continue her narrative, but suddenly she became withdrawn.

"Lucy, are you all right?" I escorted her to the sofa, where she sat next to Mina.

"I just remembered that I may not ever be chilled enough this winter to wear either shawl."

Mina placed her hand on Lucy's. "You will certainly have use for them. I can promise you that." Lucy stared at Mina's hand, and then looked up at me. After a moment, Lucy's entire body fluttered, which seemed to shake off her momentary depression.

"I hope you are well, Dr. Hemmings, for I have not felt better in weeks."

"I am happy to hear you say that, Lucy." I cast a glance at Mina, who seemed to understand why my words did not match my expression.

Lucy smiled wickedly at Mina. "Dr. Hemmings, why haven't you married?"

I could see that Mina was embarrassed. "Lucy, that is none of your concern. That question was impertinent and most inappropriate. Let me apologize for her, Dr. Hemmings."

Lucy dismissed her friend's displeasure. "Mina, I don't believe he has taken offense—have you, Dr. Hemmings?"

Mina prevented my answering. "He is too much a gentleman to answer truthfully, Lucy."

I found Mina's playing lioness especially delightful. Lucy sighed with dramatic flair.

"Oh well, I suppose it is none of my business. I hope I remain in your favor, Dr. Hemmings." With her eyes, she demanded the only answer available to me.

"Of course you do, Lucy."

"I am happy to hear *you* say that because I wish to postpone our meeting for this morning."

I had been afraid she would resist treatment after her behavior the previous evening. I began my counter argument. "But Lucy, this is a mistake, for I believe you should at least give it another try. We can—"

"I only said 'postpone' Dr. Hemmings. I *do* want you to help me, but I don't think I can speak as freely with you this early in the day. I want to come in during the very late afternoon. I would feel freer to communicate with you openly when the day begins to give over to darkness."

Mina could only shrug, while I smiled in considerable relief. "Lucy, I think it would indeed be better for you to come then."

Lucy stood as though she had just bested her opponent at cards. "Good. I will see you later in the day, then. You can tell Mina the time. I must stop briefly at one more shop before returning home."

Yates stepped into the office. "Miss Westenra, the elderly gentleman has come back for you."

"Thank you, Mr. Yates. Mina, I will send him back to collect you in a half hour or so. Until later, Dr. Hemmings." And with that she was off.

Mina was clearly exasperated. "Once more, I am so sorry for her behavior."

"Mina, as I said, there is no need for you to apologize. She must be accommodated as much as possible so that she will speak openly with me. But may I ask who is the elderly gentleman who accompanies the both of you."

He is my great-uncle, Mr. George Taltson—the brother of my maternal grandmother. We are living with my great-uncle and his wife while we are in London. Ordinarily, his wife serves as chaperone, but she is a bit of a frustrated actress prone to hysterical displays, and if she knew that Lucy and I were coming to the office of a physician whose special . . . well . . . you see."

I laughed. "Yes, I do indeed."

"But my poor great uncle claims he has all he can do to survive Lucy's antics as well as those of his wife. I'm sure she has made her shopping venture utter misery for him. She told me she wanted others to think my great uncle was her keeper in a less-than-acceptable relationship. She loves to shock and create topics of conversation. But I suppose you might have concluded that."

I had to laugh again—more at Mina's manner and expression than at Lucy's capricious personality. "Does Lucy have family in Whitby—where I assume you both have lived?"

"Her father left his family, returning once and then leaving again. I believe his desertion still affects her deeply."

"Mina, would you be offended if I made some notes."

"No. If it can in any way help Lucy, then please do."

"Thank you." I retrieved my notebook and made an entry regarding Lucy's father.

"Her mother died a little more than a year ago at her home in Whitby. At least her death was a peaceful one. She was a very gentle and sensitive woman. It is good that she never saw her daughter the way she is now."

"When did you and Lucy leave Whitby?"

"Two weeks ago."

"All right. May I ask about her grandparents?"

"She has no knowledge of her father's family. Her mother always refused to talk about them. Lucy's maternal grandparents both died several months before their daughter—the grandfather two weeks after his wife."

"So Lucy has experienced several recent losses."

"Yes, and I can add that she had an elder brother, but he died when she was three years of age."

"The father of the boy was ...?"

Mina looked at me with surprise. "Yes, Dr. Hemmings, his father was Lucy's as well."

I feared I had upset her again. "Forgive me for seeming to imply something other than that. It comes from my profession, where blunt questions are often necessary."

Mina carried on without acknowledging my apology and explanation. "Before my great-uncle returns, may I ask you some questions about your new profession?"

"Of course you may." I could tell that at present she wished to say no more about Lucy or her family.

"Is it true that Dr. Freud puts all of his patients under hypnosis?"

"Mina, his view on the benefits of hypnosis has undergone a change. A dozen or so years ago, he finally arrived at the conclusion that hypnosis was an authentic phenomenon. But now his method of analysis is what he calls emancipation from hypnosis. He now has a word for it—which he came up with only last year. He calls it 'psychoanalysis.'"

"I see." She wasn't merely passing the time with me; she was genuinely interested in learning more about Freud and the form of analysis he and I practiced. "Dr. Hemmings, I have often wondered what it would be like to be put under hypnosis. Would I look into the eyes of the hypnotizer and then see him no more? Or would his appearance change once I was in the hypnotic condition? Or what is more frightening, would mine?"

"Fortunately, Mina, your physical appearance would not alter permanently, even if you made faces while under hypnosis." I wanted to tell her how beautiful she looked to me, but I dared not.

"Lucy likes to tell me that I look too much like so many other women my age."

"She isn't serious, Mina."

"Oh, but she is. She has advised that I completely reconstruct my hair in order to stand apart from the conventional woman. That is easy for her to say—for she looks like no one else I have ever seen. Her hair is so beautifully defiant. And although her face has begun to look paler than it has been, surely owing to her illness, she still has such beautiful skin—as if it had never been touched by sun or sand but only by the light of the moon and the stars."

I was captivated by Mina's soft voice as she spoke so poetically of her friend. "She does, Mina. But I must disagree. You certainly do not look like any conventional woman. You do not look like anyone else that I have . . ." I stopped because I feared that Mina's reaction would be one of disapproval or indifference.

Mina studied my face. "I have a thought for you. Do you think Dr. Freud would find Lucy beautiful?"

I smiled—as I'm sure Mina wished me to. "Freud has told me that women to him are like a 'dark continent.' I didn't bother to ask him for further explanation—as the description seemed to sum up many a man's feelings as well as any learned and profound assessment could."

"Do you agree with him?"

Her question surprised me. I hadn't expected it, even though I should have. I moved my mouth as if to speak, but I could push nothing forth. Once more she came to my rescue.

"Well, may I ask what are Dr. Freud's major beliefs about the mind? I am very interested to know."

"You ask too much of me, I'm afraid. I have explained Freud's theories and methods only sparingly—not simply because I feel my listener would have difficulty embracing the complexity of Freud's views—but primarily because I fear I wouldn't describe them adequately or accurately enough. I am but a student myself."

"I will accept your qualification—but not the implication that I would be better off not knowing."

Above all, I didn't wish to bore her. Yet I had an aching desire to share with her what presently fascinated me. I knew I was no different than so many men who speak passionately but wearily about the theatre, the races, politics, or the sea. But in each of those areas a woman would have a basic knowledge or at least a modicum of interest. I was taking a risk, but I felt it was worth taking.

"I can see that there is no saying no to you, Mina. But before I attempt a summary, you should know that Freud's mind is always in transition—it is always shaping, re-shaping, and discarding what months ago he might have thought fixed."

"I understand. Please continue." There simply was no scaring her away.

"As you wish. One might say that there are three central ideas to Freud's beliefs. First, one must overcome the patient's resistance to any thoughts that seek to enter the conscious mind from the unconscious. The second is an understanding of even the casual significance of . . . well . . . sexual matters. Forgive me."

"We are talking science, Dr. Hemmings—in your office. We are not strolling in a park or conversing in a theatre. Therefore, the subject is allowed to be discussed in front of a curious young pupil." A New Woman she indeed was.

"I take it that you have spent very little time at the theatre, Miss Murray. If you did, you'd find the subject spoken of quite frankly and vigorously—on stage and off."

It worked. She smiled in spite of herself. "And the third of Dr. Freud's central ideas?"

"The considerable importance of early childhood experiences. The various neurotic symptoms, then, represent a give and take between sexual and aggressive drives and the often cruel demands of reality."

"And dreams?"

"Yes, and dreams. Here. Let me show you something. This is the most recent letter I have received from him." I retrieved it from my desk and handed it to her. I wanted almost desperately to touch her fingers as she took it from me.

She saw that he communicated with me in German. "I fear I am unqualified to read it—as my proficiency in other languages limits itself to French and Italian."

"Then you may return the favor and translate for me any correspondence I receive in Italian—as I barely know a dozen words of that beautiful language. Freud says here that he is getting closer to finishing his book on dream interpretation. Another year or so should find it published, he says.

"Is this a new interest of his?"

"He told me that he had been interested in the significance of dreams for some fifteen years, although he did not apply the full power of his analysis until a few years ago."

"That is most interesting." Again my good luck held. She was clearly being honest with me. She changed the position of her hands and placed them palm down on the sofa. "I should like to tell you of my dreams, Dr. Hemmings."

I resisted every impulse to agree. "You have no need to do so, Mina. You are not my patient. It is Lucy's dreams that we must have knowledge of."

"You seem disappointed by my request, Dr. Hemmings. Have I said something wrong? Perhaps I don't understand the boundaries between your familiarities and your profession."

I was horrified that I appeared as she described. I was so very far from disappointed. If she only knew how much I longed to know everything about her waking and sleeping thoughts. But the words of my Austrian friend seeped into my mind and chilled my sensibilities. "My dear Hemmings, I have concluded that for men in our profession to have sexual affairs is prohibited by both middle-class morality and medical dignity."

CHAPTER 10

Without enough patients to fill my day, I had pieces of time during which I could leave the office and assist other physicians with non-surgical matters or visit the asylums to learn more about the mind and occasionally to plead for the release of those who might be helped by talk therapy. After Mina left at mid-morning with her great-uncle, I was free from appointments until three in the afternoon. At first I had instructed Charles to speak with any potential patient who walked in inquiring about my services, even though I knew he wouldn't provide enough encouragement and enthusiasm to do much good. Therefore, I changed tactics and had a brief outline of my services printed up so that Charles could simply hand a sheet to a curious visitor, who might then ignore the unpleasant grunt as my assistant dispensed the information.

Today I took a hansom cab to a private asylum in East Putney, located to the west of my office. As I crossed over the Thames on Putney Bridge, I recalled my first meeting earlier in the year with Edward Maybrick, the medical superintendent of the asylum. I had just accepted my first patient and was moving into my current office space. He came to the door and introduced himself, asking for a few minutes of my time. Three hours later, we parted as friends and scheduled our next meeting—at the asylum in East Putney.

Since that time, I have met with Maybrick on several occasions and spent time at the asylum examining and talking to him about a number of those in his charge. But more importantly, he educated me on the history of London asylums—both public and private—and inspired me to visit others, where my observations on patient treatment were almost always ignored. Only Maybrick attempted to incorporate some of my suggestions.

As I have noted, since boyhood I had been fascinated by those commonly called the insane, or as they have also been described—the lunatics, the defective, imbeciles, idiots, madmen, and madwomen. When young, I drew exterior sketches of several London asylums and had every intention of drawing the faces of selected inmates, although I never got around to doing so. I knew that these places existed throughout the city and in other parts of England and that they housed the troubled, the dangerous, and the homicidal. What I didn't understand until meeting Maybrick was that they also lodged the suicidal. In the past several months I have visited eight of these institutions other than the one at Putney and on each visit I solidified my desire to further study the mind and treat my patients as an analyst. I confess that such determination exacted a price. My spirits sagged as I observed the worst off of the inhabitants, and it took almost an entire twenty-four hours before my mood again lightened.

Now in his mid-forties, Edward Maybrick came by his profession naturally, as his father and grandfather were both involved in the treatment of London's mentally impaired. His grandfather aided the government for both the Madhouse Act of 1828 and the Lunatics Act of 1845. His work appeared in the *Journal of Psychological Medicine and Mental Pathology* as early as 1848, and both he and his son—Edward's father—published findings in the *Asylum Journal* of mid-century. In addition, both men served on the Committee of Enquiry in 1860, which led to the Lunacy Act of 1862. Even so, by the time of Edward's birth in 1853, the study of insanity was deemed unessential in the training of physicians. Both Maybrick's father and grandfather worked hard to improve the public and medical reputation of those studying the damaged mind—a reputation that characterized these men as being on the hinterlands of reputable medicine. Until each man breathed his last, the elder Maybricks made every effort to educate the public and the government to the importance of properly caring for the mentally afflicted or deficient—to treat them as patients and not merely as prisoners—and in a number of areas their work led to reforms of the manner in which such patients were institutionalized and treated. Not surprisingly, young Edward followed in their footsteps and devoted his energies to furthering their efforts.

Yet as we neared the end of the nineteenth century, the reputation of physicians and reformers such as the Maybricks had improved only marginally. Although the public by-and-large thought of the asylums as places of treatment rather than of incarceration and punishment, London citizens still weren't keen on accepting those who were treated and then released—one result being that the number of inhabitants in these places was fast approaching one hundred thousand. I can still recall the passion of Edward's sentiments on these matters the last time we spoke.

"If only the public could get behind us and demand more forward-thinking methods for treating our patients. I can't believe how many years it took my grandfather to convince the government that mechanical restraint and isolation were unnecessary for the largest number of men and women in the asylums. Fortunately, he and my father were able to introduce into the county asylums a regimen of leisure activities as well as work-related ones. I have argued more times than I care to remember for the benefits of cards, dominoes, music, and literature—and even the occasional outing—as far outweighing the efficacy of manacles and the straightjackets. It is true that for the past forty years we have been able to educate the medical profession to see insanity as an illness and not simply as a criminal condition, but I hear far too often that we are still 'Mad Doctors' standing on the edges of the profession. It infuriates me that far too many physicians finish their educations with little or no comprehension of how to understand and treat mental illness."

I arrived at the asylum and immediately joined my friend Maybrick for a mid-day meal.

"Julian, I'm so glad you have accepted my invitation to come out. It's been well over a month since I've seen you."

"Excuse my neglect, Edward. I've been attempting to increase my list of patients."

"I hope you've had at least some success doing so."

"Some, but not enough to satisfy. Still, I have just begun with a young woman who I believe will challenge my fledgling abilities. I fear I'll be writing my friend Freud every other day for advice."

Maybrick frowned and returned his forkful of food to his plate. I guessed that he had changed his mind about encouraging me to learn all I could from the Viennese analyst.

"Julian, this young woman. May I ask her name?" He was clearly disturbed. Could he possibly know Miss Westenra?

"Forgive me, Edward, but that is information I shouldn't reveal."

"Not her full name. Please just tell me her Christian name."

I debated whether to share even that, but he now seemed almost in distress. Why, I could not possibly guess. "Very well, it's Lucy."

"I see." Maybrick swept his fingers on the surface of the table.

"Why do you ask, Edward?"

He raised his eyes to meet mine. "I will explain in due course, Julian. But for now, let's enjoy our meal and talk about the thankless lives we have chosen for ourselves."

I couldn't fathom what he was getting at; yet he seemed to regain his stride. "Julian, I suppose you have read the critical article in the *Times* regarding the cure rates in our asylums."

"I have, though I regret having done so."

"I'm sick of having to remind them that the cure rates are low because we don't get to these poor souls early enough to do as much good as we might. Because of the proliferation of those needing care, we have continued to open new asylums but the odds of hiring attendants who are well trained, conscientious, and humane decrease with the need for so many of them. You yourself have seen the effects of the worst of them."

Indeed, I had. Evidence of neglect and brutality included the utter filth some patients had to sleep in, bodies marked by scars, bruised and discolored skin, and broken fingers and toes—all the result of impatient and at times brutal attendants.

Maybrick continued as he was wont to do whenever he was frustrated by evidence of regress in this area. "The asylums, especially the public ones, are burgeoning with so many of the insane and the deeply disturbed that they have become not a place of cure but rather a repository for the incurable—those who our government believes require only watching and not treatment. So many medical superintendents have now become financial officers and managers—concerned about balanced books and profits. As I've told you, the mark of a successful asylum has become equated to the fewest suicides at the institution. Attendants are taught to spot the tricks of the suicidal and to check for knives, rope, shreds of fabric, and broken glass. Prevention of suicide marks also the success of the attendants, the attending physicians, and the superintendents.

We next discussed the recent return to more restraint and sequestration, which my friend Charles Yates applauded so vigorously. Maybrick shook his head. "The desire to shackle with a jacket, wrist bands, leather sleeves, and handcuffs—too often placed on the patient roughly and too tightly—is no less than it has ever been, regardless of the efforts men like my grandfather and father to enlighten the public and the government on the ill effects of restraint. Yet in more recent years we have what many have laughingly called 'an alternative' to restrain in a new reliance on administering drugs. One damned cynical assessment I read was that if a medical superintendent administers morphia or opium for most types of madness, he can proudly announce to the world that he has very few instances of patients being restrained or isolated. In order to assure quiet in the large wards during the night, the inhabitants are given opium, bromide of potassium, and chloral hydrate—even cannabis. Yes, one can see evidence that these drugs lessen excitement and depression, but really, Julian, what is the difference between shackles and drugs? They both seek to control the body, leaving the mind to its misery."

I said that I understood his indignation and agreed wholeheartedly with his views. "I can only hope that through analysis, we can save some of these men and women from such wretched fates." I hastened to add that it was fortunate such asylums such as Maybrick's in East Putney did exist, which were still committed to employing the most humane and imaginative methods.

It was at this moment that Edward's face again sank in an attitude of despair. I assumed he would now tell me why he reacted earlier to the mention of my treating Lucy Westenra.

"Julian, I haven't been honest with you."

"What do you mean, Edward?" I poured him a second glass of sherry. I had barely touched my first.

"I asked you to come and see me so that we might inform each other of our recent work."

"There is no need to apologize for voicing your disappointments over the lack of progress in the treatment of the mentally ill, Edward. I learn much from you even when you release your frustrations, believe me."

"No, Julian, I am not speaking of that. My real reason for asking you to come was to see one of our female patients here."

I smiled with relief. "Edward, I am happy to do so, if you think I can be of some use."

"I don't know that you can. But she has asked for you."

"For one like me, you mean?"

"No. For you specifically. She mentioned you by name."

"Does she know me?"

"I don't see how she can. She came to us only two weeks ago, after you were last here."

"Where was she before coming to you?"

"Kept in her family's home in Holywell."

"Near Liverpool, you mean?"

"Yes."

"I might have met her years ago—or in Paris, perhaps?"

"Julian, after she asked for you, she cried out and became violent, warning that you shouldn't see 'that young lady.' When I asked which young lady, she opened her mouth and started rocking her head forward and back, attempting to articulate something. Her muscles strained to speak but when she did her voice was barely audible."

"Dear God, what did she say?"

Maybrick took his time responding, as though he feared having to answer. "Julian, she said, 'No. No. No.' and ended by whispering 'Lucy.'"

CHAPTER 11

In spite of his antipathy for restraint and isolation, Edward Maybrick's private asylum did employ both when all other methods were unable to prevent the inmates from harming others or themselves. The woman I was to see had to be isolated in a cell with padded walls and that when she became violent she had to be secured in a straightjacket.

As we walked to where she was housed, I asked why she had been sent to East Putney from her home in Holywell, even though she had been under the family's care for some time.

"Initially, she had become traumatized after witnessing her husband's horrible death last autumn. It happened while they were traveling to Budapest and Constantinople following their marriage. Her husband was an official in the Liverpool city government and was sent to negotiate contracts between his and the other two cities. Since he was accompanied by his young bride, he received permission to disembark from the ship in the Mediterranean and spend a week in Milan. From there they were to take an overland route to Budapest and then southeast to Bucharest and finally to Constantinople. But somewhere between Budapest and Bucharest, they separated from their traveling party and lost their way. That's where her husband was killed in a most gruesome fashion, which tragically his wife witnessed. The account of those who came upon the scene was that he had been set upon by wolves, which all but tore his neck from his shoulders. The wife was found huddled nearby by members of their party and eventually sent back to England from the port of Varna on the Black Sea."

We hesitated before opening the door to the section of the asylum containing the solitary rooms. Maybrick insisted on telling me the full story before seeing the woman. "When she returned to Holywell, she refused to talk about her husband's death—in fact, she barely spoke and insisted on remaining inside the house. And so she lived for almost a full year until she was brought here." I asked Edward how old she was. "She is only twenty-four, although . . ."

"What is it?"

"You shall see."

Again, my friend was refusing to answer plainly. "I take it that her behavior altered, forcing her family to bring her here."

"Yes. Some two weeks ago, she engaged for the first time in violent demonstrations—breaking glass objects and ripping at her clothing and at the fabric throughout the house. She also began to speak in a profane and violent manner. She insisted that she had to come to London."

I had seen several poor souls in other asylums who behaved similarly, but I can't remember being as affected as I was by the account of this young woman. "Did she say why she felt it necessary to come here?"

"No, she only repeated that she had to come—and that she had to help."

"To *be* helped, you mean?"

"No, *to help*. She said nothing more specific than that. After three days of being unable to calm her, the family made inquiries. A physician in Holywell recommended me and this asylum to care for her, and she was immediately brought down."

"Has her behavior remained as difficult to control since she arrived?"

"It has become worse. Much worse. The night she arrived, she broke a window and before anyone could stop her, she dragged a jagged edge of glass under her ear. Fortunately, the wound was high and forward enough to spare the carotid, but after she was restrained and the wound sutured, she worked one hand free and tore at the stitches, reopening the gash. I had no choice but to restrain her more fully and place her in our one padded room. I greatly feared for her life."

"And that was some ten days ago?"

"Yes. Julian, her speech has been marked by incoherence, her thoughts flowing so rapidly that she would begin a sentence speaking of one topic and then finish that sentence speaking of another. She begged me not to let her go insane as she tore at her clothing and broke the small table and chair situated near her bed. She was in a constant state of irritability, and after a week of struggling against her restraints and railing against her isolation, she suddenly calmed and once more behaved as she did for those many months living at home after the death of her husband."

"But then?"

"Yesterday morning she once more erupted in a violent fit and demanded to be set free so that she could assist."

"Assist? Whom?"

"She gave no name until early last evening, when calmly she asked to see 'Dr. Hemmings' and then late at night mentioned the name of 'Lucy.' I had no choice but to send you a note early this morning."

"It was good that you did, Edward." Yet I had no reason to say such a thing because I couldn't guarantee that I could be of any assistance to her. I had seen much of this behavior in a number of the asylums I visited, such as Bethlehem Lunatic Hospital, St. Luke's, Munster House, Camberwell, and Hoxton House. Still, my knowing the tragic history of this poor young woman made all of her outbursts and cries more personal to me. Realizing I didn't know her name, I asked my friend who she was.

"Her name is Amelia Reeves."

"And she is twenty-four, you say?"

"Yes, but again don't expect to see someone appearing to be of that age."

We were now in front of her locked door. I listened and heard only her measured breaths.

"Good. She is in one of her calm states, but don't be surprised to see that change as soon as we enter." Edward softly called to her and opened the door.

The room was padded from the floor to a height of some seven feet, the padding made of stuffed waterproof ticking fastened to wooden frames, which were attached to the four walls. The room was illuminated only by the dim light coming through the one window covered with a wire blind to prevent Amelia from breaking the glass. The sun had begun its downward path on the other side of the building, requiring for adequate visibility the lantern Edward held in his hand. As I stepped inside, I saw near my feet the straightjacket she had been placed in when she was her most violent. I looked at Edward.

"We don't put her in it unless absolutely necessary. Fortunately, she seems composed enough now," he whispered.

Without addressing the hunched figure sitting on the floor against the far wall, I picked up the jacket and noticed that there were several incomprehensible words drawn on it with what looked like particles of dried food. I strained to identify the words as Maybrick made the introduction.

"Amelia, this is Dr. Hemmings, whom you wished to speak with. He has come especially to see you."

"Amelia." I acknowledged her the only way I could. I would say no more until she responded.

She said nothing but continued breathing deeply. Edward called to her again. Raising her head slightly as she remained seated on the floor, she pushed her back against the padded corner of two walls. She started to hum what sounded like a lullaby and finally spoke.

"Dr. Maybrick, I should like to speak with Dr. Hemmings alone."

"Amelia, I don't think that would—"

I cut him off. "No, no, Edward. That will be fine. Please."

He paused for a moment before nodding his head. "I'll be at the end of the hall if you need me. Here." He handed me the lantern and left.

I gently placed the straightjacket on the floor and turned to her. "Amelia, I have come to see you. I would like to help you if I can." I saw there was no table or chair in the room. I wasn't sure whether to remain standing or to take a place on the floor near her.

"Have you come to help me?" Her reply was almost bemused.

"If I can."

"You cannot help me—only yourself."

She kept her head down as she answered, although I could barely make out, because she was in the darkest part of the room, a bloodied bandage wrapped around her neck. I imagined it was secured as tightly as possible to prevent her from ripping at her wound.

"I would at least like to try. We want you to recover and live a happy life, Amelia. Please allow us to offer our assistance."

"Living is nothing I care for."

My heart ached for this young woman so unhinged by the violent death of her husband. I thought of other suicidal patients I had learned of and even observed—those who attempted to destroy themselves by setting their beds on fire while they lay in them or slashing their throats with scissors and panes of glass. Several had attempted to hang themselves, mainly with torn pieces of bed linen or clothing. One woman even tried to gouge out her own eyes, while shouting of her own damnation because God had abandoned her.

"Amelia, did you wish to kill yourself by cutting your throat with that piece of glass."

"I didn't cut low or deep enough to do that, Dr. Hemmings." She followed that comment with a muted giggle. It struck me that perhaps she really wasn't trying to end her life, but only to punish herself for some as yet unknown cause. Did she in any way hold herself responsible for her husband's death?

"Then you merely wanted to inflict pain on yourself?"

"You see through the obvious, Dr. Hemmings. I am so glad you are that kind of thinker. It is important that you do see through what is intended to lead you astray. You *must* see through all that, Dr. Hemmings." She paused as if she wished for me fully to absorb all she had said. Her eyes expanded as she continued. "You provide an interesting challenge, you see, and . . ."

Suddenly she winced as though in considerable pain and rose to her feet. As she rushed towards me, I put up my hands in self-defense and was about to call out for Edward, but she stopped her progress some two feet before me. The raising of my hands elevated the lantern, and for the first time I saw her features plainly.

I was aghast at her appearance. Now I understood Edward's remark about her age. Her hair was not that of a twenty-four-year-old woman. It had been cut short—likely as a way to prevent her from tearing it out or otherwise hurting herself. But the remaining hair had splotches of white all over her head, as if part of her follicles believed they were three times her age. Her hands were a mass of bruises and cuts—all self-inflicted I had no doubt, given Edward's devotion to humane treatment of everyone at the asylum. Her trimmed fingernails were cracked, as if she were a woman in her seventies or eighties.

But what horrified me most was her face. Other than the bloodied bandage wrapped high on her neck, the skin around her jaw and mouth looked as though it had been pulled away from her bones and then allowed to sag back into place. Amelia was generally emaciated, but the looseness of that skin wasn't the result of lost weight. It seemed as though something had grabbed at that skin and refused to let go. I wondered if that was the result of the wolf attack that took her husband's life, but there were no puncture marks or ripped flesh on that part of her face.

Her lips were dry and cracked, except for a reddened section of her bottom lip. I had seen that before in patients who gnawed at part of their lower lip and caused it to bleed. Her cheekbones were hollow and her forehead scraped. The cheeks themselves were hideously disfigured by lines of broken skin, not properly healed. Before her nails were cut, she must have dragged them across her cheeks until she drew blood. Or she had used a nail or a small sliver of glass to dig into the flesh.

As she stood before me, I sought some part of her face I could focus my attention on. I found it in her eyes. Although the brow area was bruised and scratched, her eyes were clear and deep blue. Once more I saw something reminiscent in this part of her face. I had only begun to search my memory to see if her eyes reminded me of the prostitute I painted when I was fourteen or of the young woman who died on my operating table when Amelia dropped to the floor. I thought she had swooned, but when I knelt down to assist her, I found that she had merely reached for the straightjacket on which were written the incomprehensible words.

While we were both on her knees, she leaned towards me and whispered, "I have done this with a broken piece of a pencil to make him think I can make no sense with my words. Here—take this paper." She handed me a half sheet folded over twice.

"What is this, Amelia?"

"You can see through things and will know what I am telling you."

"Can't you tell me what you want me to know?" I whispered also.

"I have told you—it is there, on that paper."

"Can I show this to Dr. Maybrick?"

Suddenly she threw herself against me, knocking me backwards. Lying on top of me, her whisper was full of malice. "No! You cannot show this to anyone. It is for you. Only for you!" Her breathing intensified, as her voice calmed. "I have been forbidden, can't you see? This way he will not know what I have done. He cannot know. She . . . she . . ."

"You mean Lucy?"

"Lucy!" In an enraged whisper, she had spoken the name with a horrifying expulsion of breath—a violent hiss.

"What about Lucy, Amelia?"

She opened her mouth as widely as she could and moaned. "No, no, no. Lucy. . . Lucy . . . Lucy." Amelia grabbed her throat and started to pull at her bandage.

"Please, Amelia!" I grabbed her hand. She wrapped her thin and damaged fingers around my wrist. I winced at the pressure she applied.

"I could have killed myself if I wanted. I thought that if he saw that I tired, he would . . . he . . ." Her torso arched and she fell backwards off my still prone body. I quickly jumped to my feet and tried to help her up, but she started writhing on the floor and screaming a series of profane ejaculations as her arms continued to rip at the bandage, which she finally tore free. Her fingers turned inward and she began clawing at the wound under her ear.

I stood unable to speak, staring at the blood that began to seep from her unhealed wound. I heard Edward call for the attendants. In a moment the men rushed into the room and began restraining the wretched woman.

CHAPTER 12

As soon as I entered the hansom cab after parting from Maybrick, I pulled the folded note from my pocket. I was disappointed when I read what Amelia had written. A series of four short phrases, one under the other, ran down the half sheet of paper. Unlike the nonsense words I detected on her embroidered straight jacket, these words were all decipherable on their own but made little sense together as a phrase. For instance, with pencil she had printed "bare waif omen" and "anemia brew of." Still, I decided that I would attempt some kind of explication of these phrases while I traveled back to my office.

Without question, Amelia may have considered herself little more than a "bare waif" in her present condition—and perhaps she was trying to say that she had seen an omen right before her husband's death. But then she had wished to warn me—so was the omen something I should have seen coming from her—or from Lucy Westenra? But Lucy certainly didn't present herself as a waif. The second phrase didn't lend itself as easily to interpretation. Although "anemia" could of course suggest Amelia's physical condition, was she also trying to tell me that she had ingested something from what she might, in her disturbed condition, call a witch's brew?

The third phrase, "a baron wife me," might relate to her husband, but Maybrick hadn't said he was a lower member of the peerage or that he had come from that stock. Was this an aspiration of Amelia's before she married her husband—to be married to a member of the peerage? I next considered why she wrote in such stunted syntax. Also, did the first three phrases relate to each other? Surely they must have done so in her mind. Might they be connected to form a sentence of some kind?

On the final line was the mere two-word description "bowman faerie"— "fairy" spelled in the old style. Once more the possibilities were multiple. Was she called a fairy's child or some similar endearment by her father, who would be the "bowman," a man who could trace his ancestry back to one of the archers who fought at Agincourt, Shrewsbury, Hastings, or some other important battle? Or was her father merely proficient with the bow, perhaps having taught his daughter to shoot? Again, I tried to ponder these phrases as they might also relate to Lucy Westenra. I would ask her today if there were bowmen in her family and whether she was ever called a "fairy's child" or a "waif." Perhaps Lucy had been proposed to by a baron or another member of the lower nobility. Yet the knottiest question remained: how could Amelia know about Lucy—about her background and her having come to my office for treatment? I accepted that I would have to study these phrases more carefully—and perhaps return to the East Putney asylum to speak once more with Amelia.

When I arrived at my office, I was unable to dismiss thoughts of Amelia's odd phrases and concentrate totally on my scheduled patient—a thirty-six-year-old woman suffering depression following the birth of her fifth child—nine years after the arrival of her fourth. Throughout this century, many women in her mental condition had been sent to the asylums for treatment—most leaving after a relatively short period of time. Others didn't leave at all. And still others, as Maybrick informed me, left in coffins after committing suicide. After being introduced to her by another physician, I convinced Mrs. Haney to see me three times a week. I believe we had made progress, although today I failed to serve her as well as I should have. When she stood to say goodbye, I apologized and refused payment for the session.

I shouldn't have expected to have done better, given my experience with Amelia, the odd phrases she penned, and Lucy's impending visit late this afternoon. But I also knew that Joseph Styles would soon also arrive—and I had become more concerned about his behavior as I thought further about his difficulties. In addition, I was still most curious about the way he stared at me yesterday when I returned to my office after purchasing the Chelsea bun from Bracy's cart.

"Mrs. Haney seemed disappointed, Julian." Yates stepped inside the office.

"We touched on matters upsetting to her." I never liked misleading Charles or keeping from him what I had learned from my few patients. It was a dynamic of communication neither of us was used to. Previously, I shared with him every thought I had about a surgical procedure or medical diagnosis. But because privacy was important to those I treated and because Charles wasn't supportive of my new medical ambitions, we at first had a silent agreement to speak as little of my work as possible—even though lately he had been much more open in his disagreements with me on particular treatments and on the state of "lunacy studies," as he called them.

"Styles will be arriving shortly—if he in fact arrives at all—and then you are to see Miss Westenra. Therefore, if it is all right with you, I will leave the office while Styles is here and have a bite of something and return when Miss Westenra and Miss Murray make their appearance."

He would likely have a pint of ale in addition to his bite to eat, but I never begrudged him that. Still, I found it striking and somewhat amusing that a man who constantly warned me that Joseph Styles should be put away, would willingly leave me alone in the man's company.

Half an hour after Charles left, Styles made his way into my office—again through the back door.

"I am six minutes early, Dr. Hemmings."

"You are, Joseph."

"Are you proud of me?"

"Indeed I am."

"I wouldn't want you to be angry at me, so I made sure I wasn't late."

"That was very good of you, Joseph."

Evidently pleased, his face flushed with modesty. I fully expected him to solicit further praise, but he said nothing and just stood before me.

"Joseph, please remove your coat and sit down."

He lowered his head, again in a gesture of shyness.

"Joseph, did you hear what I said?"

He raised his head and now wore the same expression he had when he stared at me from across the way. Although we had known each other less than a week, I had already become accustomed to his sudden shifts of mood, but this one left me particularly ill at ease.

"Joseph, why did you watch me from across the street yesterday afternoon?"

"I don't remember that."

"You don't?"

"If I did, it was because I wanted to see."

"Wanted to see what?"

"What you were thinking."

"Joseph, don't be silly. One cannot *see* what another is thinking."

He remained rigid in the center of the room. "Oh, it is possible to do so if you are looking for another."

"Another what, Joseph?"

He closed his eyes and dropped his head forward. "I have answered you as completely as I can, Dr. Hemmings. I'm sorry I can't do more than that."

I suppressed my frustration with him. "All right, let's remove your coat and sit you down on the sofa." I slid off his worn coat, took his hat, and led him to the sofa. As soon as he sat, his demeanor changed once again.

"You are very kind to me, Dr. Hemmings. You listen, and no one has ever done that before. It is always I who must do the listening."

I felt gratified by his remark. Freud had told me how often his patients thanked him for remaining quiet while they talked.

"I have a freedom to speak everything to you, Dr. Hemmings."

"That is what I want, Joseph."

"Yet you don't want me to act on all I say." He now sounded offended. I resolved to be patient with any subsequent shifts of mood and tone. I needed to know which responses came from deep within, which were affectations, and which were evidence of wicked longings. My Viennese friend had spoken of composite figures in dreams, and I wondered if Styles was manifesting such composites in his indiscriminate remarks to me.

"Dr. Hemmings, I do forgive you. Therefore, it is only right that you forgive me as well for all I have done or am soon to do." His eyes implored me to respond as he wanted.

"Joseph, it is not my place to forgive. I am here to listen and to help. Tell me whatever you wish. Think nothing of right and wrong. Just speak as honestly as you can."

"Can I speak of sin?"

"Joseph, I am not your confessor. Think not of what is sinful. Just speak freely."

"But I cannot remember the chronology of what I have dreamed, what has truly happened, and what I have done."

I again recalled Freud's insistence that the patient shouldn't be encouraged to speak in any logical patterns. "That is unimportant, Joseph. Just begin with what is first in your mind."

He once more dropped his eyes to the floor and took a labored breath. "Then she is the one I must kill because I will dream of her tonight, and the dream will not leave me in peace until it is done."

"Joseph, if you do dream of her tonight, we will talk about your dream and I will do my best to explain it to you."

He stood as though we had come to the end of our time. "We have nothing more to speak of today, for as I told you earlier I cannot remember dreaming last night."

"Let me make certain I understand. So you didn't dream of killing the woman you have just mentioned?"

"No. Dr. Hemmings, why do I have to murder only the pretty ones?"

"Why do you think, Joseph?"

"I don't know. Can't you tell me?"

"I want you to answer that question, Joseph."

"I just want to love the pretty ones, but I cannot. I want to feel their cheeks pressed against mine, but I can only do so after their deaths. Why is that, Dr. Hemmings? What have I done to be burdened with this responsibility? Who am I to have been given such a responsibility?"

"We will come to these answers Joseph. It just takes time."

"I've almost spent all my time. I can't purchase any more."

Freud had treated a number of patients suffering from vivid hallucinations of disgusting and fearful objects such as dead rats and writhing snakes. I would write him soon to ask if he has treated anyone who truly believed he had murdered women. But I knew what Freud would advise — that I must trace Joseph's relationship with the female sex and whether Styles had traumatic sexual experiences in boyhood or since that have led to these fantasies of murdering young and attractive women. I held firm to the view that they were figments of Joseph's disturbed mind. As I told him, members of the police and the Yard had assured me that there had lately been no reports of young women having turned up murdered.

When I was in Vienna, I attended Freud's lecture to the local School for Psychiatry and Neurology, which focused on the "Etiology of Hysteria." Present were many who were quite knowledgeable about the more disturbing aspects of human sexuality. I recall that Herr von Krafft-Ebing was in attendance—the author of a major study on the subject, which I read soon after this event. His book challenged much of what I had assumed about the topic, and although I disagreed with much of it, many of his conclusions forced me to think more seriously about sexual fantasies and perversions. Freud and I discussed the book at length, and I sided with my mentor when he disagreed with Krafft-Ebing, who had called a "scientific fairy tale" Freud's view that the root of these problems and perversions must be traced back to childhood. Freud suggested in his lecture that in sexual abuse by a parent—most often by the father—and nursemaids, governesses, teachers, and servants, one would uncover the root of these obsessional sexual neuroses. He said that a "sexual scare" or a sexual pleasure in children often led to devastating "self-reproach."

I felt a twinge of guilt commiserating with Freud and supporting his view, for I couldn't accept that *all* neuroses stemmed from the sexual experience and abuse of children. And Freud did conclude after much further thought that he was wrong to generalize about the subject the way he had. But he did say that much truth is buried in fairy tales—an obvious rejoinder to Krafft-Ebing's harsh dismissal in the spring of 1896.

Regardless, as I looked at Joseph Styles, I knew I had to delve as far back into his childhood as possible to find some cause for his insistence that he has killed and would kill young women.

"Very well, Joseph. I will see you at our next scheduled appointment." I saw the panicked look on his face. "*Or* the day after you've had your dream."

He smiled in gratitude and began to go out the back way, as he had come in. He stopped and turned to me, this time wearing a confused expression.

"Dr. Hemmings, how can I take the one I am to kill and hide her as I have done the others? I fear it will be quite impossible to do so."

CHAPTER 13

"Mr. Yates, you amuse me with your fanciful story of New York."

Charles was as convivial as I had seen him in months. "There is nothing fanciful about it, Miss Westenra. The man appeared every morning at the entrance of Washington Square and handed out love poems to pretty young ladies."

Lucy seemed as though she hadn't a care in her life. "And he was one hundred years old?"

"He was. Or he said he was." Charles was quite pleased he had delighted her so.

Lucy playfully pointed a finger at Yates. "Oh, he might only have looked that old. I can see him plainly. A mere three wisps of gray hair barely visible on his dented head. His face gnarled and twisted like the bark of some ancient tree." She placed her hand in front of her mouth, likely wishing to suppress as much of her laugh as possible.

"He once asked to show me tombstones." Charles made no effort to hide his mouth, as he was grinning ear to ear, the way an older man invariably does in familiar conversation with a beautiful young woman.

Mina, who had been shaking her head at Lucy's giggling, finally spoke. She had said little since arriving. "I've had older relatives who behaved the same way as your hundred-year-old gentleman in New York, Mr. Yates. I think they wished to frighten the young by talking of ghosts and showing us the graves of forgotten souls."

"Do you think the old man was afraid of dying, Mr. Yates?" Lucy proposed the question seriously.

"Well, I don't really know. Perhaps he feared it until he reached the ripe old age of eighty and then thought, 'I guess I'm not going to die after all, so why worry?'" Charles laughed, but Lucy gave him not even a complementary smile.

"But you have seen many die, have you not, Mr. Yates?" Although she addressed the words to Charles, her eyes stared into mine.

"Alas, I have." Charles also looked at me for assistance, but Lucy continued.

"They were alive when you began to assist Dr. Hemmings with his surgeries, weren't they?" She kept her eyes on me. I wanted Mina to interrupt her friend, but she remained silent. Charles had no choice but to respond.

"Yes, they were. Miss Westenra, if you will excuse me, I need to—"

"But they died, didn't they, Mr. Yates?"

"Some, yes. Now I think I need to get back to my duties in the outer room." Charles was visibly disappointed by the turn the conversation had taken. Before he could step away, Lucy asked him one final question, again while looking at me.

"Mr. Yates, did they catch your eyes before you gave them anesthesia?"

Charles groped for a reply. Lucy stepped toward him. I felt palpable relief that she was no longer looking at me.

"When I was a girl, I was told that the Angel of Death would someday sound his trumpet for me. When your patients died on the table, did you hear trumpets, Mr. Yates?"

Mina sighed as might a mother after her child has been too rambunctious at play. "Lucy, I think we should let Mr. Yates get back to his duties and allow you and Dr. Hemmings to speak alone."

"Very well, Mina. I know you prefer the piano to trumpets." Lucy's smile seemed almost malevolent. I recalled my recurring dream. Did Mina play the keyboard?

"Once more, if you will excuse me." Charles returned to his desk—in far less of a cheery mood than when he left it a few minutes earlier.

"Dr. Hemmings?"

"Yes, Lucy?"

"Promise me that you will share with Mina all the dreams I tell you about."

Mina shook her head. "No Lucy, there is no need for Dr. Hemmings to share them with me. They are your dreams."

"It is good you know what is mine and what is yours, Mina. But I wish you to hear of my dreams." Lucy's face reminded me of a petulant child's. "Promise me you will share them, Dr. Hemmings—or I will tell you nothing of any of my dreams."

I looked to Mina, who reluctantly nodded her head. "Very well, Lucy. I shall do so."

"It is beginning to rain and I am tired now." She whispered something I could not quite make out. It was a two-syllable word—evidently not in English. Perhaps Russian or eastern European.

I sensed that it would be fruitless at present to ask her what she had whispered. She would likely tell me soon enough. Mina excused herself and joined Charles and her great-uncle in the other room. Lucy turned her back to me and stood before the sofa. I was struck by the pronounced wavy pattern of her black hair. It almost commanded one to reach out and fondle it.

"Lucy, please sit. I would like you to speak about your childhood."

She sat and leaned back on the sofa. She made no attempt to position herself demurely.

"My childhood?"

"Yes."

"Some days I remember all of it. On other days, only bits and pieces."

"Please tell me the first memory of childhood that comes to you."

"A photograph."

"A photograph of . . . ?"

"Of my family—when I was three years of age."

"All right. How many were in the photograph?"

"My mother and father wanted it taken. I did not." Her head was slightly thrown back. She seemed as far away as she could possibly be.

"A photograph of the three of you, then."

"No. There were four of us in the photograph."

"I see. Who was the other member of your family?"

"My brother."

I remembered that Mina had mentioned him. "Of course. Did your bother wish to have his photograph taken?"

"If he could have spoken, I am sure he would have been on my side and wouldn't want us to sit for it. He was older than I—by two years—but he would have done whatever I wanted."

"He was five years old, then?" She nodded mechanically. "Was his speech delayed? Or was he born without it, or had he lost the ability?" She lowered her head and stared at me, her face wrenched by a painful memory.

"He was dead, Dr. Hemmings."

I felt both embarrassed by and regretful for my ignorance. Her parents had apparently requested a *memento-mori* photograph of the family. It wasn't uncommon, especially close to twenty years ago, when the Westenras had theirs taken. With the high cost of photography then, often a family's only formal sitting would be in a post-mortem setting, with a dead child or parent posed with the living members. When I was twelve, I was approached to paint such a *memento-mori* portrait including the body of a boy about my age. I was horrified at the possibility that my father would arrange for me to do it, but he refused the offer in my name.

I asked Lucy if she was in fact speaking of such a photograph. She again nodded lifelessly. I thought the subject worth pursuing, regardless of the pain she was evidently feeling. Freud taught me that the analyst must require patients to confront painful as well as sorrowful events from their pasts.

"Lucy, do you have that photograph now?"

"It is buried with my mother. But my brother is not with her. I tore out his likeness from the photograph before they took my mother away for burial."

"Do you still have that section of the photograph?"

Even though she didn't answer me, the care disappeared from her face. She sighed contentedly. "I was a lively child, Dr. Hemmings. Unlike Mina, who read book after book, I acted my own books—never written down but thought completely through in my imagination."

"Did you have many friends?"

"I don't think I had any until I met Mina when we were both eleven years of age. And I wasn't sure I wanted her as a friend at first. She had talents I didn't possess. She read literature that bored me, and she played the piano with great skill—whereas I couldn't bear to look at a keyboard lacking vivid colors and to play the same exercises thousands of others practice every day. But when I found that I could be what I was and that, while she would scold me from time to time, she never wanted me to be anything other than I was, I took her to my heart and we have been the closest friends ever since. She never minded when I told her I wished to be alone on my walks or in my room." Her face again dropped. "But now she doesn't wish me to be alone— and I don't like it."

I knew I should have let her speak more on this matter, but I wasn't comfortable facing the likelihood that she would begin criticizing Mina. I feared I would come to Mina's defense and spoil the relationship I needed to nurture with Lucy.

"Tell me more about your childhood imaginings, Lucy."

"I should like you to tell me, Dr. Hemmings, why I don't remember the moment when my childhood imaginings became my womanly imaginings."

"Do you think they are all that different, Lucy?"

"I don't. It's just that when we become women, we make substitutions in the objects we desire, but the longings have been there all along."

"Did anyone interfere with your childhood imaginings, Lucy?"

"No. I wouldn't let anyone do that. And no one has interfered with my womanly ones either." The last remark disconcerted me, given the alteration of Lucy's voice.

"Did you have aspirations as a young girl?"

"Of course—every girl does. Only most girls aspire to what they can never have. My aspirations were destined to be realized. I always believed that."

Her use of the past tense surprised me. I assumed that she would be confident enough—or pose herself as confident enough—to claim that she *would* get what she wanted. Yet she spoke as if recalling a goal already accomplished.

"But I assumed that I would always feel like Peaseblossom in the court of Titania."

"You mean one of the fairies in Shakespeare's *Midsummer Night's Dream*?"

Her pale yet beautiful face sagged wearily. "Yes, but I never expected to have my wings pulled off so violently."

I had not opportunity to interpret her comment, because I recalled one of the phrases given to me by the tortured Amelia Reeves: "bowman faerie." I couldn't resist asking Lucy, "When you were a child, did you have pet names given to you by anyone—by your mother or by Mina, for example?"

She pursed her lips and narrowed her expression, evidently insulted that I seemed to be ignoring her last statement about the fairy's wings. "I had many of them. From 'queen' to 'waif'—from 'Diana' to 'Medusa.'" She noticed that I had dropped my eyes and turned my head slightly to the left—the way I always did when I was attempting to recall something or to make a deduction after hearing the evidence. "Dr. Hemmings? Dr. Hemmings?"

I thought of Amelia's "bare waif omen" and I knew that Diana—or her Greek counterpart Artemis—was strongly associated with the bow. I was astounded, even if my rational faculties encouraged me to see all this as mere coincidence.

"Dr. Hemmings, I am very happy that I have given you so much to think about." She left the sofa and came to me, making it impossible for me to rise from my chair.

She shook her head gently. "I hope for your sake that you can sleep tonight." She sighed and looked toward the window. "I know I will not."

CHAPTER 14

After Charles left for home, I remained at my desk recording thoughts about today's sessions with Joseph Styles and Lucy Westenra. I wasn't happy. I had no time for any conversation with Mina before or after I met privately with her friend. In fact, it seemed as if Mina was anxious to *avoid* speaking with me. After a few moments, I shook free from my childish pique and reminded myself that Charles had dominated the conversation with his New York stories when Mina and Lucy had arrived and that both she and Lucy wished to return to the home of her great-uncle before it was completely dark. Still, Mina merely wished me a polite good night as they were leaving the office.

I chased away my self-pity, but ludicrous vanity rushed in to take its place. I fancifully imagined that Mina was feeling about me the way I was about her—and her reticence to engage me in any familiar conversation was evidence of her modesty and perhaps concern over her growing fondness for me. In any event, I knew I had entered that level of affection for a woman where every expression, gesture, and omission carried significance, regardless of the truth behind any of them. Such silliness on my part, even at age thirty-three. I laughed to help cast off these lovelorn thoughts, but the next image that came to mind erased all amusement. I visualized myself painting a portrait of Mina. When I decided to paint the face of Yvette Auger, I had purchased two canvases in case I was dissatisfied with a first attempt. I never discarded my paints or the second canvas, which now rested with the portraits of Yvette and of the young prostitute on Greenfield Street. Had I somehow believed that I would someday paint a third portrait—but this one of a woman I truly loved?

I rose from my desk and walked to the rear door. I opened it and stepped out into the cool night. I remained there for less than a minute, but it was enough to restore my senses. After all, I had my work and studies, and Mina likely had several men seeking her hand. I returned to my desk and jotted down several thoughts about Lucy.

I believe that the source Miss Westenra's condition may be found within a reasonable amount of time. Miss Westenra is evidently a young woman of cultivation and talents. At heart, likely given to charity. Vivacious, though at times stubborn. Cannot discount her cleverness. She seems in part physically strong and vibrant, but at the same time seems inevitably weakening. Full examination not yet taken, given patient's reaction to instruments. Body is uniformly warm. Admits to regular menstruation. Active vanity, yet protectively modest about one side of her face and neck and about her mouth. Considerable intelligence. Likely frequent daydreaming. Escaping into her own personal theatre. Perhaps a recent sexual encounter has stimulated memory of a childhood sexual experience. Hysteria may be the manifestation of this conflict.

I recalled On one of the last walks Freud and I took in Vienna before he left the city for his summer holiday, he told me of a woman who had been developing a series of incapacitating symptoms and ailments. Mental lapses, rapid shifts in her moods, even hallucinations about dead rats, skulls, and snakes. "She was susceptible to self-induced hypnotic states," he added. "The tales she chose to share were often sad and at times horrific."

I asked if she was eventually cured.

"All was finally traced to her father's fatal illness," Freud said. "She was a devoted daughter and his impending death gave rise to all of her physical distress and mental delusions."

I asked him if that would include the woman's morbid tales.

"Yes, my friend Hemmings, even those."

"How was she cured?"

"Through talking. The 'talking cure,' as the woman herself termed it. She described it to me as 'chimney sweeping.' I employed hypnosis, but it was through talking that she shed each of her symptoms. It was often difficult, but it was done. Again, all her symptoms were the result of her suppressing her fears and feelings concerning her father. Don't you see, Hemmings? The whole process is a vigorous struggle with the patient's resistances. We cannot win every struggle, but we will lose every one of them if we make no effort."

Could it be that the source of Lucy Westenra's difficulties lay in her relationship with her father, of whom she had not spoken, except to say that he was one of the four in the *memento mori* photograph? Lucy had mentioned her mother's death and burial, but nothing about the fate of her father.

I set down my pen and locked my notebook in the desk drawer. I made sure the back door was secure, and switched off the gas light. I went to the outer office, checked to see if everything was in its place, and was about to turn the tap to extinguish the two gas lights in that room when someone knocked. My immediate assumption was that it had to be Joseph Styles. I opened the front door and felt the blood rush from my face.

"Sir? It is you, is it not?"

Here at my office door was the young woman I had last night sought in the fog on Regent Street. I was too taken aback to respond graciously, although I felt a shudder of relief that she was alive and apparently unharmed. "Well, yes. And it is you, I see."

"May I step inside, sir?" I saw that no one was with her. I looked about, understanding that it wasn't done to invite an un-chaperoned woman inside, especially at night—and especially a woman who received money for sexual favors, as I assumed she did.

"Very well, but hurry in."

She was bundled up as if it were two months later on the calendar. As she appeared to me on Regent Street, she was without a bonnet, but she wore a man's scarf wound twice around her neck and a pair of threadbare woolen gloves. Her hair had begun to come undone from whatever configuration in which it was originally placed. I had from time to time heard others use the term "mousy" to describe women of this kind—and in this instance it could have been used again, although she had such a sweet face that had she been fortunate enough to be born into another class she might have been deemed a beauty.

I saw no reason to be impatient with her because I was happy she had escaped harm from the man standing across Regent Street. "I see you are in good health." I knew not what else to say.

"I am, sir. And I am glad you seem the same. I was worried about you."

"About me?"

The question disturbed her. "Yes, because . . . well, you see that I was concerned that in the fog the man might have robbed and attacked you." I decided not to tell her that the man had turned and began following her and that I had sought her in the fog.

"How did you know where to find me?"

Her eyes dropped and she clasped her hands in front of her. "I was told, sir."

"You asked about me?"

"No, sir."

She then lifted her uneven skirt several inches, trying to shake some mud from the hem. I looked down and saw that the laces of her shoes were of two different colors—one set black and the other brown.

"Then how could you have been told about me?"

She unclasped her hands and began tapping her fists together in a gesture I have never seen before in a woman. "I must go, sir."

I was perplexed by her behavior. "Have I said something to alarm or offend you?"

"No, sir. But I must go."

"Did you come to ask me something or to tell me something?" She shook her head from side to side. "Ah, I see." I reached in my pocket and pulled out two shillings, which I attempted to place in her hand.

"I can't. I can't." Her eyes were wet and her nose began to run as though she had been suffering from a winter ailment. The change came over her in an instant, for when she stepped inside the office there was no indication that she was suffering from any illness or discomfort. She spun about abruptly and reached for the door. Before I could open it for her, she turned to me, revealing a face particularly forlorn.

"I am afraid for you, sir." She opened the door and with her hands covering her ears, she quickly disappeared around the side of the building. I ran into my darkened office and stumbled against the wall as I rounded the corner to find the back door. I unlocked it and dashed outside to speak with her, but by the time I did, I could see nothing but a thick mist covering the entire area to the rear of my office. I made my way back to the front office, turned off the gas lights and went out the door. The night was crystal clear with the stars clearly visible. I walked to the side and rear of the building, and once more I was taken aback. There was not the slightest evidence of any mist where I had only less than two minutes ago seen it.

. . . . . .

After I supped, I went to my rooms and pulled down one of my volumes of Shakespeare. Freud noted in his last letter that he wanted me to read *Hamlet* with an analyst's eye. He wrote that he was shaping a new theory, "masterfully illustrated" by Shakespeare's tragedy. He would explain what he meant after I read the play, and he seemed enthusiastic about exchanging letters with me on the topic. He ended with his usual mordant wit—"and please don't tell me that I could find a better correspondent with whom to exchange ideas on the play. Shakespeare is England's author, after all, and I have no other literate English friends, so it has to be you." Part of Freud's humor was directed at my insistence during all of our conversations in Vienna and in all my correspondence since then that I didn't consider myself knowledgeable enough about the human mind to speak intelligently to such a distinguished thinker, author, and analyst. He charged me always with "false modesty," but there was nothing at all false about it.

I looked out my window for any evidence of mist or fog. There was none. The night was still perfectly clear—one of the most beautiful nights of this autumn season. I poured myself a brandy and began reading *Hamlet*. I found meaning in the first line of the play, "Who's there?" Is that not what I was trying to determine in my treatment of patients such as Joseph Styles and Lucy Westenra? Did Freud think this as well? Below all the deception, manipulation, and emotional upheavals, who exactly is there?

I perhaps felt more than I should have when I read in the first scene such lines as "I am sick at heart," "It harrows me with fear and wonder," and "You tremble and look pale"—the last two lines reflecting the characters' reaction to the ghost of Hamlet's father. But the first of these three—"I am sick at heart"—affected me the most. For the first time in my adult life I felt the effects of unrequited affections. How long had Mina Murray been in my presence? It couldn't have been much more than a few hours. And yet I felt I knew her always. How could that be? A boy's longing at this stage of my adult life? Was it possible that over the years I had been shaping unconsciously a woman who would free me from the memory of two other young women who so changed my life? I pushed aside the volume of Shakespeare upon the realization that in the past two days there were in reality four new young women in my life, each of whom had an impact on me. Lucy Westenra, of course—but also the tormented Amelia Reeves and the young woman I first saw on Regent Street. But Mina was the one foremost in my mind. 'Yes, it is you, my darling Mina," I pronounced to no one there.

I opened the large wardrobe across from my bed. On the floor in the back was a large and sealed portfolio case. Inside were several of my best boyhood sketches and the paintings of the prostitute whom I saw at fourteen and the young woman who seventeen years later died on the operating table after having kissed me—and one empty canvas. I took the portfolio to the large desk, which once belonged to my father, on which I had been reading the opening of *Hamlet*. I began to unwind the thick string that latched the portfolio. I was driven to do so by an overwhelming yet inexplicable sense that I would see Mina's face in both portraits. I had completely unwound the string when I thought I heard a soft feminine voice whisper "No." The voice didn't come from within me—I was certain of it. I looked about and saw nothing. I went back into the bedroom. Still nothing. I returned to the desk and wound back the string. I hadn't looked at either portrait since I painted them, and I would not look at them now.

CHAPTER 15

The following day I remained perplexed by the events of the previous night. Did I actually hear a female voice? Had the voice sounded exactly like Mina's, I would gladly accept that I had manufactured it. But it was a voice I believed I had never heard before, yet somehow I couldn't help thinking it was reminiscent of a voice I did know.

Without any appointments for the entire morning, I resolved to write Mina. I did so for two reasons—first to sustain my relationship with her, especially if there was no time for us to speak when she accompanied Lucy; and second to release some of my pent-up feelings through a form of appropriate communication.

I began the letter with general assurances about my commitment to seeing that Lucy would improve and would after a time be cured. I then turned my attention to Mina.

I hope you are made comfortable while you are waiting in the outer office. If there is anything you would like while you wait—whether it be a special tea, something to eat, or a book or periodical—please let me know.

I was now at the place where I would state my regret at not having more time to chat with her, but I was reluctant to say so directly. Regardless, I couldn't let the letter end without making an attempt to express that view.

I so enjoyed our conversations when you came by yourself to speak about Lucy. I believe we hold enough in common to justify another chat.

I re-read the passage three times to be sure it was appropriate to send. I smiled, for now I recalled that Mina had shown a genuine interest in my work.

And there is much more I would like to share with you about the work I do and what I have learned from Sigmund Freud.

Now I felt emboldened to be more specific.

The one consolation of having so few patients is that I have time for such pleasurable talks as I noted above. Therefore should you wish it, I would most enjoy meeting you and your great-uncle or aunt here in my office or wherever you would prefer so that we may converse about these matters.

I wrote my closing and looked over the letter twice more. It was stilted prose to be sure, but I hadn't the liberty to make it more satisfying. Would I have the courage to send it? Other men would deliver it themselves and wait patiently for an answer, but I wasn't that way. After all, I really had no experience in the game of courtship. I called for Charles.

"Yes, Julian?"

"Charles, has The Dasher been in this hour?"

The Dasher was a twelve-year-old boy, whose real name was William something, but he favored the name "The Dasher" given the speed with which he delivered messages and letters throughout the West End. We were part of his circuit, and he would come by every hour or two to deliver or to take for delivery all forms of brief messages, letters, and books. He was a lad with a seemingly inexhaustible supply of stamina. And in addition to his value as messenger, I had taken a strong liking to the boy.

"He should be arriving soon, Julian."

"When he does, send him back here. Oh, Charles—how many will I see this afternoon?"

"Only two—unless Joseph Styles bursts in unannounced."

"And Miss Westenra is scheduled for late this afternoon?"

"Yes, as you requested. Tell me—how often do you plan to see her each week?"

"Four or five times I would think."

"You only see your other ones two or three times a week."

"They are all milder cases, Charles. Freud sees the more troubled ones six times a week."

"Seems excessive. I'll send in The Dasher as soon as he arrives."

Less than ten minutes later, the lad stepped into my office holding a book I had asked him to pick up for me and a letter sent this morning by Edward Maybrick. The Dasher therefore had a hand free to guide a large piece of spice-cake into his eager mouth.

"Well, Dasher, are you getting ready for the ice, wind, and snow of the coming winter?" I had to wait several moments before he was able to chew and swallow the spice-cake.

"I like it better in winter, Dr. Hemmings. Less citizens to push my way through."

I laughed at his ruddy and exuberant face, pock marked with crumbs from the spice-cake. "Very good, Dasher."

"Sir, can I ask a question of you?"

"Go ahead, my boy. What is it?"

"Yesterday afternoon, when it was getting dark, I was making a delivery across the street from here and I saw two young women and an old gentlemen squeeze into a hansom cab in front of your building. But before they got in, one of the young ladies saw me across the street and stared at me. Not like she knew me, but like she wasn't happy I was looking at her. The other young lady pulled her toward the cab and they got in. But when they came past the place where I was standing that first young lady stared at me looking out from the cab and turned her head as they passed so she could keep looking at me. I thought I had done something to her, but I don't see how I could have. She frightened me, Dr. Hemmings."

I put my hand on the lad's shoulder. "Dasher, I wouldn't be concerned about it. She was upset when she left here," I lied. "She was probably just reacting to her difficulties without thinking of frightening you."

He smiled and was apparently satisfied that Lucy meant him no harm. Still, I thought it best not to ask him to deliver the letter to Mina, because he might well come face to face with Lucy. I said that I just wanted him to come back to my office for a chat about his winter plans.

"Oh, I will do as I always do, don't you fear, sir."

"Dasher, that's what I hoped to hear. All right, I won't keep you, but just remember that the lady who stared at you is having troubles in her life and is really very nice to know."

He seemed embarrassed. "Well, she was very pretty, and I liked the dark blue dress she wore. Now I have to go. I'll be back next hour if you have anything for me."

I placed my hand on the back of the desk chair to steady myself. Yesterday, the color of Lucy's dress was mauve.

.   .   .   .   .

I spent the next several minutes pacing in my office, constructing several contrary explanations for the scene The Dasher had depicted. I simply refused to believe that Mina would have looked so harshly at the boy. If anything, she would have only smiled warmly at him. Might Dasher simply have been confused about the color of Lucy's dress? After all, he saw both the blue and the mauve. If it truly was Mina who looked at him, might his sight not be keen enough at that distance, even at such a youthful age, to tell the difference between a smile and a frown? Again if it was Mina, might she have been suddenly saddened by a thought or a memory and was reflecting her feelings in an expression not really directed at the boy? Yes, that had to be it. I stopped my pacing and sat at my desk chair. I looked at my letter to Mina. Perhaps my assurances about Lucy would comfort her. I resolved to hand her the letter when she arrived with Lucy later this afternoon.

I opened the correspondence from Edward Maybrick. I feared he was informing me that Amelia Reeves had taken her life during the night.

Julian, I am writing you this morning about Amelia Reeves. During the night she erupted in a violent fit that forced me to come from my home to the asylum. She had been demanding to speak with me and wouldn't accept that I would see her in the morning. She spoke the most profane language and threatened to do physical harm to the most sacred part of her anatomy if I didn't come. The attendants managed to subdue her with the jacket. They told me that she continued to writhe on the floor until I arrived. When I did, she stopped her movements and the shouting of her vile epithets.

I felt safe enough to kneel in front of her. She stared into my eyes for several moments and then spoke to me in a voice I wasn't prepared for. I will try to be as accurate as my memory allows. She sounded as though she were on her death bed, attempting to communicate one last time with her loved ones. "Dr. Maybrick, you must find out if Dr. Hemmings has translated what I gave him." Julian, she would not tell me what she meant by that. I can only hope you understand her meaning. She then said, "I fear he has found out what I have done and will punish me for it." Can you make any sense of this? What might you have found out, Julian? Why would she think you would punish her for something? She begged me to go to you to see if you have "translated" what she has given you. She added that it was very important to you. "His life depends upon it," she whimpered and then closed her eyes and fell asleep.

Amelia slept through the night, and as I am writing this at eight in the morning, she remains asleep. She is breathing normally, but if she has another violent incident when she wakes, I fear her heart won't last through the day. I now send this along with other correspondence to my brother's shop in the Strand, and he will give it to your messenger boy.

I took Amelia's note from my desk drawer and read over the four phrases once again: "anemia brew of," "a baron wife me," "bare waif omen," and "bowman faerie." I had already considered possible meanings of each phrase and discovered possible connections to Lucy, but I had not yet attempted to read them as part of a full sentence. Commencing a rearrangement of the words into a coherent statement of some kind, I halted when I looked at "bare waif omen." I thought of the young woman on Regent Street, who had come here to my office the previous evening. Much about her reminded me of a waif, and her head was without a bonnet and therefore "bare." She *had* warned me of the man on Regent Street, and her odd behavior when she came to my office was also consistent with someone wishing to warn me: "I am afraid for you, sir." Was she too warning me about Lucy? Did Amelia tell me in her own code that this "waif" of a woman was coming to so warn me? I folded the note and returned it to my desk. I wasn't in the right frame of mind to study it further. For the first time I compared my current state to that of only a few days ago, before Mina came to see me about Lucy. So much had happened that was beyond my power to alter or to understand.

CHAPTER 16

"I will prepare some tea and see to Mr. Taltson." Charles excused himself, leaving me alone with Lucy, who had arrived half an hour late. Mina had not accompanied her, and I was bitterly disappointed.

"Is Mina not feeling well today, Lucy?"

"I have no idea. I've not seen her at all. When I awoke, she wasn't in the bed."

"Did you look for her elsewhere in the house?"

"No."

I was concerned for Mina's safety. "Do you have any idea where she might have gone?"

Lucy gave me an icy look. She was evidently displeased by my interest in the whereabouts of her friend. "She's not gone back to Whitby, if that is what's worrying you, Dr. Hemmings."

I felt appropriately chastised. "I'm sorry. This is your time, Lucy. So tell me—how do you feel in comparison with yesterday?"

She took her place on the sofa, but remained silent until she was certain I would be giving her my full attention. That was impossible, considering my concern about Mina, but I did my best to make it appear so. Finally, she seemed satisfied.

"I am warmer."

"May I touch your forehead?"

"If you wish."

Her forehead was indeed warm and especially moist. But there were no other signs that she was suffering from the common ailments often associated with late autumn. She was still pale, but she wasn't coughing or experiencing chills.

"Have you been eating well, Lucy?"

"What I've needed."

"Have you kept your food down?"

She seemed annoyed by the question. "Yes, Dr. Hemmings."

"Does your head hurt at present?"

"Not where one normally feels pain."

"Then touch the place on your head where you feel the pain."

She now looked at me with impatience. "I cannot reach inside and touch my mind."

"All right, one more question. Are you unusually thirsty?"

Her mood shifted. She smiled and shook her head as if she pitied me. "Such a question, Dr. Hemmings."

I couldn't help thinking that she was enjoying my confusion and discomfort. Yet everything she spoke and every expression she manifested were clues to understanding what was driving her behavior.

"Have you had a disagreement with anyone last night or today? Mina, perhaps?"

"Again, Mina." She closed her eyes and turned her head away from me.

"Mr. or Mrs. Taltson, then?" I was curious to discover how she felt about Mina's great-uncle and aunt.

She reopened her eyes and looked directly into mine. "They are my enemies."

"Why do you think that, Lucy?"

"I overhear what they say, though it isn't difficult. They are old enough to have lost most of their hearing and they must shout to converse with each other."

I suppressed a smile. "Did you and Mr. Taltson have a conversation on the way here this afternoon?"

"He never speaks to me—only to Mina. But I spoke to him."

"About?"

"About why he forces the three of us to crowd into a hansom cab. I told him if he cannot secure a carriage, then we should come here in two hansom cabs—Mina and I in one and he in another. He always turns sideways so we may all fit, and always his backside is toward me. I dislike being near such an old fellow in any event."

"Coming over today without Mina must have been especially difficult for you, then." I made the statement with a smile and an inflection to suggest that whereas I sympathized with her plight, it was in truth a rather humorous situation. She didn't find it amusing, however.

With an extended sigh reflecting inevitability, she changed the subject. "The night comes sooner each day."

"Yes. We are now in the fall season." She reacted as though she had experienced a jolt of pain. "Lucy, are you in any discomfort?"

"Yes."

"Will you tell me where?" I was never able to forget that I was a physician and had several times advised and examined my few patients when they had medical complaints.

"No, I will not."

"Very well." I waited until she seemed more comfortable. "Did you dream last night, Lucy?"

"I do not wish to speak about my dreams."

"But Lucy, we already agreed what you would tell me of them. You even instructed me to share them with Mina. Do you remember?"

"Yes."

"Then why won't you share your dreams with me?"

"My fears prevent me."

"What do you fear, Lucy?"

"I fear I will betray."

"Whom would you betray?"

"I fear for myself."

"Why do you fear for yourself?" I'm sure she sensed the increased level of concern in my voice.

"And I fear for you, Dr. Hemmings." Now it was three young women who feared for me.

"For me?"

Lucy quickly sat up on the sofa and leaned toward me, raising her chin to stare deeply into my eyes. "For you!"

The sound of her voice was deeply menacing, as if every ounce of violence and hatred within her had been expressed in those two simple words. Not having sat, I took three involuntary steps backwards as she expelled her exclamation. What could she mean? She was afraid for both herself and me. Could this erotically beautiful young woman be fearful that she might harm herself and the man trying to help her discover the source of her problems? Freud advised that I take nothing said to me personally—even if it demonstrated insensitivity and ingratitude. But it was difficult to do so at this moment. Lucy now seemed to be part of the triumvirate of disturbed women who were concerned for my safety. I could easily imagine that Lucy would end up in an asylum--like Amelia Reeves—but I couldn't let that happen. As I contemplated the scornful look on her face, I tried to think of a way to delve more deeply into this side of Lucy without pushing her to a more violent and contemptuous reaction. But I was spared by her latest change of demeanor. She sat back into the sofa and threw back her head, looking at the ceiling. After several moments she lowered her head and offered me the most pleasant smile I had yet seen from her. Yet it was done with her mouth completely closed, and I saw that her hand was ready to cover her mouth. I was tempted to ask if she had a bad tooth she didn't wish for me to see.

"I am happy to tell you more about my childhood, Dr. Hemmings. It was a happy time. You will be pleased to know that you have brought from me a memory of my father I did not have before. I remember that he did come back home once. He did. Four years after he left home--when I was a girl of eight."

I took my notebook and sat in my chair. "Do you recall the reason why he returned?"

"Perhaps he had forgotten something."

"Perhaps he did, Lucy. But do you have any memory of speaking with him then—the night he came back?"

"No. I don't remember that night."

"No? But you just told me that—"

"I don't wish to . . . I don't remember." I was too busy writing to notice that she had been staring out the window. "It's getting dark."

I was most anxious to learn more of her relationship with her father. "Lucy, you don't remember? Or is it that you don't wish to remember?"

"Someone else."

"Someone else?" My voice betrayed my eagerness. "That night? Someone else came with your father?"

"Someone else." Her eyes had an opiate glaze to them. She was apparently lost in her recollection.

"You said that you were eight years old when your father left. Then you would be twelve when he came back that one night."

"Did he come back for my birthday?"

"Perhaps he did. You also said that there was someone else. Can you recall who it—"

"When I was twelve, my grandmother thought I was fourteen. Strangers thought I was fourteen."

I fully realized how important it was to sharpen her memory of that time. I was charged with excitement over having uncovered as much as I had in the past few minutes. I couldn't help thinking that Freud would be proud of his disciple. "Lucy . . . Lucy, do you recall if . . . do you recall if . . ." My self-pride vanished at my inability to phrase the next question.

Lucy again shut her eyes. "He . . . comes."

Surely she meant "came." But was she speaking of her father or that someone else? What had happened to her when she was twelve?

"In my dreams."

I responded with the first question that came to me. "Lucy, did you dream when you were a young girl?"

"Always. Sweet dreams." She remained in her trance-like state.

"After your father left, when you were eight, did you still dream?"

"Yes. Sweet dreams."

"And after your father came back. With that . . . When your father came back, did you still dream?"

"I don't know." Her head trembled as if she were waking from a nightmare.

"Can you try to remember, Lucy?" I was afraid I was losing my chance to learn more.

She sighed—again as if she were awakening from a troubled sleep. "Do you dream, Dr. Hemmings?"

"I have . . . at times. But Lucy, my dreams have no meaning here." Frustrated, I knew the moment was gone. Could I recreate it when next she came?

"Oh, but your dreams do have meaning here, Dr. Hemmings. They do. Has Mina told you that before she did not dream?"

I was startled by the mention of Mina's name. I cautiously replied, "But we must only talk of your dreams, Lucy, because—"

"Oh, she dreams now, Dr. Hemmings. Mina will forever live in dreams now."

CHAPTER 17

An hour had passed since Lucy left with Mina's great-uncle. I had recorded my observations in my journal and begun a letter to Freud about Lucy. Charles had just returned to the office and invited me to take a pint with him as soon as I was finished with my work. What I didn't know and what he now told me was that he had gone to the Taltson residence to deliver a recipe from his wife for Christmas plum pudding that Mina had earlier requested. His real reason, of course, was to see if Mina was safe at home. He too was concerned when she didn't arrive with her great-uncle and Lucy, and Lucy wouldn't respond to him when he asked if Mina was well.

"Was Mina there, Charles?"

"The old woman sent word to the door that she wasn't at home. I came right out and asked the servant if she knew where Miss Murray was, but I received no answer"

"Perhaps we are unnecessarily worried, Charles. She has a life to tend to, after all." The calmness of my response hardly reflected my true feelings.

"You may be right. Does she have a fiancé, Julian? If so, she and the young gentleman could be spending the day and evening as an engaged couple might."

"I don't believe she has a fiancé." My jealousy painted blackness into my face at the very idea of her being engaged to anyone but me. An immature thought and reaction, yet no less keenly felt. "Charles, did you leave the recipe?"

"I did. Perhaps she will stop by here tomorrow to thank my wife for it."

I was momentarily soothed by the image of Mina preparing a Christmas pudding. I fancifully conjured a scene right out of Mr. Dickens' *Christmas Carol* with the two of us playing the role of the Cratchits.

"Julian, have you noticed Miss Westenra's habit of leaning her head to the left as she passes by?"

"I have. She might be sensitive about a blemish or scar of some kind." I wondered if that habit and the inclination to hide her teeth suggested a low self-esteem or a desire for perfection that would also be contributing factors to her problems. Freud had spoken to me of noses and aspects of displacement, but I recollect that for him displacement was the shifting from what was unacceptable or dangerous to what was acceptable and safe. Still to me, Lucy's apparent "secrecy" regarding her neck and mouth appeared to be, if anything, shifting from one thing unacceptable and dangerous to yet another. But perhaps I didn't completely understand Freud's meaning of displacement. There was indeed so much more to learn.

Charles offered a patronizing laugh. "I can read your thoughts, Julian. Owing to the influence of your Austrian friend, you have now completely dismissed such a rational medical cause of Miss Westenra's modesty about her neck and have placed some psychology behind it."

My present mood was serene enough not to take offense. Rather, I thought it the right moment to have some fun with my assistant. "You might benefit from a more liberal acceptance of what Freud has been advocating. For instance, what did you tell me you have begun noticing about yourself lately?"

"What do you mean? That I have three times misspelled your last name? Why I left off the second 'm' in 'Hemmings' I can't understand."

"And you have begun to misplace papers and forms."

"So?"

"Freud believes these are all little messages that cry out for decoding. They are all hints about your desires and anxieties, Charles."

"No, Julian. They are empirical evidence of advancing age—and that is all."

"You are only in your forties, Charles."

"And you are a lad still in your early thirties—and you might remind yourself of that, Julian." Our verbal skirmish was doing much to brighten my mood.

"Charles, tell me what you dreamed last night."

"Oh, this is absurd."

"Then you must fear telling me."

"I fear nothing of the kind. My dreams are of the normal variety."

"Are they now?"

Charles was getting red above his collar. "Yes, they are, *Dr. Hemmings—*

with two m's."

"Come now, Charles. You are suppressing a description of your dream out of fear."

"I am, am I? All right. I dreamed I was walking through a large ball room in some home I don't remember ever having been to before. It was, I suppose, in the middle of the night, as I had a lit candle in my hand for illumination. I remember that I dropped the candle—but that the light didn't go out. When I bent down to pick up the candle, I found that it had broken in half."

I responded with my best bit of mock horror. "Oh, don't tell me that, Charles."

"What? What is it?" It was wonderful. Charles was genuinely concerned.

"And you are sure that the candle was broken?" I asked as though I had hoped he had misspoken about the candle.

"Yes, it was broken. What are you trying to tell me?" I shook my head as if I would never tell him. "I ask you again, Julian. What does it mean?"

"Well, if you insist. And you are insisting aren't you?"

"Yes, damn you!" I feared he would strangle me when he learned that I was merely having fun at his expense.

"A sad conclusion, Charles. Were Freud here now, he would tell you that the broken candlestick is always a suggestion of a flaccid . . . well . . . you know. And that your dream denotes a fear of impotence."

"Why that is . . . that is . . ." He was unable to get the next word out.

"Please, Charles, there is no need to explain. But as you said just a moment ago, it may only be empirical evidence of advancing age—and that is all." I burst out laughing like a puckish schoolboy. Then surprise of surprises—Charles found the whole dialogue as amusing as I did.

"Seriously though, Julian, such interpretations of sexual matters have no chance to succeed in any civilized society that refuses to hear them."

I was delighted by his perceptive remark and the sincerity with which he made it. "But such work as Freud's has opened a few ears, Charles. And more will be opened as we discuss more frankly the psychological and as well as biological effects of human sexuality."

"But surely you must see that some have gone far beyond the limits of decency in an attempt to discuss the topic. What is that recent work you have kept off your shelves out of embarrassment and shame at having purchased it?

"More out of prudence than shame, Charles. You are speaking of the book I brought back with me from Vienna. Krafft-Ebing's *Psychopathia Sexualis*."

"A fancy Latin title—merely a thin disguise for a book about sexual perversions." I knew it couldn't last. Charles was back to being his fully cynical self.

"And a popular seller, Charles. Don't forget that. It only proves Freud's point that in general the populace is far less prudish about sexuality than the government and the church insist they be."

"And how old was this Klaus Eberling fellow when he published this book?"

"Krafft-Ebing. In his mid-forties, I believe. About the age you are now, Charles."

He leaned toward me and stuck his finger in my chest. "More empirical evidence of advancing age—and that is all." I laughed heartily along with my friend over his observation. When our laughter died down, we heard another voice chortling in the short hallway leading to the rear door.

Charles gritted his teeth. "Come in here, Styles." I thought my friend was going to take the man by the scruff of the neck and toss him out the door through which he had just come. Styles almost crept into the room. He rubbed his worn hat with both of his hands, as he looked about. I held Charles back from rushing him. Now Styles trained his eyes on me. "She haunts your dreams, Dr. Hemmings."

I feared he would identify Mina as the one about whom he thought I dreamed. "Joseph, I must ask you to leave. Come back at the appointed time."

"It will be best. Then you can sleep and never dream of her again. You wish to kiss her again and bring her back to life. It cannot be. It must not be."

I was horrified. It wasn't Mina he was speaking of but rather the young woman I could not save—Yvette Auger. "My God, Joseph. How could you know about . . . ?"

"I must not say. I fear what may be done to me. But I know." He turned to Charles while pointing at me. "He wants the young woman, who will give *him* life."

I was mortified that he was now clearly speaking of Mina. I could only imagine what Charles was thinking.

I replied quickly before Styles could say any more. "That is enough, Joseph." Charles looked at me for permission to throttle the poor fellow, who was aware of my assistant's foul mood. Styles moved toward the hallway.

"But there is nothing you can do, Dr. Hemmings. Nothing. Your knowledge cannot save you. There is something stronger than what you think you know."

Yates bolted forward and grabbed Styles by the collar.

"Charles, please!"

Terrified, Joseph called out, "Dr. Hemmings, I want to laugh with you. May I laugh with you?"

"Charles, wait."

"Julian, this man must be put in an asylum. See your friend Maybrick tomorrow and get it done." Yates began dragging Styles to the hallway. "Come on, you lunatic. Get out!"

Styles cried out to Charles, "He does not want you to hurt me! If you do, he will hurt you!"

Charles lifted his large hand from the clothing and clenched it around Styles' throat. It was all I could do to pry it free. "Charles, what in God's name are you doing?"

Yates released his grip and Styles sank trembling to the floor.

CHAPTER 18

When I returned to my rooms after sharing two pints with Yates, who admitted shame for having reacted to Styles so violently, I resolved to go out to the asylum in East Putney the next day and speak to Edward Maybrick about housing Joseph. I accepted that for now I couldn't reach Styles merely through talk therapy—at least in my office. I would tell Maybrick that I would come out to East Putney, if he agreed to take Joseph and allow me to continue my sessions there. I still had little concern that Styles would kill anyone, but for the first time I feared he might harm himself. He had curled up on the floor after Charles had released him and sobbed before muttering that he hadn't long to live. It took him a good ten minutes before he was able to rise. He then left without another word. I shortly concluded that he would be much safer under the benevolent care of Edward Maybrick.

But I wished to go out to Maybrick's asylum also to speak further with Amelia Reeves. I had to know more about the phrases she had given me. It was possible she would be in no humor to speak or to speak coherently about what she had written, but I had to encourage her to try. In addition, I would ask more about her life before entering the asylum. Perhaps, like Lucy, she would recall something she would be willing to share.

．　．　．　．　．

The following morning I arrived at my office at half-past eight. The only scheduled appointment I had was at ten with Mrs. Haney, the woman I had ill-served when she recently came about her depression following the recent birth of her child. I would allow her to remain half an hour longer without charge, to make up for my inexcusable inattention previously.

Lucy wasn't scheduled for this day, which meant that I wouldn't see Mina. Perhaps Mina would at least send word to Charles thanking his wife for the recipe. But if it came after noon, Charles wouldn't be here. This morning he informed me that the late hour at which he returned home—after drinking two pints at our favorite pub—had raised his wife's ire. Therefore, he promised to arrive home early from his duties and do what he could to mitigate her anger.

I had already sent a short note to Maybrick by way of The Dasher, informing him that I'd come out to East Putney at 1:00 p.m. to talk about Styles. I hoped as well that Amelia would be more likely to converse with me at that time. She would have slept, been fed, and if she allowed it, bathed. I followed this correspondence with a short letter to Freud announcing that I would soon write him at length about Lucy Westenra. I next pulled open a drawer and took out the letter I had written to Mina. I decided that when I returned I would wait in the office until four and then go to the Taltsons and ask them to deliver my correspondence to her. That way, I would know if she was at home, and I would one way or the other discover if she had returned at all last night. It was possible she had gone someplace other than Whitby with other friends or relatives—perhaps up to Oxford or over to Bristol or down to Brighton. I felt that if I couldn't see her, I at least had to know where she was.

．　．　．　．　．

"Julian, I am very happy to see you again after so short a time." Maybrick smiled and handed me a glass of Colheita Port, which he had brought back with him after spending two weeks with his wife in Portugal and western Spain. "This is a special port from a single harvest. Let me suggest you take it with some cheese. Now this is Cheshire, but is actually from North Wales. It's colored with annatto, which gives it the orange tinge." It seemed incongruous that a man who devoted his hours caring for the mentally ill at an asylum still possessed a keen knowledge and appreciation of life's culinary pleasures.

"Julian, since I received your letter this morning, I have been observing Amelia. She has remained quiet since she awoke and took her bath without protest. I was informed that she said, 'I must look my best today.' I dare not hope for too much, but this seems to me a positive sign. I haven't told her you were coming to see her. I think it best that we go to her room and simply announce your presence."

I wasn't sure we should surprise her in that way, but at least she wouldn't have time to dwell on my coming and react violently against it. Maybrick gestured for me to sit.

"Now as for Joseph Styles, does he have family?"

"I have asked him and he has said nothing about them except that 'they are where they are and I am where I am.' Besides, he added, 'they would have nothing to do with me if I told them I dream of killing young women.'"

"I see." Maybrick surely had dealt with patients making similar or related claims. "Julian, it would be helpful if we could locate a family member, receive permission, and have Styles him committed that way, but until we do, I could house him here—if you think it would benefit him."

"I didn't want to believe that at first, Edward, but I'm afraid I do now." I truly was disappointed and perhaps a bit embarrassed to have given up hope that frequent sessions in my office could at least temper Joseph's imaginative and violent assertions. But again, seeing him wallowing on the floor of my office made me realize he was at a state where he needed to be protected against self-harm. In addition, I had no idea where he spent his nights, and there was always the chance he would share his dreams with others who might have him arrested or who might take it upon themselves to avenge the murders which I was fully confident were only fictions.

"Julian, is there a possibility that you could convince him to come out here with you?"

"I believe I can." I knew it might be difficult to restrain him once he realized where I had brought him, but for his sake I was willing to make the attempt.

Maybrick nodded. "It's settled then. I have a good room available for him if you can bring him out here within the week."

Because the male section of the asylum was usually full, I felt that my decision about Styles was even more justified. Maybrick had one further caution.

"I again ask you to locate any family members, if at all possible. The government will support our taking him without family approval, but it's always best to have it."

"I understand."

Maybrick finished his port, and I followed suit. "All right, Julian, it's time to visit Amelia Reeves."

. . . . .

"Amelia, I have brought a visitor to see you." Maybrick had stepped inside Amelia's room. I waited out of sight upon his suggestion.

"A visitor you call him?" Amelia's voice sounded serene enough for me to be encouraged. I would ask her more about the four phrases, but perhaps I could also glean information about her past and her journey toward Constantinople. For the first time I felt that I might truly be able to help her. But I wasn't expecting her next comment to Maybrick.

"Please tell Dr. Hemmings to come in, Dr. Maybrick." How could she know I had come or was even coming? Even if she could see out her window the view was not of the main gate of the asylum, from which I made my way to the front door. Maybrick's expression as he stepped back out and beckoned me made clear that he was as surprised as I was. I made my way inside the room, without enough time even to shape a smile.

"I knew you would come and see me again, Dr. Hemmings. They have given me a bath." I noticed a wet towel on the ground near her feet. It had the shape of the cloth she wore around her neck when I saw her last. Now she had a dry one around her neck to take its place.

"I am happy to see you once more, Amelia."

She was standing as primly as her ragged and emaciated appearance would allow. Her left hand attempted to brush back from the top of her forehead strands of hair that were no longer there. She reminded me of one who was about to speak with someone, while fearful that others might overhear. Regardless of her weary smile, Amelia's still attractive eyes danced with nervous energy. I was determined to put her as much at ease as I could.

"Edward, may I converse alone with Amelia?" I could see that he wasn't in favor of leaving me with her, knowing how quickly volatile she could become. He looked at the straightjacket propped up against the corner of the room.

"I will be right outside."

"Forgive me, Edward, but might you at least walk down to the end of the hall?" I was certain Amelia would be unwilling to speak freely if she knew he could listen in on our conversation.

"The same as last time then. Very well." He whispered, "I certainly hope you know what you are doing."

Amelia brushed her hands down against her smock. "And could you close the door Dr. Maybrick?"

"I don't think that would be a good idea, Amelia."

"Please Edward," I interjected. "It will be all right." Now it was my turn to whisper. "It will be unlocked." Maybrick was enough satisfied to agree. He turned and left the room, shutting the door gently.

"Have you eaten today, Amelia?"

"Some. But I have come to see little sense in it."

"But you must eat to get stronger." I regretted not bringing two chairs. Amelia was leaning slightly against the padded wall, but I stood erect in the center of the room. I feared my legs would give out on me.

"Food will not help me, Dr. Hemmings."

I looked into her eyes, which seemed to be pleading with me. I had to give her some hope, some assurance. "I will help you, Amelia. I only need for you to speak honestly with me."

She averted my gaze and leaned her head further back against the wall. I thought of Lucy reclining on my office sofa.

"Will you speak openly to me, Amelia?"

"Dr. Hemmings, have you understood?"

"Understood?" I wasn't sure what she meant.

"Have you understood?" She asked this time with an intensity that startled me. Her eyes bore into mine. "Have you?"

I knew now that she was referring to the four phrases and that she wasn't going to mention them specifically—likely out of a fear that Maybrick would overhear and chastise her for writing them. "I understand what you mean, Amelia. But I have not understood what those—"

"Shhhhhhhh." She sustained the sound until her breath no longer supported her voice.

I stepped closer and began to lean toward her left ear so I could whisper something to her. She bolted from her place against the wall and collapsed on the mattress where she slept. She covered her ears with her hands.

I tried to calm her so that our conversation could progress. "Amelia, I am sorry to have upset you. I won't mention . . . . that again."

She took her hands from her ears and sat up on the mattress. She looked about the room, apparently listening for something. She began to cry.

"Amelia, what is wrong?" I reached for my handkerchief, which she took and pressed to her eyes.

"Please Dr. Hemmings, try and understand. Try again. Try again."

"I will. I will." I knew it was futile to ask her directly what she meant by those four phrases. I would have to study them without any assistance from her. Of course, they may well have meant nothing at all as they pertained to me, but I couldn't afford to ignore them if I wanted to discover the person underneath her shattered exterior. "Amelia, can I ask if you remember your childhood?" There it was. Our conversation would either proceed or terminate on that question.

She looked at me quizzically, rubbed her fingers across her cracked lips, and wrinkled her nose the way a small child might when asked to recite her full name. "Yes, I remember it."

I sat on the ground next to her mattress, which was also flush against the floor. "What are some of the things you remember?" Once more I had Freud's advice in mind. "Just allow the patient to talk and meander as he or she sees fit."

"I remember summer stars; and riding alone through a nearby orchard; and blowing the feathers from dandelions."

I was both delighted and considerably surprised she mentioned three such pleasant images. I fully expected her to recall things more sad and dreadful. But the mention of stars, orchards, and dandelions only made her present state more tragic. "Did you have playmates?" I wanted to keep the recollections happy ones for the time being.

"I had no sisters to play with. My brothers never wanted to play with me. I wished to please them but couldn't."

I was disappointed that I so quickly brought depressing thoughts to her mind. "You said you loved to ride alone through the orchard. What kind of a horse did you have as a girl?"

She ignored the question. "I married thinking it would please my brothers. My father died three months before I was born. My brothers were my father. Then Mr. Reeves my husband became my brothers."

That quickly she had taken her story to the horrid moment when Reeves was attacked by the wolves between Budapest and Bucharest. How could I ask about that day? Was it even wise to allow her to speak of it? At any moment she could become hysterical and dangerous to me and to herself. But I couldn't turn back now.

"Amelia, do you trust me?"

"I want to help you."

Was she simply quoting what I had said to her? "Do you trust me,

Amelia?"

"I want to help you."

I needed to move forward without getting that assurance from her. "Amelia, were you happy when—"

"Yes. When I married Mr. Reeves I felt I had done what was expected of me. He was pleased. My brothers were pleased. I was no longer their responsibility."

She had already given me much to ponder, but I couldn't suppress my desire to take her further—to the event that had so unhinged her. As Freud emphasized, the analyst must make a reasoned decision at moments like this. Was the risk worth taking? Might the information best be gleaned with more patience? Or could a confrontation with that which was deemed too forbidden or too traumatic lead to a beneficial psychological breakthrough?

"Amelia, I know that you must miss your husband. What you saw was dreadful, I know."

"What I continue to see." I paused, fearful her motionless response would immediately give way to an unrestrained one. But her face remained dispassionate.

"I thank God you were not hurt by the wolves." I tried to imagine how she and her husband had separated from the traveling party.

"He wouldn't let them hurt me. He would care for me, he said."

I found her words, as calmly as she uttered them, rather odd in that Reeves would hardly have added that he would care for his wife while confronting several wolves. Even so, I felt most fortunate to have taken Amelia, without incident, this far in recalling that horrid day.

"He would care for me, he said." Upon the reiteration of her remark, it struck me that she wasn't talking about her husband at all. She was referring to God. I had just mentioned God before she said "he wouldn't let them hurt me." Therefore, she was likely speaking rationally—remembering the prayers and religious lessons of her youth. Could she still have faith in the Almighty and could that faith be an aid to pulling her free from the memories that tormented her?

"Yes, Amelia. God cared for you and would not let the wolves harm you."

"God? What had God to do with that day?" I sensed a rising indignation in her voice. I knew it could momentarily lead to a full emotional outburst.

"You are right, Amelia. I apologize for saying that. Perhaps we can talk about—"

"Are you here to speak to me about God, Dr. Hemmings?" I had never heard her speak with such an incredulous tone. I was losing her.

"No, I am here to speak about you, Amelia."

"He laughed when the wolves tore my husband apart. My husband was not right for me, he said. I would be his for eternity. For eternity!" She returned to speaking irrationally. But I saw no point in assuring her that God did not laugh at her tragedy or utter anything that suggested such perverse possessiveness of her. Amelia's voice had risen to the point that I could hear Maybrick starting down the hallway. "And he has left me like this!" She paused for only a moment before speaking again—her voice further rising in both volume and speed. "But he will come soon and take me—but it will not be in love as he had promised!"

Amelia threw herself at me and clutched my throat with her marred and bony hand. I couldn't believe there was so much strength in such a frail woman. Unable to cry for help, I grabbed her wrist but couldn't budge her hand from my throat. I thought I would die at her hand. The door flew open, and Maybrick and an attendant pulled her fingers apart. I rushed from the room while they restrained her. As I staggered down the hallway I heard her screaming, "No, no! You must understand! Dr. Hemmings, you must understand!"

CHAPTER 19

When I returned to the city, I walked for over an hour to relieve my stress and then attempted to eat something—but my stomach wouldn't permit it. Instead I took a small glass of brandy as soon as I returned to the office. I remained seated in the outer area, trying to steady myself before I went to my desk and studied the four phrases Amelia had given me. I had just finished a second glass of brandy when I heard the front door open. It was exactly 4:00 p.m.

"Have I come at a bad time?"

I immediately stood. "Mina, I am so very glad to see you." My worry over her whereabouts and surprise over her appearance altered my normal demeanor.

"Are you all right, Dr. Hemmings?"

I was more emotional about seeing her than I should have been, but I had an explanation that while truthful only partially explained my uncharacteristic expression. "I had a difficult experience earlier this afternoon at an asylum in East Putney."

Mina's face registered concern. "With a patient there?"

"Yes, a poor miserable young woman who had witnessed the death of her new husband. He was—"

"Please don't tell me. I'm afraid I'm particularly squeamish when it comes to stories of real violence."

How like Mina to sense the horrible truth of the man's death. I had not said it was violent, but Mina could see that by my manner and the fact that the young wife was traumatized.

She appeared most uncomfortable, and I regretted informing her about Amelia Reeves.

"Mina, now I'm the one who must ask if *you* are all right."

"Forgive me, Dr. Hemmings. I am far too sensitive to such things, I fear."

"No, you are exactly as you should be, dear Mina."

She looked at me with gentle surprise. I waited to see disapproval cross her lovely face, because I had unwittingly called her "dear Mina." What would she think of me for daring to say it? I awaited her verdict.

"Please tell me that you missed my presence yesterday when Lucy and my great-uncle came."

Perhaps she didn't hear me say "dear Mina." I only hoped that she did, because if so, what she just asked me was undeniable proof that she had some affection for me. My heart accelerated. I could no longer doubt I was deeply in love with her, regardless of how briefly we had known each other.

"Of course I missed seeing you yesterday. Just as I missed not being able to speak with you when you were last here." It finally occurred to me that her great-uncle had not yet entered my office. I looked out the front window and saw him standing between the steps and the hansom cab down at the street. Mina must have asked him to remain there. She evidently wanted to see me alone. "Mina, please wait here a moment." I went to my desk and retrieved the letter I had written her. When I returned to the outer office, she was nervously pacing. I knew she felt it was time to return to the cab. "Before you go, please take this. As coincidence would have it, I had planned to leave at this very hour and deliver it to the Taltson residence. Please read it with sympathy and understanding. I smiled to suggest that I was being self-effacing, but she seemed disheartened as she took it.

"I sincerely hope this doesn't say that you think I should no longer accompany Lucy. Have I made you upset with me by coming alone today?"

I barely contained myself from stepping toward her and taking her hand. "Nothing could be further from the truth. This letter asks if you might find it possible to have some conversations just with me—in the company of your great-aunt and uncle of course."

Mina appeared genuinely relieved, which flattered me. But as before, her demeanor soon shifted to something more serious.

"You will want to know why I didn't come yesterday—and why I spoke little to you the time before that."

Could it be that she was deciding between me and one of her suitors? Had I won the contest for her heart? Had I lost? Or was the question still unsettled?

She continued. "I didn't wish to speak to you until now. I have begun to dream vividly—of things I have never imagined before. I want to share those dreams with you and have you explain them to me. May I? I will pay you, never fear. I cannot talk to anyone about this but you."

I was flabbergasted--and sorely disappointed. And I felt completely foolish. I wished to wrench the letter free from her hands and tear it apart. She didn't want attention and affection from me, but rather professional treatment. I looked into her eyes to seek something more than that, but I couldn't see anything past the forming tears and the apprehension her eyes reflected. I couldn't deny her request, regardless of the sudden dissolution of all my romantic assumptions and hopes.

"Mina, I will listen and do all I can to assist you. When would you like to meet?" I could see she was casting glances at the door, very much concerned, no doubt, that her great-uncle would come up the steps to get her.

"I can return in an hour if you are free then."

"Yes, yes, I will be free."

"At five then?"

"Yes, at five."

She looked at me for a moment and then extended her gloved hand. I took it and kissed it as gently as I could. All my confusions and frustrations of the last several hours disappeared with the exquisite feeling of Mina's gloved hand against my lips.

She smiled and left the office with my letter in her other hand. Rather than watch her join her great-uncle, I lifted the hand that touched hers and smelled her still lingering fragrance.

· · · · · · ·

The Dasher came by soon after Mina left, and I sent him for some sweet treats to offer Taltson when he arrived with Mina. I would make tea and provide the old gentleman with reading materials to keep him occupied while Mina and I were conversing in my office. I also wished to share a few words with the elderly man. So far he had merely nodded when Mina first introduced us. I could see he regarded me with suspicion, which I understood. I could only imagine how dismayed he and his wife were over Lucy Westenra's difficulties and likely outbursts during the night. But if he saw me as a hope toward ending Lucy's distress, I might be able to win him over.

Upon his return with the treats, The Dasher appeared dismayed.

"What is it, my boy?"

"Can't say for sure, Dr. Hemmings, but it's the strangest sunset I can ever remember."

"What do you mean?"

"It seems darker than usual at this time of day. It was fifteen minutes until five.

"Day are getting shorter as we head into late fall, Dasher. You know that."

"No, Dr. Hemmings, that's not what I mean. There seems to be a mist blocking the light that usually comes up from the top of the setting sun, and the streets are darker at this time than they were yesterday."

Again I tried to allay his concern. "It's also that time of year when the fog creeps in upon us."

"I know that too, Dr. Hemmings. But what I mean is that the mist isn't all over the area as you look west. It's just in the spot covering the open street where you can see the sun disappear. The mist is no wider than the street."

Had I not seen evidence of the curious mist when I followed to the rear of my office the young woman I met on Regent Street, I would have rejected what the boy claimed he saw--but I couldn't.

"Just a quirk of the weather, Dasher." I hoped that would satisfy him.

"Not any quirk I've ever seen. Well, is there anything else you'll be needing, Dr. Hemmings?"

"No, Dasher. Here's for your troubles." I placed two coins in his hand and almost pushed him out the door. I didn't want him to see Mina and confirm for me that it was indeed she who gave him such a cold stare the other day.

. . . . .

Mina arrived promptly at five. Her great-uncle came in with her and once more nodded to me. I encouraged him to take one of Bracy's Chelsea buns and some tea, but he shook his head no. He did accept my invitation to peruse one of the books on my shelves, choosing Mrs. Gaskell's novel *Wives and Daughters,* a book the author left unfinished at her death and completed by another. I found it a most unusual choice for man of his advanced years. I had the book in the outer office mainly for wives or daughters who might be waiting for a loved one or a friend I was treating. I couldn't imagine old

Taltson would be interested in a domestic tale about a young woman raised by her widowed father, who then marries and introduces a step-sister into his daughter's life. From what I could glean by my own rapid skimming of the book, the two sisters were quite opposites in levels of sophistication and personalities. I seemed to recall that their lives were touched by scandal and the like—but that was all I could remember.

Mina informed Taltson that she would speak with me for half an hour, and I added that he was free to help himself to tea and the sweet treats should he change his mind. I smiled imagining how quickly he would exchange the Gaskell book for something else more to his liking.

Mina went immediately to the sofa and I to my chair. I didn't bring my notebook. I saw this as a one-time only session. I decided against asking where she had gone if she in fact had left the Taltson residence the day before, because I feared the question would upset her. And that any answer would likely upset me.

"Mina, please tell me what you've been dreaming and what you've been thinking about after you've had those dreams."

"Before I hardly ever dreamed, or rather hardly remembered anything I might have dreamed, but in the past two weeks I have been recalling my dreams—and in the past several days they have become terrifying." She paused and I nodded for her to proceed. "In my dream last night I awakened to find myself alone on the grounds of the house. The dream was so distinct that I can still feel all the sensations. The wind, the mist, the touch. It . . . it was so unlike the one I had in my dream of two nights ago, and yet . . ." Her lips formed a pathetic smile. "But I should tell you about that one first, shouldn't I?"

"There is no need to be chronological. Just tell me about them in any order you like."

"No, I must start with the first one two nights ago. My dream was frightening and yet parts were so beautiful. I was lying face up under a flowing stream, which was sprinkled with flowers petals. My face was only a few inches under the surface. I could feel my arms lift above the water and my hands open for someone to help me. I could feel the water gently moving across my face. It was cold. So very cold. Then I felt someone holding my hands, rubbing them softly. Suddenly I sensed my entire body lifting. The water parted on my face, and I was placed on the grass next to the stream. Parts of the grass were green; other parts were brown. My body was completely dry—except for my lips, which were still wet. I moved my head slowly from side to side so that the water would run off my lips—but they remained wet. I opened my eyes to see who had pulled me from the stream and saw no face but only the back of someone walking away from me."

"A woman?"

"No. It was a man."

Again, Freud had spoken to me at length about the intricacies of dream production but stressed that a dream is a "wish fulfillment" and that the interpreter cannot take the components of a dream literally. Dreams serve to disguise what is in essence a fervent wish of some kind. I would have to think long on what the cold stream, the flower petals, the wet lips, and the man walking away all truly meant. Even Mina's physical activities—the raising of her arms above the water, the opening of her hands, and the lifting of her body—were disguises for something more profound. Yet I felt so unqualified at this moment to articulate what her dream could mean. It might take me weeks or months. I regretted even more that Freud's book on dreams had not already been published.

"All right Mina, now tell me more about your dream of last night." I could think of no other response to her first dream.

She dropped her head into her open hands. "I am so ashamed."

It was all I could do to remain seated in my chair. I wished so very much to sit on the sofa and take her hand. "No, no, Mina. You cannot feel shame."

"You don't understand. I have never felt such shame in all my life. I will not be forgiven."

I dared not imagine what she visualized in her second dream—and I dared not insist that she tell me. I couldn't risk adding to her shame and embarrassment and subsequently placing further distance between us. Trying to have it both ways, I promised confidentiality. "Mina, I swear to you that I will never breathe a word of what you tell me—not to anyone. Remember that it was a dream and nothing you necessarily wished to have occur. We are passive agents when it comes to dreams."

"Surely, you don't believe that, Dr. Hemmings." In truth, I didn't, but I knew not what else to offer except "You can trust me, Mina."

"Then you must promise to suppress your judgment of me if I tell you. I must have that assurance."

"I have no right to judge you, Mina. I want to help you. Telling me your dream will at least lessen the shame."

She turned her eyes from mine. "There was another man. I don't know if he was the same one as in the first dream, but I couldn't help thinking that he was. His face was all too visible to me. There was a deep scar on his forehead." She took a long and painful breath, her torso rising higher than I had ever seen in a woman. "This man held me down. Both my arms were pinned with just his one hand. The other hand grabbed me by the back of my neck. I saw blood on my nightgown. It came from a thin stream of blood that ran down his front. He was pressing my face toward that trickle of blood. It was so real to me. And his mouth . . . No, I cannot."

I was staggered by jealousy and dread. I was unable to devote any part of my mind to a rational interpretation of this dream. I couldn't bear to conclude that she was imagining a romantic tryst with a man she barely knew. I was conscious that I was violating one of Freud's first rules for the analyst—the need to keep an emotional distance from all patients, even if they happen to be friends. Still, I was helpless to interrupt or terminate her account.

"Please, Mina. Continue."

"No!"

I had not expected such a powerful reaction from her. Her voice sounded cruel and almost wild. Her beautiful features were shaded in tones of passion and guilt. I stood and pleaded for her to go on.

"Could you see his face in your dream?"

Her intensity finally abated. The shadows lifted from her face and her voice sank to softness. "His eyes were aflame, and his mouth . . ."

"Mina?"

"It was a dream, was it not, Dr. Hemmings? Only a dream, yes?"

My strength had left me. I fell back into my chair. "Yes, Mina. Only a dream."

"When will you see Lucy again?" Somehow she had regained her composure and sounded exactly as she did the day we first met.

"Tomorrow afternoon."

"Before dawn she began feeling pain here." Mina touched her stomach. "She cried out that his child was coming. Perhaps tomorrow she will tell you that."

"The poor girl. Most likely she was experiencing another frightful dream."

Mina stood and prepared to leave. "She was not asleep, Dr. Hemmings."

"I see. Mina, this is what is called a hysterical pregnancy. It's not unheard of. It is like other puzzling symptoms—painful joints, chills, vocal and muscular spasms, including even severe facial neuralgias."

"Would this include certain odors that others cannot smell?"

Once more Mina comported herself like an eager student. I began to relax. "Yes, yes. Had Lucy smelled something others were not able to?"

"Last night when she was in bed and right before I blew out the candle, she said that she had the most intense sensation of being able to smell something I could not detect."

"What was it she smelled, Mina?"

"Blood."

CHAPTER 20

I remained at the office for an hour after Mina and her great-uncle departed. Mina didn't offer her hand this time, surely for the reason that Taltson was in the room with us. The old gentleman hadn't touched any of the sweet treats I left for him, but he apparently read through a number of pages of *Wives and Daughters*, because the book was left open on a side table. At the top of the left-hand page was a description of the girl Molly Gibson. My curiosity prompted me to read to the end of the paragraph:

. . . but all the girl thought of was how little they wanted her in this grand house; how she must seem like a careless intruder who had no business there. Once or twice she wondered where her father was, and whether he was missing her; but the thought of the familiar happiness of home brought such a choking in her throat, that she felt she must not give way to it, for fear of bursting out crying; and she had instinct enough to feel that, as she was left at the Towers, the less trouble she gave, the more she kept herself out of observation, the better.

I was struck by the similarities between Gaskell's narration and Lucy Westenra's current situation. From my conversations with Mina and Lucy, I concluded that they had been in London since the end of the third week of October, some two weeks now. Had the Taltsons made Lucy feel unwelcome? As a result, had Lucy begun thinking more about her father since coming down from Whitby? Was she only now recalling with regularity that part of her life when she had a "familiar happiness of home"? And would Lucy eventually leave the Taltson home without announcing her intentions, even to Mina? These questions only made me lament not having seen Lucy today.

But the passage from Gaskell's novel also reinforced in me the notion that the more devoted one is to an idea, the more he sees reflections of that idea in so much he observes. Passages in books, unrelated conversations, and a host of incidents all seemingly comment on the object of one's intense thought. With some mortification, I recalled how Mina's every word and expression seemed to remark upon my feelings for her—as if she could possibly know the intensity of my affections. Yet I didn't wish to be evaluating every nuance of this evening's meeting with Mina as they pertained to her feelings for me. Accordingly, I sat at my desk and recorded further observations about Lucy. Although I hadn't met with her today, Mina's comments about Lucy's "pregnancy" allowed me to speculate further about her condition.

It may be that as a girl, perhaps at the age of twelve and perhaps as young as seven or eight, Lucy had a sexual scare—that is, in her pre-sexual period of development. Perhaps it was more than a scare. It might have had something to do with her father or perhaps with a man her father might have brought home with him when he visited after a four-year absence. She might have had a later or a very recent experience of sexual pleasure and that encounter might have stimulated considerable self-reproach, leading to her hysteria. I do not know. It is only what I am thinking of at present.

I reached for two pieces of blank paper and opened my desk to retrieve the four phrases Amelia Reeves demanded that I understand. I wrote down all twelve of the words in "a baron wife me," "bowman's faerie," bare waif omen," and "anemia brew of" and placed them indiscriminately on the page—in the hope that a sentence of some kind might emerge. Since there were no verbs among the twelve words, I despaired of coming up with a coherent thought. I tried combining the words differently to see what that might reflect. I could see in such combinations as "a bowman's omen" and "a bowman's brew" the best chance for a different interpretation, especially when I considered that "bowman" might mean a sailor or boatman in the bow of his ship rather than an archer. "A bowman's omen" then might allude to a sign of disaster at sea. Could Amelia be warning me not to set sail? Did she believe she was given the gift of prophecy— that she was a modern-day Cassandra, as it were? But I had no immediate plans to cross the channel and head for Vienna or sail the Atlantic for a visit to America. Was that all the four phrases were supposed to tell me? It was impossible to believe such was the case.

I next wrote the four phrases the way Amelia had written them. I looked at all four again separately, but my eye kept going back to "bare waif omen." I imagined the "w" in "waif" pushing its way to the front of "omen"—forming the word "women." I then studied "bowman faerie" and saw even more easily that the word "women" could also be culled from the phrase, or rather in the singular form merely from the word "bowman." An initial look at "a baron wife me" and "anemia brew of" suggested that my theory was incorrect, but upon further study I saw that indeed each of the letters for "women" was in these phrases as well. I began to think I had solved the riddle: Amelia was warning me of the dangers of the female. Again, I included her, the young woman I met on Regent Street, and Lucy Westenra. Each of these women could cause me harm in her own way—Lucy might have the power to shake my confidence in my professional beliefs, as well as expose my ignorance or inexperience; Amelia might harm me physically; and the young prostitute on Regent Street might well damage my reputation if she continues to visit me as she did the previous night. And then there were two other women from my past and the continued effect each has had on my life—not to mention my developing love for Mina. Yet I was puzzled as to why Amelia believed she knew me well enough to issue such a warning. Besides, such a warning wasn't at all profound—men have been warned about women since time immemorial.

After tearing up the paper on which I had written Amelia's phrases, I was about to do the same to the paper she gave to me, but I decided against it—at least for now. Placing the list back inside my desk, my eye caught the other piece of blank paper I had reached for. Staring at it for a moment, I picked up a pencil, touching its tip to the paper without knowing what I was about to do. Rushing into my mind was the sound of Mina's voice, telling me of her dreams. I had no desire—or the strength—to resist the thought. Therefore, I closed my eyes so that the memory would seem as palpable as possible. It was as if she was speaking to me from over my shoulder. I didn't even feel my hand move the pencil.

I don't know how long I sat at my desk with pencil in hand, but when Mina's voice went silent in my head, I looked down at the paper before me. On it I had drawn the front of a woman's torso. I hadn't drawn a face to accompany it, but I had added a trickle of blood on the partially opened nightgown.

. . . .

I left the office as soon as I locked the sketch in my desk. Because it depicted the torso of my darling Mina, I couldn't tear or burn it, even though I would never show it to a soul. It was the first depiction of a woman I had done in over two years. Although I hadn't drawn Mina's face, I was stimulated by what I had sketched, and the thought, now that I was walking in the cool night air, troubled me. In her dream she spoke of the blood as the violator's, but I couldn't help seeing it as her own. I wrestled with both fear and longing. Fear of losing her to another to whom she would offer her uninhibited passion, and longing for a shared passion with her.

Driving those images from my mind as I began to walk toward my rooms, I reflected further on the changes in my life from the time Mina and Lucy first came to see me. Amelia's peculiar emphasis on "women" in her note led me to consider that I was being hemmed in by the female sex. I had attempted and was attempting to aid them—Lucy, Amelia, the woman on Regent Street, and tonight Mina. I was supposed to save the young woman who died on my operating table two years earlier. The only one who did not need my assistance was the prostitute I observed on Greenfield Street when I was fourteen. Had I felt guilt all these years because I didn't try to assist her—even though she didn't require or want my help? It was absurd to think that I might have rescued her from a life of sin had I pulled her away from her customer—yet I couldn't help feeling then and since that it was my duty to do so. Perhaps then her face wouldn't have remained in the forefront of my mind, as it had since that day.

But I hadn't walked far from my office when I was nearly knocked aside by a large animal coming unseen from an access lane. It bolted across the street and disappeared between two buildings as it headed in the direction of Hanover Square. From what I could tell from the blur as it nearly collided with me and the quick glance I had of it as it reached the other side of the street, the animal resembled a breed of dog depicted in a picture shown to me by a Russian acquaintance, who called it a Siberian Chukchi. This particular breed resembled a smaller version of the wolf. But the animal that fled past me seemed much larger than the Chukchi, which the Russian told me grew to an average of fifty pounds. It appeared to me three times that size. Could it have been a wolf? Although the species was as far as I knew extinct in England, it might have been brought to London and escaped its handler or released for the purpose of creating mischief. If so, it would be a serious threat to life in the city.

With little regard for caution, I ran across the street and reached the spot between the buildings where the animal had disappeared. I remained against the front corner of one of the buildings and listened for any sound or movement, but I heard nothing. I slowly moved my head past the front corner and snapped it to the left for a quick look. My vision was obscured by a collection of mist that filled the alley way. Once more, no other evidence of fog was apparent anywhere else my eyes could see.

. . . . .

I arrived home and drafted a letter to the city authorities warning them of the possibility that a wolf might be running loose in London. I would have The Dasher deliver it in the morning. As I reached for a book, one of Amelia's four phrases slipped into my mind—"bare waif omen."

"Waif" and wolf. The phrase had an "o" in it but no "l." Such was the case with the other three phrases, which I had now committed to memory. What was wrong with me? Was I attempting to determine if Amelia was warning me of a wolf instead of women? I had to put those four phrases out of my mind. Amelia was deeply disturbed, and the odds were very good that each of the phrases meant something to her but had absolutely nothing to do with me.

I no sooner opened the book when I heard a knock. I knew it couldn't be, but I wanted so badly to see Mina's lovely face when I opened the door. There was no one there.

I was tired and without patience for anyone wishing to disturb my quiet. I shut the door behind me and went outside to find the culprit who had knocked. I saw no one. Considerably annoyed, I turned and headed back up the steps to the front door.

"I still cannot dream, Dr. Hemmings. It's as though I no longer have to dream."

I didn't need to turn around. It was Styles. "I am happy to hear that, Joseph. But I said that you could come here only if you had the dream again. We will meet tomorrow. Please excuse me until then. I should wish to sleep now." I still hadn't turned to face him.

"Sleep will no longer be the same now that he has come."

I tried to prevent sarcasm from influencing my reply, but was powerless to avoid it.

"So you have found religion now, Joseph?" Many like Styles had claimed to have seen the light through an acceptance or renewed commitment to God—or held the belief that Christ had returned to judge the quick and the dead—but in most all cases the light was extinguished within a few days.

"Will you not face me, Dr. Hemmings?"

"Forgive me, Joseph. My fatigue has made me forget proper civility." I wearily turned toward him and saw that his head was covered by a black hood.

"Joseph, why are you wearing that hood?"

"I am cold, Dr. Hemmings."

I recalled Joseph's earlier dreams and Mina's recent one.

"Joseph, please go. Tomorrow—tomorrow we will talk."

"What is tomorrow? There is only now. No yesterdays. All that you have believed. All that you have thought was a dream is not." He lowered his voice to a whisper. "All interest has been directed at you, Dr. Hemmings."

I was becoming quite annoyed by his observations and demeanor. "I want to sleep, Joseph. Please go."

"She is no longer as you knew her. She is gone from the world you have trusted. She wanted to go. Deep within her was the longing."

"Good night, Joseph." I made a futile attempt to open and close the door before he spoke again. I had become afraid of his words.

"But the other one, Dr. Hemmings. The one you want in your dreams does *not* want to go. But she too has the longing. Deep within her. Deep within her."

Unnerved, I left him standing before the steps, shaking his head in pity. But by the time I reached the door, his voice had reclaimed its normal tenor.

"I must do as I am told. I have no choice, Dr. Hemmings. Forgive me. Please forgive me."

When I climbed into bed, I was too exhausted to read or even think. I closed my eyes and within seconds fell asleep. I had a dream but not like others I had experienced. There were flashes of images that visited my mind and quickly left—as if I were glancing at a stack of photographs. Some of them were devoid of persons—for example, a cobblestone street, a syringe, a mountain range, an empty operating table, the sea, and a half drunk cup of tea. As I did often in my waking thoughts, I visualized the face of the woman on Greenfield Street. The same look she had given me almost twenty years ago. I saw my own face looking at her. But I was no longer fourteen but rather the age I am now. I briefly saw another woman's lips—but not the one who died on the operating table—in the attitude of a kiss, but the lips were deathly pale. I saw Lucy Westenra reaching out her arms from a hansom cab, apparently calling for me. In another image, Amelia Reeves stood inside her room at the asylum staring into the eyes of a wolf. And finally I visualized Mina in the middle of an empty street clutching my sketch of her torso to her breast. Her eyes were cast heavenward, and blood came from her nose.

. . . .

It was barely dawn when I left my rooms and headed for my office. But I hadn't taken two steps down from the front door when I saw the figure of what I assumed was a man lying against the corner of building next to mine. I had seen more than my share of the recently deceased lying on the streets and in alley ways, but in two cases my examination of the body showed that the one man and later the one woman were still alive. In both instances, I did what I could for them and had them taken to hospital, but neither lived out the day. Perhaps I could save this one if he were still breathing.

When I reached the body, I saw movement in the feet and lower legs. I reached for the ragged gray blanket that was covering the head area down to the knees and slowly lifted it. It was Styles. He had evidently slept the night outside my rooms. For the first time I gave serious thought to his having spent every night wherever he could. But surely he had always sought some kind of shelter rather than sleeping against the corner of a building, subject to the elements. It had rained a bit during the night and the blanket was quite saturated. I noticed that the black hood he wore when he confronted me last night was missing. Had it been taken from him while he slept—or had he traded it for the blanket or something to eat? Why hadn't I invited him inside to spend the night?

"Joseph, Joseph. Come, wake up, man." Styles' eyes popped open and he looked at me with great sadness.

"I wanted to die during the night, Dr. Hemmings. I hoped that someone would kill me before I awakened and harmed someone else."

That was all I needed to hear. After I cleaned him up, clothed and fed him, I would take him out to Maybrick's asylum this morning.

.   .   .   .   .

I asked Styles many questions about his family and earlier life during our breakfast and while we traveled out to East Putney. He deflected many of them by saying he couldn't remember much about his past. But I persisted, and he offered some information I found intriguing as well as disturbing.

"Dr. Hemmings, I must of course have lived at some residence in Grimsby when I was a boy, but I don't remember anyone taking care of me."

"No father or mother, Joseph?"

"Not until a few weeks ago."

"What do you mean?"

He frowned and shook his head. "No, I am not supposed to explain my meaning of anything."

Joseph, you forget that you have been seeing me about your problems and your dreams."

He leaned toward me so that the cab driver wouldn't hear. "That was then, Dr. Hemmings. There is a brand-new now that takes precedent. All is as it must be."

"Joseph, do you know where I am taking you?"

"Wherever it is, it is where I must be taken. I know that and am content."

What had caused this startling change in his perception of things? No longer was he the embattled and depressed soul weeping and pleading in my office. "Are you having better dreams now, Joseph?"

"All dreams become better once you accept what cannot be changed, Dr. Hemmings."

"I'm happy that you have become a bit of a philosopher, Joseph."

"I am no philosopher because philosophers teach. I only learn. Happiness can only come from learning and doing what you must do."

He stuck his head out of the cab and allowed the breeze to rush against his face. He seemed like a young boy coming back from a joyful Christmas celebration in the country.

· · · · · ·

"Hello Joseph, I am very happy to meet you." As always, Maybrick did his best to make his new inmates as comfortable as possible. "Dr. Hemmings and I think that you should remain here with us for a time. We think you'll be more comfortable here. You'll have plenty to eat and with the winter coming, you'll have a warm place to sleep. Does that sound satisfactory enough for you?"

Styles looked at me. "Is this where I'm supposed to be, Dr. Hemmings?"

"Joseph, I really think it is—at least for now. I will come and see you and we'll talk about your dreams and whatever else that's on your mind."

"The next time I will see you, but I can't promise you will see me."

"No, Joseph," said Maybrick. "I assure you that whenever Dr. Hemmings comes out here, I will make sure he sees and talks to you."

Styles sighed. "My meaning is lost on you, Dr. Maybrick. True meaning is lost on all educated men—especially those that study the mind. But no matter. I will wait here in this place for instructions."

After Joseph was taken to his room, Maybrick poured me a sherry. "Julian, I don't believe I have ever committed any man as compliant as your patient Styles. Women are usually like that, but no man I have brought here. You seem to have done some good for him. Congratulations." Maybrick held up his glass to toast me, but I felt more confused than delighted by Joseph's behavior.

"Thank you, Edward. I only hope he remains so." Because there had been no gradual lessening of Styles' violent imaginings and disruptive behavior, I feared he would soon come undone—perhaps as early as this evening. "Can you send a very brief daily report to me until I come back out later in the week?"

"Of course, Julian."

"May I ask how Amelia Reeves is getting on?"

Maybrick certainly expected me to ask about her. "Since you were here last, she has been perpetually worried about you. Yet she has exhibited no aggressive or otherwise excitable behavior. My guess is that you wish to see her while you are here, but I would advise against it, given the fact that she is now calm."

"No, I agree, Edward. It wouldn't do to have me see her today."

"Thank you for understanding, Julian. So, how do you like the sherry?"

Before I could answer one of the attendants entered Maybrick's office.

"Sorry for barging in, Dr. Maybrick, but it's Amelia Reeves again." Edward and I shared a despondent look.

"What is it, McCarthy?"

"She's walking rapidly around her room repeating the same two words over and over again, sir."

"What words," I asked.

"He's here. He's here. He's here. He's here."

Maybrick's sigh suggested his disappointment. "Somehow she's found out about your arrival. Forgive me, Julian, but you should leave now."

I couldn't protest Maybrick's desire. I could only make matters worse by staying.

CHAPTER 21

Upon my return, I found Charles speaking to a husband and wife about the services I could provide. After the introductions, I took stock of the wife. She seemed in her later twenties or early thirties. She was neatly and properly dressed for a woman of her station, and not a hair was out of place. Her demeanor seemed quite serene and pleasant. The only evidence of her troubles was the hopeful if not pleading look on her face. I couldn't help guessing at what was tormenting her. I feared it was the loss of a child.

"Dr. Hemmings." Her voice was soft but even—not quite a monotone but apparently not given to excitement. "Mr. Yates has told us that you might be able to help. You were recommended to us by a physician we consulted in Gillingham, where we live."

"I am flattered that he would recommend me. Now, would you both be up to traveling—what is it?—thirty-five to forty miles to London for your sessions—perhaps several times a week?"

She touched her husband's arm. "We are. We don't mind train travel, and my husband's brother lives here. We can stay with him if necessary."

"Very good, then. I can begin today, if you'd like." Since Styles was now residing at Maybrick's asylum, I had no other appointments scheduled until Lucy arrived late in the afternoon.

The woman seemed very grateful for my offer. "Yes, yes. The sooner the better." Yet her husband seemed somewhat reluctant, and I feared he wouldn't allow his wife to see me for her problems.

"Charles, would you take some information down, while Mrs. Pendry and I go into my office."

"Julian?"

"Yes, Charles?"

"It's *Mr.* Pendry who is the prospective patient."

. . . . . .

When the Pendrys left forty minutes later, I had to contend with Charles's impish grin, prompted by my embarrassing mistake.

"Julian, it seems that you wanted the wife to unravel her deepest thoughts rather than the husband. Do you wish me to change the sales strategy and advertise your trade as 'Mind Physician for Women Only'?"

"Very amusing, Charles." I wasn't about to tell Yates that the mistake was inevitable, considering the number of women who had taken up residence in my mind of late. Still, his joke wasn't far from the mark. I did indeed feel more comfortable and helpful with my female patients. Perhaps I was emulating Freud in this, since he had spoken to me most enthusiastically about the women he saw. Still, my Austrian friend laughed at himself for devoting so much time to researching the "feminine soul," as he put it—without much to show for it. He spoke of the women in his life as a possible motivation for studying the sex. During one of our discussions he brought up the well-known beliefs of my countryman the late gynecologist William Acton.

"Acton shared my interest in pondering the habit of masturbation," Freud remarked, "although our views greatly differ. For him, our bodies can only produce so much energy in the course of a lifetime, and therefore the release of too much semen—primarily through masturbation—was detrimental to overall health. His belief also encouraged the mistaken and absurd notion that masturbation leads to blindness." I nodded my head in agreement, for my father had endorsed Acton's view on masturbation in his serious talks with me in the two years before our falling out when I was fourteen. My desire to engage in the hedonistic practice increased after the encounter on Greenfield Street, and I suffered much guilt over having wanted to do it and felt considerable frustration when I refused to engage in the activity.

But Freud was most in disagreement with Acton's argument that women were not given to pleasurable sexual thoughts and desires for sexual satisfaction. Women, Acton observed, engage in sexual intercourse with their husbands out of duty only—with the obligation of childbearing being paramount. Acton was willing to concede that moral women could feel some desire when they menstruated, but beyond that, any active thoughts of sexual pleasure were evidence of nymphomania. I can still see Freud sitting at table savoring his favorite boiled beef and Italian artichokes, while he rejected Acton's claims and forwarded the contrary view that men and women were similarly responsive to erotic stimulation and therefore as sexual creatures, men and women were the same. He confided in me with a twinkle in his eye that his wife Martha believed these ideas of his were a kind of "pornography."

These and similar conclusions of his intrigued me the most. I now gave more thought than perhaps I should have to female sexual response. No longer could I dismiss the aloof yet erotic expression of the woman on Greenfield Street as merely reflective of her desire for payment. I felt twenty years earlier that there was more to her look than that, but Freud has made me see that my instincts might well have been correct. Since going to Vienna, I have even judged differently the kiss given to me by the ill-fated Yvette Auger. Knowing that she needed me to save her life aroused more than my strong desire to save her. I had even briefly imagined that we might have a romantic relationship if she recovered from the surgery. Lucy Westenra has of course stimulated my curiosity about her sexual desires, and even the emaciated Amelia Reeves induced me to imagine her as a vibrant and beautiful young bride. And was my attempted act of gallantry in behalf of the prostitute on Regent Street prompted primarily by her youth and helplessness, in spite of her occupation? I couldn't deny that it was possible. Finally, there was my love for Mina Murray, but with her I dreaded learning about her sexual imaginings. It's not that I didn't desire her—I did without any qualification—but I was fearful of the destructive effect on me should she admit to sexual thoughts involving another. Her dream had so affected me that I was compelled to draw her torso with the blood on her nightgown. What might I do if I had clear evidence that she experienced the kinds of active thoughts Freud talked about?

"Julian?"

"Yes, Charles?"

"Since you have no appointments until Miss Westenra arrives, I wonder if I might be excused for an hour or so? My wife is going to have a tooth filled by Sam Arnold and has demanded that I accompany her. She is certain that Arnold will pull the tooth to save himself time and effort of filling it if I am not there to make sure he is going to try and save it."

I couldn't help laughing at Charles's predicament. "Assure your wife that Sam Arnold has been filling savable teeth with silicate cement for over fifteen years. But you should be with her nonetheless."

"I tell you that I'd much rather be right here, Julian. Everything about Arnold's office gives me a fright. That's why I won't go myself. One looks at those instruments and bottles—and that infernal chair—and it's all one can do not to have nightmares."

"Charles, how can you be afraid of all that? You have handled even more frightful instruments and stood next to operating and post-mortem tables with bodies lying on them."

"It's not the same, Julian."

There he was—a large middle-aged man speaking like a boy lost in a graveyard. "Well, it's fortunate you have good teeth, Charles, or else I'd have to ask you to find employment elsewhere."

It did my soul good to banter with Charles the way we used to do when I was a surgeon. I still held out hope that he might yet become reconciled to our new situation.

．　．　．　．　．

Charles hadn't been gone ten minutes when I heard the front door open. I went into the outer office and immediately my spirits were further elevated by Mina's appearance.

"My great-uncle has chosen to remain in the cab, Dr. Hemmings. I told him I wouldn't be long. May we go into your office?"

This was the second time she went in with me without a chaperone or Charles sitting in the outer office. I gestured for her to sit. She looked more beautiful than ever, even now with her eyes closed and her hair not as perfectly secured as usual. I was most curious why she had come. She seemed reluctant to speak. My vanity therefore overcame my caution.

"Mina, have you read the letter I gave you?"

With her eyes still closed, she dropped her head. "Forgive me, but I have not."

I should have let the matter lie, but I was too afraid she was about to announce her departure from London. "May I ask why you haven't?"

"In spite of what you said yesterday afternoon, I am afraid to read any phrase that might suggest your indifference to me. You see, I am not presently in a state where any rejection would be endurable."

My sense of relief was considerable. "No, Mina. I have not nor will I ever view you with anything remotely approaching indifference—I promise you."

"Not ever?"

"Not ever." I threw off all caution and allowed myself to revel in the thought that she cared for me.

"Dr. Hemmings, will you—"

"I would prefer that you call me Julian. We are friends and similar spirits, after all."

"Will you hypnotize me?"

I was taken completely aback by her response. "Mina, why do you ask of me such a thing? For what purpose would I hypnotize you?"

"I must know what I cannot now understand. Perhaps I will reveal something to you that you may then inform me of. In truth, I have misplaced something that I must find. I couldn't sleep at all last night trying to determine where it was."

I now saw that her eyes were pink and somewhat sunken. "Then you didn't dream last night." My response was insensitive and therefore unforgivable. Why did I refer first to her dreams? "But more important than that, I am so sorry for your difficult night."

She paused several seconds before continuing. "I cannot sleep again until I find what I have misplaced. Will you help me find it? Will you?"

"What is it that you have lost, Mina?"

"I have too much shame to tell you. Only ask me what it is when you have hypnotized me. Do you know how to do it?"

Freud had shown me several of the techniques he had used, even though he had already moved away from hypnotism in the treatment of his patients.

"Yes, I believe so." In fact, I had never attempted to hypnotize anyone.

"Will you use a swinging watch?"

I smiled. "No, Mina. That is more the stuff of stage hypnotists, who care only for the theatrics of it."

Freud had educated me to the history of hypnotism in our own century—noting that it ran afoul of those believing in the "animal magnetism" theory of the Mesmerists. Many early practitioners employed hypnotism to treat "hysteria," especially in women, but Freud made clear that many female patients suffered from sexual tension, not hysteria. He frankly shocked me when he told me of the medical practice of manual and mechanical clitoral stimulation as a temporary relief for a woman's sexual frustration. I'll admit that as a surgeon, I had never heard of such a thing, and was dubious of Freud's pronouncement, which has also been called "pelvic" and "vulvular" massage. I stopped Freud when he began speaking of the popularity of repeat visits and the physician's abuse of the remedy. He laughed at my ignorance of the treatment and my general squeamishness. "You'll have to get over all that, my dear fellow, if you wish to be successful at talk therapy." He punctuated his remark by blowing a perfect smoke ring from his cigar.

My Austrian friend also spoke of his earlier experience with hypnosis. He said that he attempted to lead the patient into a state of relaxation so that the man or woman would be receptive to a series of questions focusing on the experience or the thoughts that led to the patient's troubling symptoms. Often the symptom would vanish if the patient could be encouraged to articulate what the experience or thought was that led to a particular behavior or feeling. But again as he told me, Freud came to find that for him hypnosis was generally unnecessary, because almost all could be accomplished through talking.

"Will it take long, Dr. Hemmings? My uncle will soon get impatient."

I wanted simply to speak with Mina and see if I could influence her to identify what she was looking for, but she seemed insistent on hypnosis. Perhaps if she thought I was indeed leading her into that state, she would feel free enough to open up to me.

I was disappointed that she continued to call me by my professional designation, but I had no time to encourage her to use my Christian name. "Mina, do you have any fear of being hypnotized?"

"None. Please hurry."

"All right. I want you to feel as comfortable as you can. Remove all thoughts from your mind and listen to my voice only. I want you to allow what is inside to come to the surface." Freud noted that hypnosis requires a willing subject, and I had no doubt that Mina qualified on that account. "Mina, what is the first pleasant image that comes to your mind." I best recalled from my talks with Freud the following technique. "Tell me what you are thinking of."

"Holding an infant in my arms." It was all I could do to remain detached. I imagined her now as an angel—holding a child of our own. "Fold your arms in front of you and slowly rock the baby back and forth, Mina. Slowly say 'Trust me' ten times to the baby."

She did as I instructed.

"Now open your arms and let the baby go. It is older now. Now slowly say 'Go to bed and sleep' ten times." I gave her several other pleasant images and verbal reinforcements and then asked, "Do you remember something you've lost?"

"Yes."

"Will you tell me what it is?"

"Yes."

"Do you want to find it?"

"Yes. I must."

"Why, Mina?" My voice remained steady and mildly authoritative.

"I must know if there is blood on it."

CHAPTER 22

I heard Mina's great-uncle enter the outer office shortly after Mina, still under hypnosis, began taking herself through the rooms of the Taltson house. I remained silent as she continued her monologue, asking herself if her nightgown was in each room and answering with a slightly elevated voice, "No." She had just pronounced that "It's not in the house at all," when Taltson knocked on the inner-office door. I did nothing to "awaken" Mina; rather, she reassumed her normal manner on her own—seemingly satisfied that she had located the whereabouts of the garment, although she didn't mention anything about it as she wished me a good afternoon. Her eyes seemed once again clear and she touched her hair and appeared embarrassed that it wasn't done up as neatly as always. My only consolation was that after she said her formal goodbye, she whispered to me. "I'll read your letter now, Julian." I was so affected by her behavior and desire to find the nightgown that it wasn't until she left that I realized she had used my Christian name.

Anticipating Lucy's arrival between 4:30 and 5:00, I chose a brisk walk to clear my head. I closed the office and headed north and then west through Cavendish Square, then over to Wimpole Street, finally making my way to Bentinck Street—some half a mile from my office. I often enjoyed going there to see where Dickens lived over sixty years earlier, when he was working as a court reporter. Here too the great historian Gibbon wrote most of his *Decline and Fall of the Roman Empire.* And as an added literary connection, Conan Doyle's more recent *The Final Problem* had the detective Holmes nearly killed in this area by a two-horse van "furiously driven." Naturally, I recalled almost being knocked down by the wolf or wolf-like creature that dashed past me the previous evening. I assumed that by now it had been located and either shot or caged. The coincidence was further manifested by thoughts of Amelia Reeves and the horrific experience of watching her husband set upon by wolves, likely somewhere in Romania. How had she escaped a similar fate? Might it not have been better for the poor woman if she had perished along with her husband? I hoped Maybrick would inform me soon about her condition. I hadn't planned to go back out to see Joseph Styles for a few days, wanting him to get acclimated to his new surroundings, and given Amelia's most recent reaction to my arrival, I knew it was best to refrain from seeing her at present.

Feeling a pronounced chill in the air and observing that it had gotten darker, I momentarily feared I had allowed several hours to escape my awareness, but a glance upward revealed that the sky was thickened by rain clouds, yet they were much blacker than usual on rainy afternoons. I remained stationary, waiting for the first drops to fall, but I felt nothing until I crossed Wimpole Street and started into Cavendish Square. The rain whipped furiously into my face as if it had come horizontally—yet I couldn't detect any wind or breeze. I stopped by the statue of Lord George Bentinck on the southern side of the square and walked around it to see if it might block the horizontal direction of the rain, which was stinging my face. But as I made my way around the statue, the rain changed its direction as well, therefore preventing my face from escaping its cruel lashing.

I lifted my arm to protect my face the best I could and started eastward, even though I was almost completely blinded by my arm and the pelting rain. But as soon as I stepped from the Square proper, the rain ceased. It hadn't abated; it just stopped. I turned back to see if it was still raining in the Square, and there, next to the statue of Lord George Bentinck, stood a woman. No rain was falling in the Square.

I stared at her for several moments, hoping to purge the thought that I knew who she was. But it was useless. I did know her. It was the troubled young woman whom I met on Regent Street and who later came to my office.

I headed back to where she stood, half-expecting the rain to begin again. She made no move away from or toward me, but simply kept her bare head bowed. When I reached her I saw that not a strand of her hair was damp.

"What are you doing here, young woman?"

"Wishing to see you." Her answer was ripe with reluctance. Had she been forced by someone to talk with me? Or had she violated a promise not to speak to me?

"May I ask your name?"

"Hannah, sir." Her voice trembled, but she smiled and seemed grateful I had asked. I could see that her clothing was the same as it was the two other times I had spoken to her.

"Hannah, can you tell me why you came to my office?"

"I wished to see you."

"I know that." The repetition of her words frustrated me. I was perplexed not only by her earlier visit, but also by her disappearance into that odd mist behind my office building. And how had she come to be standing in a place I had just left—not having been touched by the unusual rainfall.

"This will be my last meeting with you, sir." Once again she bowed her head.

"And why is that Hannah?"

"I was told not to speak with you the last time, and I will die for doing so this time."

My impatience with the young woman evaporated as I looked upon her as another deeply troubled soul whom I could assist with talk therapy. I knew she probably couldn't pay me, but as I had done with Joseph Styles I would take her on to gain experience in my new craft as well as to help her through her difficulties.

"Hannah, would you consider being my patient?"

"That cannot be."

I now had more time to examine her face. Her matted hair precluded a general appreciation of her attractiveness, but her lips were well formed and her other features were balanced and more than respectable to the eye—even in her present state. My heart was quickly going out to her—another result, I was sure, of my being in love with Mina.

"No, Hannah. It *can* be. You have only to come and talk with me. In the morning or afternoon—several times a week if you wish—and without cost to you." She began to cry. "Hannah, don't cry. I am happy to do it."

"No, you cannot!" Her severe declamation startled me. "You will not see me again after today. I am here to warn you one last time. You are in danger. Leave London for a time. Escape, please!" She quickly turned and ran out the western side of Cavendish Square. I took several initial steps in pursuit, but halted. Her ominous words held me fast. She and Amelia Reeves were insistent that something would happen to me. But who in God's name could wish me harm? Could these two women be suffering from the same kind of dreadful experience and present hysteria—the only difference being that one was inside an asylum, the other out on the streets? Regardless, I was thoroughly shaken—far more by Hannah's warning than by my dampened condition.

. . . . .

I had a change of clothing in my office ready for whenever I might be caught in the rain, and my fear lessened and my spirits rose when I was again dry and warm. Charles came in a short time afterward, and I spoke with him about his wife's dental appointment and about my plans to see more patients gratis. He asked if I intended to include prostitutes.

"I think it would be helpful to me as well as to them if I did, Charles."

"I hope you will reconsider, Julian."

"Charles, I know you're not in favor of my doing so. I remember your objections when I determined to perform surgery on a 'fallen woman,' as you prefer to call them."

"Yes, I did, but now the effects would be without question destructive."

"Oh, come now, Charles."

"I am most serious. Spending time alone in your office with one of them cannot in any way enhance your reputation in the medical community. People will talk—and you know they will—and soon you'll have no one respectable seeking your assistance. I'm warning you that if you do this the results will be disastrous to you."

Yet another warning. With Lucy and Mina shortly to arrive, I wanted Charles to calm down so that he could be at least somewhat attentive and charming to Mina and her great-uncle while I spoke with Lucy. Therefore, I thought it prudent to concede something to him for the sake of peace.

"Charles, I promise to think carefully about what you have just advised."

He seemed disarmed. "You will? Good. Just be sure that you do."

. . . . .

Lucy didn't arrive until nearly five. I greeted her and waited for Mina and Taltson to come in—but Lucy had come alone. Charles was also disappointed, though not nearly as much as I by the absence of Mina. Yet I didn't expect him to excuse himself to Lucy and ask to see me in my office.

I waited until he closed the door. "Charles, what are you doing?"

"You shouldn't see her alone, Julian."

"I won't be alone. You'll be waiting out there."

"No, I just have a strong feeling that you should reschedule this appointment. Make it for tomorrow—earlier in the afternoon."

"Charles, if you need to get home to your wife, then by all means go. I'm a physician. This won't be a physical examination; therefore it's proper for me—alone—to chaperone my female patient. I will speak with her and then see that she gets home. I'll accompany her myself if need be."

"It's just wrong, Julian. Given Miss Westenra's manner, if nothing else, it just won't do to see her after I leave. And damn it, Julian. I *have* to go home. My wife's nephew and his fiancée are coming for supper at six. I assumed that the old man and Mina would be here. But I am most serious when I say that you should reschedule. I can call a cab to return Miss Westenra to the Taltson residence."

Charles's nervousness and insistence were very much out of character for him. I grabbed both his arms and assured him that all would be fine.

"Go home, Charles. Send my regards to your wife and her nephew—and his fiancée. Now go."

I was relieved when Charles finally capitulated. He wished a hasty good evening to Lucy and left.

"I thought you would leave me standing out here all night, Dr. Hemmings." Lucy seemed far more bemused than aggravated.

"My apologies for all that Lucy. Please come into my office and take your place on the sofa."

"Of course. Have you both been sharing delightful thoughts about me?" I feared her evident playfulness would inhibit her ability to speak seriously.

"So, Lucy, how have you—?"

"You want to know why Mina didn't accompany me, don't you?"

"That wasn't what I was going to say, but if you wish to tell me, please do so." In truth, I most certainly wanted to know.

"She will not willingly come to me now."

"Why do you say that, Lucy?"

147

As was now her custom, she leaned her head back and placed herself in a relaxed position on the sofa. "Although she fears going with me, she will soon join me. She mightily fights her desires, Doctor Hemmings. That is the difference between us."

I couldn't bear to hear Lucy slander Mina. "Why have you come alone? Did no one accompany you here?" I hoped that at least a hansom cab was waiting outside or would return to collect her.

"I am never alone. Not ever again. If you must know, I came in a cloud."

"On a cloud, you mean?" I would play her game of metaphors.

"No, *in* one."

"And you will return to the Taltsons in the same cloud?"

"I will never return to the Taltsons, Dr. Hemmings."

We gazed at each other in silence, but her eyes had the expression of triumph. She held me captive with her look and remained silent for several long moments before she again spoke.

"Dr. Hemmings, you want to know if Mina has found something, don't you?"

Had Mina shared her dream with Lucy? Or had she cried something out in the night?

"We are here to talk about you, Lucy."

"But you are also here to learn something important about Mina."

"No, I want to speak only about you." My words barely fell from my mouth.

"She has found her nightgown."

"I see."

"It was lying outside—in the rear of the house. It has blood on it."

Unable to endure the expression on Lucy's face, I cast my eyes downward as I asked the next question, too weak to bend the discussion away from Mina.

"Lucy, do you . . . do you know how the blood came to be on her nightgown?"

I heard her gasp and lifted my eyes to see her slide off the sofa to the floor. She remained with her body and head leaning back—but now against the bottom edge of the sofa cushion.

"I need blood, Doctor Hemmings. Can't you see how pale I am?" Yet she didn't sound at all frantic.

I leaped to my feet and leaned over her, "Lucy, we can get you a transfusion. Now, if you wish."

She rolled her head and laughed, but without humor. "I look at children now, Dr. Hemmings. Some are as pale as I."

I desperately tried to salvage what I could of this session. "You have dreamed of children, Lucy?" She merely stared straight ahead. "Can't you see? When you were a child, you were frightened. You saw yourself in the glass. The paleness came from your fear as it is doing now." I had to believe that was the cause of her blanched complexion. Yet she remained enticing and alive in a way I had never seen before. I shook free from that thought and suddenly felt a surge of confidence in my analysis. "Lucy, listen to me. I will explain it to you. When your father came back, there was someone with him, wasn't there?" Lucy remained motionless. "You have told me so, correct?" I had no time to take her through her experience slowly. I sensed that I had the true cause of her behavior within reach. "Or was it that to you your father was now 'someone else'? Lucy, you must tell me, did your father—"

She interrupted, but without agitation. "He said he had been there before. He has been everywhere and will continue to be throughout time. He remembered me, Dr. Hemmings. Even though I was very young and I must have certainly changed, he remembered me. I was his own, he said, since he first saw me, but I had to wait for him to come back. Seven years."

My heart ached for this poor girl. In spite of Freud's recent cautions regarding the effect of the father's cruel or unspeakable treatment as a major cause for the mental suffering of those like Lucy, he still held that in many cases all misery can be traced to examples of physical abuse and incestuous acts caused by the father.

"Lucy, your father had no right to touch you in that manner." I knew my words would provide little comfort.

She turned her head and looked into my eyes. She seemed momentarily puzzled. "My father? Why do you think I was speaking of my father?"

Then it was the man who accompanied her father when he returned. "Lucy, forgive me. I see now that it was the *other* man you were referring to. Did you tell your father what he had done to you?"

"He did nothing to me but lift my chin and run the back of his fingers down the side of my face. He only promised me that I would be his someday."

I helped Lucy to regain her place on the sofa. Momentarily too confused to speak, I made my way back to my chair. "Then nothing happened to you which caused you pain when your father came back with that man?"

"Oh, no. My soul fluttered with anticipation from that day forth. Each day was filled with the same thought. When would he come back and claim me as his own?"

Now it struck me that she might have separated her father into two men. The one she loved and wished to be with and the one who had done something vile to her.

"Lucy, did your father and this other man speak together in your presence?"

"No."

Once again I felt creeping exuberance over the first bit of evidence that my theory was correct. "Did they walk together?"

"My father couldn't see him."

"Even in the light of day?"

"I only saw him late at night."

My mind was replete with horrific images of her father coming into her darkened room while she slept. Would he have been so despicable as to have worn a disguise—a mask of some kind as he engaged in the most unspeakable of acts?

Before I could ask her further about the other man, she again gasped loudly. Almost with a sense of majesty, she stood this time, fully in command of her movements.

"Blood. I must have it. The children. I see them. The poor children."

"Lucy, these are but your dreams. They are telling you something else. I want you to let me find out what they are really saying to you. I want to hear all of your dreams."

Her left hand moved to the side of her neck, which was, as always, completely covered. Pain registered on her exotically enticing features.

"I don't dream any more, Dr. Hemmings. I have been mistaken. I now see things before their time. But perhaps I always did."

How many other physicians would have had this young woman committed to an asylum without caring to know what drove these thoughts into her mind? I couldn't let this happen to her. She had to be assured that I wouldn't abandon her—as had her father.

"Lucy, keep telling me what you are feeling. Know that I am your friend and will be there whenever you need me."

Her expression of fatigue and resignation transformed into one of acute awareness. "All will soon be. After tonight. No. *Before* this night is through it will begin. What I have seen and long known will begin."

"You must tell me what you have seen and what you have long known."

"You will see and you will know without my telling you. I will not warn you as others have. Yes, the blood of children will sustain me so I will not be cast away." Her smile dropped. "I deeply fear being alone throughout time, Dr. Hemmings."

"No, Lucy. You must believe me when I say that the blood of children is your blood. Your blood when you were young. Remember that I am here for you. Mina is here for you."

Lucy stepped toward me. I had not budged from my chair since she had stood. She was now standing over me.

"Mina is not here, Dr. Hemmings. Never again for me. She is wanted now. And I fear being replaced and forever alone. Hunger and love. That, after all, is the true philosophy."

I was aghast. These were Freud's words, spoken to me in Vienna and repeated in a recent correspondence. Was this young woman that clever and audacious as to have come into my office and looked through my correspondence while Charles and I were away?

"Lucy, how could you have—"

"I will die and then live forever. I see now before me the crucifix. The host."

"Yes, yes. That is true." Her orthodox religious assertion was a sign of rationale thinking and I had to encourage more of it. "Think of the crucifix; think of the host."

"No! No! No!" Her scream filled the room and drove me deeper into the cushions of my chair.

"Lucy, what is it? What is it?" I pushed myself upright and reached to comfort her. Her eyes flashed such hatred that I was truly frightened for my own safety. Was this what Amelia and Hannah had warned me of? She repelled from my touch and moved to the narrow space behind the sofa.

"It will be Mina and *not me*." She was in a trancelike state. She had thrust her body against the rear wall with her head arched upward. The wrap around her neck came loose and slipped down several inches. I saw them now. Two spots of blood on her neck. I dared not approach her.

"Are you speaking of more dreams, Lucy. Are you having visions?"

"You have had them and will always have them. You hope she will come

151

into your dreams and kiss you. That she will cure you. That she will save you. But she will die and you will not save her. Then you will fear the very thought of closing your eyes. You will fear sleep and what it brings. Dreams. Dreams that will never end. Dreams of a young face. A beautiful face. With eyes closed. Never more to open again." She had said all this in one sustained breath.

I was helpless to maintain control of my emotions. The intensity of the moment was unendurable. "Lucy, please stop this. Think of how much Mina and I care for you and want to help you." As her body sagged against the wall, she reached for the back of the sofa to steady herself. Her head dropped and her unloosened black hair fell over her like a cascade. Still I hesitated to come to her assistance. I could only call her name softly. She said nothing but took four or five heavy breaths—the room was completely hushed otherwise. Finally she lifted her head, and I watched her hair once more fall in luxurious waves to the side and rear of her head. She touched the side of her neck, and slight trickles of blood escaped from the two puncture wounds.

"Un-dead, I will lie there—in the coffin—alone. I will see the faces, Dr. Hemmings. I will rise up and want to kiss. My open red lips will want to kiss. Such cruelty and wantonness. The desire for the taste. The need to take and the wish to live."

I couldn't bear it. I fell back into my chair. "Please, Lucy."

She came from around the sofa and once more stood over me.

"I want to be forever in the land beyond the forest."

I saw blood on the tips of her fingers. She must have touched her wound as I collapsed into the chair. She breathed heavily again. I looked up to find what was in her eyes, but I couldn't see them. They were looking straight up. Slowly, she spread her arms out to each side and uttered a single word I had never before heard.

"*Nosferatu.*"

CHAPTER 23

How Lucy returned to the Taltsons—if she did return—I cannot say. Too overcome by the memory of her alluring yet contorted face and eyes and the frightful modulations of her voice, I remained motionless in my chair, my thoughts traversing unbridled—unable to shape an analysis of all Lucy had said. Not even Amelia Reeves in her worst moments had so astounded and intimidated me.

Finally, though, my thoughts settled and realigned, and I was able to consider Lucy's behavior more rationally. I first considered the peculiar word she uttered moments before she left me—*Nosferatu*. I would write a linguist acquaintance of mine at Cambridge and ask for a translation. Again I thought of Amelia Reeves and her odd phrases—but also where she had witnessed her husband's death. Could the word Lucy uttered be of Eastern European extraction? Bulgarian, Romanian, or Serbian? Lucy's exotic appearance now suggested to me that she might have bloodlines from one of those countries. Could *Nosferatu* been a formal name of some kind—or an equivalent of father—or ravisher?

She said she wished to be "in the land beyond the forest." Such a place could be anywhere—in London or anywhere else in Britain. Or she could have meant many places in Europe—or even in America. Perhaps she was speaking metaphorically of heaven, although her unnerving behavior and speech suggested something more of hell. But she had mentioned a crucifix and a host, leading me to believe that she was of the Roman faith and perhaps more superstitious than I at first imagined. My head ached. I refused to remain in my office any longer pondering Lucy's words and behavior. I was tempted to go to the Taltsons to see if she had arrived, but I couldn't bear the possibility of seeing her as she was when she left my office—or of not seeing Mina. I wanted a long walk in the cool night air to clear my head, stimulate an appetite, and tire me enough for sleep.

IN MIND OF THE VAMPIRE

I removed from my desk Amelia's four phrases and the sketch of Mina's torso in order to take them to my rooms to assure that neither Charles nor anyone else would discover them in my desk. Folding them once, I placed them in my coat hanging in the outer office. As I did so, I heard a rapping on the front door. I knew immediately who it was by the five quick knocks repeated once. I opened the door and let in The Dasher.

"I was going to hold these until the morning, sir, but I saw the light inside your office and thought you might be in." The Dasher handed me two sealed letters bundled together by string. "The gentleman who gave these to me said to tell you that Dr. Maybrick wants you to read the top one first—that is, before you read the second one."

I smiled at Dasher's superfluous addition. His appearance had calmed me further. "How is the evening going, Dasher?"

"Busier than usual for me, Dr. Hemmings. I've been running from The Strand to Gloucester Square and back again."

"Then you've made some good money."

"It's money, Dr. Hemmings. But how good it is depends on your outlook. Not everyone is as kind to me that way as you are."

"I wish I could do even better by you. But . . ."

"Ah, don't worry, Dr. H. You'll soon have more customers than you can handle. Just today I've seen seven or eight odd ones on the street you might like to get your hooks into."

"Perhaps I need to hire you as an agent, my boy."

"I could do it—easy as turning a spit."

I handed the lad an extra coin for brightening my mood. "Take it and buy yourself something special to eat tonight."

"Thank you, kind sir. Want me to bring in one of the odd ones tomorrow to add to your list?"

"No, that won't be necessary, Dasher. Tell me. What are the conditions outside?"

"Getting colder. The wind isn't blowing though. I may have also felt a rain drop or two."

"Any fog or mist?"

"None that I've seen tonight. Well, good night to you, Dr. Hemmings."

"And to you as well, Dasher."

As soon as he left, I sat at Charles's desk and opened the first letter from Edward Maybrick.

All goes well with your patient Styles. He seems content enough, although that isn't uncommon for even the most troubled souls upon first arriving. He sits on a chair and leans his back against the wall and looks straight up unless someone speaks to him. He seems to have slept soundly and he ate a good breakfast, although he hasn't eaten anything since. I trust he'll be hungry sometime tonight. I'd allow him at least another day—perhaps two—before you come to see him. He hasn't asked for you by name, but he has said to me and to the attendants "He has instructed me" and "He has told me what to do." That appears to be a good sign—that Styles has taken whatever advice or instruction you have given him.

I couldn't remember sharing any specific advice with Styles or giving him instruction when we rode out to Maybrick's asylum or right before we parted. I only recall reminding him that he would be better off and that I would not abandon him. I read on.

Julian, you will also want to know about Amelia Reeves. We managed to calm her soon after you left, but since then she has been filled with dread, the cause of which I do not yet understand. She begged me for paper and pencil, which I initially refused, for fear she would harm herself, but she promised that she would not and continued to plead to the point that I had to give in. An attendant stood within inches of her, ready to grab her hand if she attempted to jab the pencil into her eye. I agreed to let her place the note to you in an envelope and assured her that I wouldn't read it. I don't know what it says but I am sure it further reflects her tortured state. If I can do anything to help you translate the meaning, do let me know.

As I opened the second envelope, I wondered if Amelia had given me an explanation of the four phrases or a better clue to their understanding. Or had she written four new phrases with which to plague me further? I opened the note.

Understand me! A name. A name! HE is not he as you think.

That was all she had written. "Understand me" she had said to me before. That meant I must understand the four phrases. "A name. A name!" Was she saying that I needed to identify "women" in each of the four? I hadn't told her that I had made that discovery. But "a name" could well refer to the "HE" she capitalized. Had I been on the wrong track all along in believing she was warning me about the female sex? "HE is not he as you think." Her full meaning, though, eluded me. Did I know a "he" who was in truth a woman? It seemed preposterous. The only possibility would be The Dasher, who at age twelve still had the voice of early youth—it hadn't yet changed. Was Amelia Reeves warning me about The Dasher, who was in reality a young girl? I laughed at the utter absurdity of such a possibility. Still, I brought to mind one of the four phrases, "bowman faerie," and made sure that the Dasher's name wasn't hidden inside the two words the way "women" was. There was no *d, s,* or *h* in the phrase. But then I recalled that I didn't know Dasher's surname. With that thought I slammed the palm of my hand on Charles's desk and muttered a profanity at my misguided concentration. I slipped on my coat and went out into the night.

I decided to walk east on Oxford Street until I reached Soho Square. I would then turn back and return to the intersection of Regent and Oxford Streets. I planned to dine on some roast chicken before returning to my rooms for further reading and then—I truly hoped—a good night's sleep. But I didn't quite make it to Soho Square, as I could feel my body giving out much earlier than I anticipated. Not wishing to follow the same route back, I walked north for a bit and then made the turn to the west. I then passed All Saint's Church, a structure now some forty years old, which I had sketched as a boy, to the acclaim of my father and of those to whom he showed it. I always felt a sense of inspiration when I came here, although at this moment it seemed less impressive and meaningful to me. This impression had to be the result of my recent experiences with Lucy Westenra, Amelia Reeves, Hannah, and Joseph Styles. Had my faith in God been shaken by my recent experiences? I was never devout, but I never doubted that I believed in all I had been taught. I quickly walked past All Saint's and continued westward.

When I arrived at Regent Street, I looked across the road in the direction of Cavendish Square, where I had recently seen Hannah and experienced that bizarre rainfall. I was thinking about that poor girl, when from the corner of my eye I saw The Dasher running toward the Square. I feared someone was in pursuit of him and I bolted across Regent Street to come to his assistance. When I got to the Square I saw several others standing in a semi-circle near the statue of Lord George Bentinck. The Dasher was among them.

I ran up to where he stood and squeezed my way next to him so that I could easily see what everyone was gawking at. Still others were coming up to swell the ranks. All were staring at the body of a woman, whose throat and face had been ripped open. Even as a surgeon I had witnessed nothing to compare with these ghastly wounds.

Some gasped as they stood mesmerized by the gruesome sight; others ran away wailing or crying. The Dasher glanced up at me for an explanation I couldn't provide. I stepped closer to the body and looked more closely at the ravaged throat and face. It was clear to me what had happened. The woman was attacked by an animal which ripped her flesh apart with its teeth. My stomach so tightened that my torso bent forward involuntarily. The animal that had earlier rushed past me was certainly a wolf, and now it had done what I feared it might. What I had warned the city of what it might do—and yet I had heard nothing from anyone official relating to the beast. I stepped back and felt The Dasher's arms grab at one of my own.

I turned to the others. "Please, everyone. Return to your homes or to some shelter until the morning. Please don't run or speak loudly. The animal could still be in the area."

The others did as I suggested just as two members of the Metropolitan Force arrived. I told them of what I had previously informed the city officials, as The Dasher continued to hang on to my arm.

One of the officers asked if I knew who the woman was. I was about to say no when I took another look at the body and saw the unfortunate woman's worn shoes. The lace on one of the black boots was brown. My body became numb. The wolf had mutilated Hannah's care-worn but gentle face beyond all recognition.

As the two members of the Metropolitan force consulted with several other officers who had just arrived, I spotted the edge of a piece of paper under Hannah's torso. I sent The Dasher on his way, warning him to stay in the middle of the street and near as many persons as possible and to warn them about the wolf as he headed to his home. Because he lived in the direction of the Taltson residence, I instructed him to go there and implore the family not to venture forth during the night. The Dasher was reluctant, but assured me he would do as I asked. No one watched me as I bent down and retrieved the folded paper.

On the outside of the note was my name, misspelled and written in pencil. I stood back up immediately and slipped the note inside my coat before the other members of the police came to question me. One of the officers found a block of wood lying seven or eight feet away from the body. Soon he found a stub of a pencil near the block of wood. I was horrified to think that Hannah was in the process of writing the note, using the piece of wood as a miniature desk, when she was attacked by the beast. It was my duty to hand the note over to the police, but I simply had to read it first.

When I returned to my rooms, I placed the note on my desk, poured some brandy, and read the almost illegible hand. It took some effort to make my way through the many grammatical errors and misspellings, but I believed I understood all of what she meant to convey. Hannah wrote that when she left me on Regent Street, the man she thought was following me came up to her in the fog—just as I had feared. She said it was like a dream, and she felt powerless to run away from him. He did something to her she couldn't describe, but it made her feel important. He made her promises that excited her sensibilities but after he left she began to visualize "horibel" things happening to her and to others, including me. The note ended, "I have to worn you spesficaly of." That was all she had written, and I imagined she either heard the wolf approaching or was set upon as she reached that point in her message to me.

That a man would approach a woman like Hannah and flatter her wasn't unusual. I'm sure she had heard at least a few men—sincerely or otherwise—praise or at least note her attractive qualities. I could easily imagine the man in the fog making promises that would turn her head—for it wouldn't take much to elicit such a response from her, given her situation. This man may have been important or claimed to be so. A governmental official, perhaps. She might even have recognized him. Her visions of horrible things happening to her, to me, and to others were likely part of a larger pattern of mental illness. What left me most puzzled, though, was her writing that this man had done something to her she couldn't describe, yet had made her feel important. Had the man performed some variation of the sex act she found novel and pleasurable? Was she still young enough in the trade to believe that he had engaged in a novel form of sexual stimulation only with her? Or had she simply imagined all she described to me in the unfinished note? Sadly, I would never know the answer to any of these questions.

I placed the paper inside my desk and pulled from my coat Amelia's four phrases and the sketch I had done of Mina's torso, with the streak of blood on her nightgown. I no longer wished to read, as was my custom before falling asleep. I wanted something intimate with Mina, with the woman with whom I had fallen so much in love. Did I need her tenderness and steadiness in the midst of what I had seen and listened to in the past several days? I couldn't doubt it was so. But I needed more. I desired her touch and her passion in exchange for mine. I was half-temped to make my way to the Taltson residence and tell her everything I felt for her. Understanding my present vulnerability owing to my heightened emotions, I knew such a visit wouldn't do. Giving further thought to the wolf running loose somewhere in London, I trusted the animal would be found and shot before daylight. How often in this city had it taken an incident of a particular violent nature before the authorities would take appropriate action?

Since I had no photograph or miniature of Mina, only one course remained open to me. I took out a large piece of heavy-weight drawing paper from the portfolio in the wardrobe, cleared my desk, and sketched an oval—the first step in drawing the human face. I had not done so much as this in over two years, when I had depicted the face of the young woman who died at my hands. I stared at the oval for some time, hesitant to go further but knowing I had little choice but to do so. Mina's exquisite features were so deeply etched in my mind that no photograph could have assisted me in the task of drawing her likeness. Yet I remained daunted by the prospect of fully depicting her. Why was I afraid to do so? The associations of the other two women I had drawn continued to torment me. If I brought out every detail of Mina's face, would something dreadful happen to her? Or would I lose her to another? It was impossible to fend off this illogical fear. I decided merely to draw the outline of her eyes, nose, and mouth on the paper in their unfinished states. I hoped that would be enough to satisfy the intense need for some kind of intimacy with her.

It wasn't—and I had to add something to what I had sketched. Instead of adding the requisite detail to her eyes and mouth, I began drawing her luxurious black hair. But I made no attempt to place it in the chignon, but depicted it loose and flowing across the basic shoulder design I had made.

Even though I had never seen her hair down, my imagination was so strong with the image that drawing it in its fallen state came easily. When I was done, I felt a significant release of frustration and some of the intimacy with Mina I had desired. For what seemed like many minutes, I contemplated the partially constructed face and the fully realized and loose hair, feeling that I had taken steps toward the kind of intimate relationship with her I so desired. Yet, she was incomplete—the meaning inherent in her eyes still unknown—and her mouth was yet to provide me with an indication of her affection for me.

I set the sketch up against the wall at the rear of my desk and continued to stare at it until my eyes closed. When I awoke, my head was down on the top of my desk. The sketch had fallen to the floor, face down. I lifted it carefully to prevent any dust or dirt from smudging it and placed it in the portfolio, where I had kept the two portraits I had painted. I climbed into my bed contented and fell fast asleep.

CHAPTER 24

When I arrived at my office the following morning, Charles was in conversation with a member of the police, who had come to speak with me further about the tragic incident in Cavendish Square. I answered his questions truthfully and completely but didn't volunteer that I knew the woman or that she had written me an unfinished note.

"Has the wolf been captured or shot?" I asked the officer.

"I am disappointed to say that it has not been. And sad to say that some dozen large dogs were shot by mistake during the night. We've had reports that the animal was seen heading in the direction of all four points on the compass—down across the Thames, over west toward Hyde Park, east all the way to Bethnal Green, and north near Highgate Cemetery. We can only hope that daylight will help us discover where it is and then we can dispatch it. Well, I must be off. Thank you for answering my questions, Dr. Hemmings. No need to be troubling you further."

"Still, I would appreciate your sending me word when the wolf is caught or killed."

"We will, Dr. Hemmings. Good day to you."

On my walk to the office this morning I had given thought to the ghastly coincidence between Hannah and Amelia Reeves. I wondered if Amelia's husband had his face and throat ripped apart as savagely as what I had seen the previous night. To come upon it in the aftermath as I had done with Hannah was one thing, but to have witnessed the very act itself would be beyond all descriptions of horror.

"Charles, when The Dasher comes by, tell him I'd like to speak with him." I headed into my office to jot down a series of questions to ask Lucy later today, assuming that she would return as scheduled. Although Freud advised that I must allow the patient to speak freely without agenda, I had to prevent Lucy from controlling the session and weakening my resolve to speak further about her more recent past. But I had no sooner sat down at my desk when Charles entered.

"Yes, Charles?"

"May I have a word, Julian?"

"Of course. But first let me say that I am most grateful for your efforts to acclimate to our new situation, even though I know it was not what you would have preferred. You are such the good friend to me."

"Julian, I'm afraid that . . ." He was evidently uncomfortable with what he was about to say.

"Charles, if you need to leave early today, I understand. I have but two appointments after the noon hour. I can manage."

"Julian, I believe the time has now arrived that I have dreaded these past several months. My wife has completely exhausted her supply of patience, I'm afraid."

Oddly, I attempted to postpone the inevitable with elementary humor. "'Supply of patience.' As I have sent away my own supply of *patients*, as you have been quick to argue." Charles was unable to muster even a smile. "It's a pun, don't you see, Charles? A quibble on the word 'patience.' Freud says that quibbles have meaning when they appear in dreams." I had now run out of diversionary remarks. "You wish to make a change, don't you, Charles."

"It is not a desire of mine, Julian—only a concession. It's true that my wife wants me to part from you, but in truth I can no longer come here every day and witness what you are doing to yourself and your reputation by devoting so much of your energies to these mental . . . well, there is no need to slander them further. I fear my own nerves have been frayed to the point that I have begun applying the fanciful imaginings of your patients to my own sensibilities and that I can no longer manage my anger, as my unacceptable handling of Styles the other day demonstrated."

I had expected this moment, especially of late, but had held out hope that Charles would come around to find some interest, if not fascination, in what I was now doing. But why should I ever have believed such a thing? It was pure vanity and selfishness on my part. Out of loyalty and friendship, he had given up doing what he did best—and I couldn't provide him enough satisfaction in return.

"I understand, Charles. You need to go. Please offer my apologies to your dear wife and tell her I have always appreciated her kindness and hospitality. And of course I stand at the ready to write you a reference, although the respect with which you are held by others in the medical profession will make any words from me superfluous."

"Thank you, Julian. I will come tomorrow and work with whomever you choose to succeed me. But if I may beg your indulgence for today, I have an appointment with a surgeon in an hour."

"I sincerely hope it's for a position as his assistant and not for any procedure."

Charles smiled and shook my extended hand with both of his.

"Charles, given my schedule for tomorrow, I see no need for you to be here. I will let you know when I employ someone new and then, if you have the opportunity, you can come by and instruct him."

"May God bless you in all you do, Julian." Charles left and I felt relieved that this moment had passed gently and amicably. I realized that I was now free of the guilt I was harboring each day as I watched this vital man relegated to mere office duties. I would miss him, but it was for the best—for the both of us.

Within a minute, The Dasher came into the outer office.

"I saw Mr. Yates in the street, Dr. Hemmings. He says you want to see me."

"I do Dasher. Here is a note that I want to have sent up to Cambridge." It requested the translation of the peculiar word Lucy had uttered at the end of her last visit.

"I'll be sure it's sent up before the end of the day."

"Good. Now, is there any word on the wolf?" I hoped that he might have just learned something.

"Nothing but that in this city the animal seems to be everywhere at once."

"So I've heard. Dasher, I've been thinking about that poor girl and wondering about arrangements for her burial."

"She'll be placed in a pauper's grave somewhere in or around the city, I would imagine. If she was a lady of the street, she'll surely end up in one of them." The Dasher jumped up and sat on Charles's desk. "I shouldn't wish to be buried—ever."

His swinging his legs to and fro as he uttered his startling comment delighted me. "What would you prefer, Dasher?"

"Burn me to ashes is what. I've been told by someone who buries bodies that the remains begin to rot right away but can take up to eighty years to fall completely from the bone."

"Well, Dasher, the truth is—"

"No, that's what he said. Six feet under the ground you are rotting away while others only inches away are doing the same. You might be resting on top of someone who has a fifty year jump on you in the rotting process. From what the man also told me, the coffins or bags they put you in can't hold out the water—so you have the added misery of drowning while you're also rotting. No. I want to end up a bunch of dry ashes—that's my wish."

The Dasher amusing depiction of the post-mortem state had nevertheless reflected what a growing number of physicians and scientists had been arguing for close to fifty years. These men—and surely the many women who held similar views—thought that a more sanitary, convenient, and respectful handling of the human body would come in the form of cremation. One physician even wrote that it was a "beautiful method of disposing of the body." There was a strong case made for free urn burials of the very poor, because, as one critic of the current practice noted, "the mode of burying paupers" in London is "an abomination and a disgrace."

I took out another piece of paper and began writing. "Dasher, take this note to Mr. Henderson at this address. Ask him where the body of the unfortunate woman killed last night in Cavendish Square has been taken. Tell him to read it immediately and to get back to me as soon as possible. I wrote in my note,

If possible I should like to pay for a more respectful burial for the poor woman.

I realized that I would have to explain my interest in a woman given to prostitution, but I couldn't bear to imagine her buried anonymously with other wretched souls. I wanted to be there to see her properly laid to rest. I felt it was the least I could do for her.

．．．．．

After jotting down a series of questions I would ask Lucy regarding her family background and later childhood, I felt fully the absence of Charles Yates. It is true his unease and unhappiness had increased ever since I altered my profession, but I feared the events of the last several days forced his hand—regardless of what his wife may have insisted on. I had to conclude that he wasn't being completely truthful with me when he used his wife as an excuse to be away from his duties of late. He likely had appointments in the past few days to discuss the availability of a position with several surgeons. If so, I couldn't blame him. Again, the situation between us would only have gotten worse.

My close friends were otherwise limited to Edward Maybrick, who was too committed to his work to socialize with me on any regular basis, and of course Sigmund Freud, whose residence in Austria limited our socializing to brief paragraphs in our correspondence. He had invited me to join him in Vienna during the spring, and I was hopeful of doing so. The thought pleased me all the more when I fancifully imagined bringing my new wife Mina to meet him.

With Freud on my mind, I continued the letter to him, detailing Lucy Westenra's odd and at times frightening behavior of the previous day. I would put this letter aside and finish it after I saw Lucy late this afternoon—in some six hours' time. I was most anxious to speak with her again, in spite of my palpable fear of doing so. I wanted especially to inquire about the strange word she had uttered at the end of our last session—*Nosferatu*—yet I feared it might stimulate a violent reaction of the kind of which Amelia Reeves was capable.

It struck me that I had thought of Mina, Lucy, and Amelia in the span of several seconds—as well as poor Hannah previous to that. I wondered how often during a single day I thought exclusively of the female sex. Were half my thoughts so devoted? Surely more than that. It had been that way since I witnessed the woman on Greenfield Street and became haunted by her look. When I was a surgeon, I particularly desired to assist and save female patients, and since becoming a talk therapist, the same held true. Freud had tried to draw me out on the subject, but I was hesitant to speak about it. I recall his chuckling, "Your hesitation tells me more than any words you could speak. Just remember this, my friend, all sexual excitement that finds no satisfactory release makes a transformation into anxiety. Simply put, repression causes anxiety." I had never felt his words more than I did at this moment. And I recalled his answer to my remarks about Henry Ridland, who trained me years ago. I told Freud, "When I assisted him in removing a bullet from the shoulder of a winsome bar maid who worked in an East London pub, I turned my head in embarrassment when he exposed part of her breast. I apologized for doing so. Dr. Ridland told me, 'My boy, don't apologize. All men are afraid of pretty women.'" Freud slammed his fist on the table and roared, "He's right!"

. . . . .

"Are you certain you wish to cancel for today?" I looked at the young woman sitting next to her husband in the outer office. It was evident she was conceding to his wishes or his insistence that she cease her visits after only one session.

"Tell him, my dear." The husband was both embarrassed and annoyed.

"Dr. Hemmings, I thought I would gain much benefit from seeing you, but my husband . . . and I have thought better of it since we talked last."

Apparently when she first came last week with her mother, she hadn't told her husband she was going to seek my assistance. At first, it was difficult to extract the true reason she wanted help, but at the end of our session she confessed to considerable displeasure in performing the "marriage rites," as she called them. She said it was nothing physical about the act that displeased her, and she asserted that the expected physical discomfort she felt on their wedding night had nothing to do with her subsequent feelings. I looked forward to treating her and thought of similar patients Freud had spoken with, but without her husband's approval, I stood no chance of convincing her to remain under my care.

As they rose to leave, her husband extended his hand though not his well wishes. His wife looked back at me as they stepped toward the door and mouthed the words "I'm sorry." Now I had one less patient to treat, and the prospect of other husbands or fathers thwarting their wives' and daughters' plans to see me seemed an insurmountable barrier to my success—a likelihood Charles Yates no doubt considered as he made his decision to move on. I wondered how content I'd be if I were limited exclusively to male patients. The thought left me cold. Yes, it was the female sex that I wished most to assist, and I couldn't imagine carrying on otherwise.

But my lowering spirits did not affect my appetite. Accordingly, I decided to leave the office early and have my meal. It was 11:45 a.m. I would take with me a pencil and a sheet of paper on which to list as many ideas as possible about advertising my services. I hadn't done much on that account since I began treating patients with talk therapy. I had relied exclusively on the recommendations of others in the medical community who were sympathetic to my controversial methods, as well as the occasion advertisement in the papers. I needed to be more active and creative in my pursuit of new patients.

I would also go out tomorrow and talk to Maybrick about this matter and then see Joseph Styles and perhaps Amelia Reeves.

"Are you leaving the office, Julian? Should I come back at a later time?"

As the poet Wordsworth might have said, "my heart leaped up" when I beheld Mina standing in the doorway of the outer office. She wore a green dress with yellow highlights, which were an exquisite complement to her dark brows and lush black hair, now perfectly done up in the chignon. Her face held no evidence of worry or unhappiness. She seemed as serene a young woman as could possibly be.

"Mina, this is a wonderful—no, a splendid—surprise. Can you stay or is Mr. Taltson waiting for you below?"

"I'm afraid my great-uncle is tending to his wife, who isn't feeling well. I was accompanied here by a gentleman who lives nearby. I assured him that I was coming to speak to you about Lucy and convinced him to return in a half-hour's time."

Now I was relieved that the young woman and her husband had canceled her appointment. What would I have done had Mina arrived while I was about to begin a session with the wife? No, I knew what course I would have taken. I would have begged out of it, as awkward and unprofessional as that would have been. I was about to smile at the thought but then I imagined the gentleman who brought Mina.

"May I ask if this gentleman is a contemporary of Mr. Taltson?"

"Or whether he is a man closer to your age?"

Mina was teasing me of course, but I felt the presence of the green-eyed monster. "Well, if you wish to tell me."

She offered an enigmatic smile. Was she conscious that she was tormenting me by remaining silent? I looked into her utterly magical eyes but couldn't read them. Suddenly she broke into a wide grin.

"He's in his sixties—a full thirty years older than you, I would imagine."

What she thought of the visible manifestation of my relief I could only guess.

"May I sit?"

I was mortified. "Forgive me, Mina. Please." I pointed to the sofa in the outer office.

"I would prefer sitting in your office, since I wish to speak to you about Lucy . . . and about me, I'm afraid."

I closed the door behind us as Mina took her place on the sofa. She sat in a formal manner, being sure that her dress was appropriately positioned. "Please sit in your chair, Dr. Hemmings."

"Mina, do call me Julian."

"But we are about to speak professionally and not socially."

"Indeed. All right, tell me what you've been thinking and dreaming."

"I want to speak about Lucy first, if that is all right."

"If you wish." I reached for my notebook and my "eyedropper-filler" pen, which, unlike most others of its kind, barely leaked. I looked down at the paper and not into Mina's lovely face, so that I might maintain my professional demeanor. "How is she, Mina? I was deeply concerned for her after our session yesterday afternoon."

"She is worse. She will not see or speak with me. She remains locked in her room, although . . ."

"What is it?"

"Although I saw her outside my window last night. She was walking in the small garden at the rear of the house in her night clothes with her hair undone. She seemed unaffected by the chill in the night air or by any noises that came from the street."

"Mina, I believe she came and went from here yesterday without a chaperone or companion."

Mina nodded, her expression being one of tender sadness. "Has Lucy been coming later each time, Dr. Hemmings?"

"Yes, she has. It's almost dark when she comes and completely dark by the time she leaves. Will you or her great-uncle accompany her this afternoon?"

"I will not, for she will have nothing to do with me now. My great-uncle won't either. Lucy's presence in the house has contributed to my great-aunt's illness, I'm certain of it. I fear for the old woman's life. If Lucy comes today she will come alone, or . . ."

"Mina?"

"No, I meant nothing." Mina delivered her words in a lifeless monotone, so unlike the usual soft lilt and variety characteristic of her speech.

Perhaps I could assist Mina as well as inform myself if we spoke about Lucy's past. "Mina, tell me what you know about Lucy's history—her ancestry and more about the years you two have been friends."

Mina took her time before responding. "Lucy and I became fast friends when she returned to Whitby when we were both thirteen, which was eight—

almost nine— years ago now."

"Came back? Where was she before you both met?"

"She had spent two years in Europe with her mother."

"Were they traveling or visiting?"

She again hesitated. "I cannot recall for certain."

It was evident that Mina had difficulty articulating an answer. She seemed to be debating whether she should respond truthfully to what I asked. "Remember that I am only trying to help Lucy, and knowing more about her past would assist me greatly. Was her mother English?"

"No." Her reply came immediately.

"I see. What of her father?""

"English."

"Was Lucy born in England?"

"Yes."

"Then after her father left, his wife took Lucy to her homeland?"

"Yes." Mina spoke her answers so quickly that I supposed she refused to allow any time for any internal debate about whether she should tell me these basic facts.

"Did they go to Central or Eastern Europe?"

"Yes."

"Can you recall where?"

"Many crosses standing alongside the road. Beyond the forest."

She had repeated Lucy's exact words—"Beyond the forest." Mina's eyes were wide open—her body motionless, as if she had suspended all breath.

"Mina?"

"Shade and shadow."

I stood and came to her. "Mina, are you all right?" She immediately reacted to my concern.

"Yes, yes I am. Forgive me, Dr. Hemmings. I was lost in thought."

"I understand. Can I get you anything?"

"No thank you. Please continue." She seemed perfectly fine now.

I returned to my chair. "You said that you became friends with Lucy after she returned from Europe."

"Yes. I knew of her before then—that is before she left Whitby, but we had barely ever spoken until she returned. As I might have said, we were both thirteen."

I did a quick calculation. The incident with Lucy's father's return with the "other man" occurred when she was with her mother in Europe. "Mina, tell me about your friendship with Lucy."

"From the beginning, we relied on each other for our delights and shared all of our secrets—or so I then believed. Lucy would hold my hand and tell me that she always wanted to remain somewhat a child and regretted that we hadn't been intimate friends since our infancy." Mina sighed. "And now she tells me behind the closed door of her room that we are no longer friends but rivals."

I wrote "rivals" in my notebook and would return to that matter after learning more about the friendship between them.

"Did you both like living in Whitby?"

"As I got older, I found less pleasure in the fall and winter there. Everything was so gray—the gray rocks, the gray sea. But Lucy disagreed. She would say, 'No, Mina. All is so beautiful here. You judge Whitby only in the daylight. That is why you cannot know its beauty.' At first she refused to come with me to London. She said she feared I would find it to my liking and abandon her."

"Then she agreed to come because she was afraid of losing you?"

"I fear it was not that." Mina's body sunk further into the sofa and her eyes averted mine. I decided not to pursue her meaning. I was vainly proud of myself for not succumbing to my desire simply to look into Mina's face and tell her how deeply I had fallen in love with her. Would I ever do it?

"Mina, what amusements amused you and Lucy?" I immediately realized I had committed a grammatical *faux pas*. I'm sure my face flushed with embarrassment as Mina gave me her best schoolmistress look and shook her head in mock disapproval. I so reveled in her playfulness at moments like this.

"Well, I suppose the *delight* that *delighted* us the most was my reading passages and poetry to her." How easily Mina smiled at her gentle teasing reply. It was such a contrast to Lucy's reluctant and always veiled smile.

"I imagine that you have always been a most expressive reader."

"I don't know about that, but it was always difficult getting Lucy to read to me—or to read at all. I told her that she might improve herself by reading more than she did, but she would always say, 'No Mina, I would much rather be read to.'"

"What were some of your favorite pieces to read to her?" I wondered if Mina and I had a shared interest in certain literary works.

Mina appeared quite at ease in her recollections. "Lucy would always insist that I read her aphorisms and single and memorable lines. She had little patience for long passages. I always believed she had authored her own novels in her imagination and that anything I read her could never equal what she thought up herself. Yes, Lucy would always make me read to her—when all I wanted was to hear her voice."

I could see that Mina was becoming wistful again. "Did she have a favorite quotation?"

"Indeed. It was from Pascal. 'The state of man: inconstancy, boredom, anxiety.'"

"That seems strange for someone as lively and imaginative as Lucy Westenra."

"No, you see she wanted me to repeat the words so she could devote her life to avoiding what Pascal claimed to be the state of man."

I smiled, more than content with the discussion I was having with Mina. This is how our evenings would be if we were man and wife. But I refused to allow such delightful thoughts to divert me.

"So Lucy didn't care for poetry—preferring only single lines or quotable couplets?"

"No, there was one poem she adored and made me read to her at least once every two weeks. In fact, she would join me so that we both read the same piece to each other."

"And that would be?"

"A poem about a woman called Porphyria."

"That's by Mr. Browning, is it not?"

"It is. Then you know it?"

I was tempted to nod yes, but I couldn't lie to her. I only hoped she didn't judge me deficient in literary knowledge—which I was not, generally speaking.

"I'm afraid I don't, Mina. Can you educate me about it?"

She seemed most pleased to do so. "Porphyria comes on a horrible night to the place of the man she loves. As Mr. Browning writes, 'She shut the cold out and the storm, / And kneeled and made the cheerless grate / Blaze up, and all the cottage warm.' Wet from the rain, she removes her outer clothing and lets her 'damp hair fall.' She sits by her love's side murmuring how she loves him but she was 'too weak' to set her heart's 'struggling passion free' and give herself to him forever."

IN MIND OF THE VAMPIRE

I could well understand why Lucy wished Mina to read to her. I felt immediately that the account was real and not merely literary. "You have memorized most of the poem, then?"

"All of it—as has Lucy. But there is more. Porphyria knew then that she truly worshipped him. That moment she was his, his, 'fair, / Perfectly pure and good.' Lucy would always recite the next part. And then, with her sitting next to him, in his hands he took all of her hair and wound it 'three times her little throat around.' Then I would say, 'And thus they sit together now, / And all night long they have not stirred.'" Mina's face took on a lovely sadness. "Lucy then completed the poem, 'And yet God has not said a word.'"

We both sat in silence. The moment was to me almost sublime, in spite of the basic horror that characterized the poem. The man knew through his act that Porphyria would never leave him. He had made her his forever.

The literary moment was broken by the sound of footsteps in the outer office. I thought it might be Charles. Perhaps he had had a change of heart. Or it was the gentleman who had brought Mina—arriving earlier than both I and Mina expected.

"Mina, excuse me for a moment. I'll be right back." I felt almost guilty, as if I were harboring a mistress. I had no reason to feel that way, for I had done nothing untoward, but my friend Freud would have associated this uncomfortable feeling with what I had thought, not what I had done. I looked back at Mina before I opened the office door. She nodded.

"I will stay. There is more we must speak of."

Much relieved, I stepped into the outer office. My relief was enhanced by the sight of The Dasher.

"Dr. Hemmings, this is for you. I was told to tell you that you need to read it immediately."

172

CHAPTER 25

"Will I need to take back an answer from you, Dr. Hemmings?"

"No need at this time, Dasher. Here's for your efforts. Is there any word on the wolf?"

"None, sir. They hope he was frightened out of the city during the night by the gunshots that killed the dogs."

The Dasher left the office, and I took a quick look at Edward Maybrick's brief note.

Do all you can to come here tonight after your last session. Very important. No need to reply. Just come as soon as you can.

I could only assume it was something relating to Joseph Styles. Had he struck out in a violent manner? Had he injured himself—or worse? I was sure Maybrick wouldn't invite me out again if Amelia Reeves had simply desired my presence.

I placed the note in the pocket of my coat and stepped back into my office. Mina was standing over my desk.

"Excuse my curiosity, Dr. Hemmings, but I see you have started a new correspondence to Dr. Freud."

"Yes, I have. As you can see, I am sharing my thoughts about Lucy and asking for his assessment." I hoped Mina wouldn't think I was violating Lucy's privacy by doing so. "It's physician-to-physician, you see, and therefore—."

"I understand, and I see nothing wrong with your doing so. I think it is most admirable as well as fascinating that you have found much inspiration and purpose in the teachings of Dr. Freud."

"I have indeed. Mina, the state of the mind affects so much. It can rip apart as well as repair. Muscles, bones, and organs may all deteriorate because of the mind. I believe we are still in the infancy of our understanding. This next century will mature us in ways we cannot now possibly foresee. We will then have a better chance of eliminating the devastating effects of fear and superstition."

Mina took a sudden swallow of breath and her eyes broadened, as if she were frightened by what I had just said. In a moment, she was herself again. "I want to know more about the mind."

"I am happy to hear it."

"And I have finally read your letter. You offered to speak with me about the subject—or have you forgotten?"

"No, Mina, I have not forgotten. Yes, of course, I will speak to you about the mind. I am so delighted you have read my letter." Joyfully anticipating my teaching her all I knew in the days and weeks to come, I wanted now to schedule our first formal discussion, but she seemed absorbed in the letter on my desk.

"Well at any rate, I will finish the letter to Freud after I see Lucy later today."

"If you do see her." I saw Mina's fingers begin to curl—a typical reaction to anxiety.

"Yes—if. I will try to bring her out about why she had put distance between the two of you, if you would like."

"I have full confidence that you will do what you think is best, Dr. Hemmings."

I was frustrated by her formal way of addressing me. "Mina, you are not sitting on the sofa now. Can you not call me Julian at least while we are standing here?"

The twinkle had returned to her eye. "You should know that society frowns upon a young woman addressing such an important man as you by anything but his fully-titled name. Isn't that right . . . Julian?" How broadly I grinned, I could only guess. Her cheerful tone further elevated my spirits. "Please don't be put off by my boldness, Julian. Lucy believes I have decided to begin living in the new century before the old one is even out. She has teased me by saying that I don't wish to finish, as they say, in the back of the pack when women begin running with their more natural and quicker speed—and with their shoes off."

It was so splendid sharing a laugh with this incredible young woman. I must admit that the image of her running without shoes was a most stimulating one. Previous to meeting her, I always deemed all my sensual imaginings furtive at best. How could I live now without Mina? I wanted desperately to reveal my heart, yet I so feared hearing her check me with "But you have known me but a few days."

"May we speak professionally now, Dr. Hemmings?" Mina's eye had lost its sparkle. Her features had turned serious—almost intimidating.

"Yes, of course. Please sit on the sofa."

She sat as she did before, taking care to position herself and her dress as would a lady of elevated rank.

"I want now to speak further of my thoughts and dreams."

My anxiety returned. I felt as though I was about to learn something that would separate us. I had no choice but to hear her, even though I was violating the warning of Freud about the dangers of allowing personal feelings for the patient to interfere with analysis. I just couldn't risk losing her by adhering to professional scruples.

"Speak freely, Mina."

My words elicited a start from her. She involuntarily took another deep and quick breath. "Freely," she replied—almost with a whisper of terror.

"Yes. Please. Go on. You can trust me."

She leaned her body back on the sofa and slightly elevated her head. "Lately when I have dreamed, I see myself running in a direction with the wind at my back, but the terrain isn't level. During these dreams, I fall into a pond or ditch and listen to the wind as it rushes over my head. I return to my feet and look back to where I began my journey, but nothing appears the same as it did when I initially ran past. The hills have disappeared as have all the cottages and streams. I begin to run again and hear the wind behind me. I stop and try to understand if the wind has circled back around me or if this is a new wind—just one of a series of winds that will never stop."

"Do you again fall into the pond or ditch?"

"Yes, and the same thing happens. I look back, see that all is different, and hear the new wind rushing up behind me. Nothing is ever resolved. Only when I awaken or shift into a new dream does the wind finally stop."

I was so taken by her account that I had forgotten to jot down details about her dream. But it was doubtful I would ever forget any part of it.

"Mina, do you want me to attempt an explanation of your dream."

"No. I want you only to listen. Promise me you will only listen."

"I promise."

Her insistence on this matter surprised me. I had assumed she wanted me to help her understand the darker visions she was having.

"I have again dreamed of the man I told you of earlier."

I didn't wish to think of this figure or of the blood Mina said was streaked on her nightgown. Would she speak of finding the garment outside the house?

She waited to see if I would reply, but I said nothing, honoring her request that I only listen. Satisfied, she continued.

"He stood before me—but he didn't touch me. My eyes were tightly closed, afraid to look into his face. I didn't want to hear him but I had to listen. He said, 'Mina, you are to me a woman of your time. Your beauty will never fade, for I will make you perfection.' He then began slowly to whisper 'Lucy—Lucy—Lucy' in a haunting and a taunting manner. I begged him to stop, but he repeated her name again. 'Lucy—Lucy—Lucy.' I was brought to tears, pleading even more ardently for him to stop. He breathed deeply—the sound of which was unlike anything I had ever heard before. Now he whispered 'Mina—Mina—Mina' in the same haunting and alluring voice. I opened my eyes and looked into his. His look held me fast."

My fingers gripped at the notebook in my lap. The emotional agony of hearing her speak of this male figure was almost unbearable. My temples throbbed from the pressure of my discomfort.

"He took my hand and held it before his mouth. 'You have always wished to be like Lucy,' he said. 'To have her passions and express them as she has. Dearest Mina, you read books, but you know yourself so little. You rely on knowledge and reason to sustain you, but they only obscure who you really are. I can show you who you are and have always wanted to be. I can show you how futile are all demonstrations of sophistication. Are you ready to learn from me, or will your misguided pride force you resist?'"

How could she have recalled all these words from a figure in her dream? Or was she for the first time creating these words as she sat on the sofa in my office? Her face remained elevated, but her feet were no longer crossed at the ankle.

"He then touched my hand with his lips. 'You think to hear the holy music I cannot know. But deep within you sounds the melody I have played for centuries. And you have heard it. You have responded to its harmonies in ways others cannot.' He rubbed my hand across his half opened lips. 'It will always be the same,' he whispered, 'The want, the hunger, the longing.' I couldn't control my voice. I responded slowly 'Yes—yes—yes.'

Barely able to take a breath, I desperately wanted her to cease. I couldn't endure what I was feeling—the hurt and the growing rage emanating from my jealousy. But I said nothing.

"He released my hand and stepped away from me."

Thank God I was allowed some abatement of my pain.

"He spoke of the end of this century. 'You will always remind me of this great time, in which man has advanced his machines and ideas but an era which could not efface his many superstitions and fears—nor suppress the deep desires of its women. I wonder, Mina, will all mystery and romance be forgotten in the coming time, with its new logic and ambition?' Suddenly I felt his breath in my ear. I never saw him move from where he stood, yet now he was behind me. I could feel his body pressed against my back. His arms enveloped me."

Fighting through my misery was my continued amazement at her recollection of this dream. Or if not that—the incredible vision she was articulating for the first time.

"He spoke again and I inhaled the odor of blood. 'In my world, all passion is un-dead. It always seeks and is always satisfied. All logic and learned wisdom cannot destroy or completely suppress what is deep within the soul of all men and women. You know it is true, my lovely Mina. It will always be so. And I will prove it to you.'"

My heartbeat had accelerated to the point that I feared for my well-being.

Mina expelled a sigh tinged with reluctance. "Then the dream ended. I awoke and stood by my bed, as if I were waiting for someone."

I had to break my silence. "Lucy?"

"No, she was alone in her room. But I must have fallen asleep while I stood, for I found myself in another dream. But this one was so very brief. He again stood before me. He caressed my face with the back of his hands and asked, 'How do you come?' I answered, 'Freely.' I then awoke and found that I was sitting on the edge of the bed. And on my lips and on my chin and on my cheeks was . . . No, I can't. I can't."

I sprung from my chair and came to her. She was evidently in distress.

"Mina, Mina? Speak to me." I placed my hand on her now lowered head. She threw her body rearward and looked at me with terror.

"Do not touch me! I am unclean! I hear the words 'Flesh of my flesh. Blood of my blood!'"

I lurched backward, completely stunned by her reaction. With labored breath, she slowly stood and held out her hand to me. Cautiously I took and

177

caressed it between both of my closed hands. The tears dropped unimpeded down her cheeks.

"Julian, I did not want to stop him. Forgive me. Please forgive me."

My anguish disappeared with these words. She wanted me to forgive her for her horrendous dream and for her behavior in it because she didn't wish me to think less of her. I dared to believe at this moment that her asking for forgiveness meant that she loved me.

"Dearest Mina, there is nothing to forgive. You only had a terrible dream."

Her eyes bore into mine. "You will not forget what I have told you. You must promise me that when I leave here, you will not forget."

"Dearest Mina, I will not ever forget."

There was a polite knock on my office door. Mina pulled her hand from my tender grasp and touched her hair. "I must go now. The gentleman has come to take me back."

I could think of only one "gentleman"—the one in her dreams. I opened the door and saw an unremarkable-looking man with gray hair and beard.

Mina's voice was unsteady. "Dr. Hemmings, this is Mr. Kincaid. He has kindly escorted me from my great-uncle's home and will now take me back."

I extended my hand. "It is a pleasure to meet you, sir."

Kincaid looked at Mina as we shook hands. "Are you all right, Miss Murray?" he asked. He looked at me, but what could I say?

"Yes, Mr. Kincaid. I am just deeply concerned about my friend Lucy."

He seemed satisfied with her reply and wished me a pleasant afternoon. I was almost desperate to ask Mina when I would next see her, but present company made that impossible. But she looked back as she reached the door and whispered "I will prove it to you." At first I felt exhilarated by the possibility that she had just promised to prove her love for me, but the distressed expression on her face and my realization that she was quoting the figure from her dream disabused me of my initial assumption. When I heard the outer door close, I immediately lamented not having kissed her hand—or her cheek—before Kincaid's arrival. Would she come back tomorrow? I shook off my feeling of helplessness and self-pity and resolved that if she didn't visit me the next day, I would go to her. Nothing would keep me from loving her or telling her so the next time we met.

CHAPTER 26

Having several hours to myself before Lucy's scheduled session, I had the choice of sitting at the front desk in the hope of speaking to a potential new patient who might walk in or leaving for a meal. Even though the emotion of seeing and speaking with Mina had suppressed my appetite, I knew it would return once I began walking. I would take the time to ponder all Mina had said to me, as well as try to analyze further Lucy's recent behavior. I gave thought to going to Maybrick's asylum and eating there, but he specifically said to come this evening. Besides, if there was a complication regarding Joseph Styles, I might not make it back in time for Lucy's appointment—again if she came.

As I headed south on Regent Street, I thought of the unfortunate Hannah, whom I had first seen the last time I walked in this direction. I still hadn't understood why she felt she had to warn me. Had she known of me before our first meeting or had her warnings been the direct result of mental illness? I was of course aware of several instances of a woman or an older girl becoming inordinately and disturbingly infatuated with men of respected place or position, although given my allotment of patients, my position could hardly be attractive enough for such misguided devotion.

As I crossed Regent Street and headed toward Berkeley Square, I passed a man and two young girls of probably fifteen or sixteen years of age. The girls were engaged in private conversation, laughing every few seconds, while the man—the father of one of the girls, I supposed—scanned the *Times*. I couldn't help imagining Mina and Lucy at that age speaking in the same delightful manner. What had now come between them?

Given the details of Mina's dream, it appeared to me that the friends indeed had a rivalry. Had they both been enamored of the same boy when they were younger? Did Lucy envy Mina's intelligence, self-assuredness, and manner? The disturbing figure in Mina's dream suggested that she lacked the same "passionate" expression of which Lucy was capable. Did Mina desire to be as open about her feelings as was Lucy, and did they have a falling out about that very matter? I believed it was more than possible. Yet I couldn't believe Mina's envy to be such that she would have precipitated the breach between them. If Lucy continued to deteriorate physically as well as mentally and died as a result, Mina would never forgive herself for not reconciling with her friend. If Lucy came late this afternoon, I would do what I could to find out more about the disagreement between them and then try to encourage reconciliation.

By the time I reached Berkeley Square, my hunger had returned with a vengeance. I stepped inside a dining house nearby and claimed the last table available. The waiter was upon me like a flash and began his litany of all that was "just ready." I would have preferred a printed menu, but the elderly man insisted on the old style of listing everything from which I might choose. Because I knew it would be impossible to recall every item he was likely to mention, I decided to order the first thing that struck my fancy. The fourth dish the old waiter listed was roast veal, and I stopped him with "Very good. I'll have that." I could see he was disappointed that he never got to mention the boiled pork and rump steak pudding.

My knife, fork, and spoon were deftly placed before me, and I selected some bread from the small assortment offered. It was only then that he asked if I would like something to drink. I could see that he was momentarily confused by having failed to follow the proper order of service, but I put him at ease and asked for a pint of pale ale. Was his momentary forgetfulness the result of his age or had he been suffering from some emotional or psychological difficulty? I had never felt such empathy for strangers when I was a surgeon and artist. I couldn't help feeling that my love for Mina had only enhanced this growing feeling within me.

While waiting for the beverage, I overheard two gentlemen speaking at the table behind me. They were speaking of the wolf and Hannah's death.

"I still hold that it was a mastiff that ripped into that bunter," by which the gentleman meant a woman or girl who was part whore and part beggar.

The other man countered. "No, mastiffs don't attack with anything close to such ferocity. They are by temperament gentle, especially for their size. They are trusted around small children. At most he would have leaped on the girl if she posed any threat to its master. It had to have been a wolf."

"Whatever it was, it hasn't yet been found as far as I've heard."

"I wouldn't worry," the second man responded. "It's likely miles away by now." He chuckled. "I don't think the species is attracted to the sound of gunshots. There must have been a hundred blasts throughout the city last night."

The waiter delivered my pint of ale and I tried to ignore the conversation behind me so that I might think further about Mina's dream. But the man who believed Hannah was killed by the wolf then revealed something to his companion that astounded me.

"My sister's husband, who assists in post-mortem examinations of violent death, told me something about the wounds on the girl."

"They were horrific if all reports are true."

"Indeed they were. But they found something very peculiar on a piece of torn flesh. Apparently the beast clamped on to her throat and chewed his way through to the spine. But the flap of skin on the left side of the throat was merely sheared and remained intact. And on the un-torn flesh they found two puncture marks. They can't understand how the animal bit into the neck at that spot but apparently let go without tearing through it. Based on the condition of the wounds, the beast moved directly from the throat to the face. They say that the two puncture wounds were not post-mortem. All rather curious, I must say."

I somehow managed to finish my meal, along with a second pint of ale. I couldn't help believing that those visible puncture wounds on Hannah's neck were exactly like the ones I saw on Lucy's. What on earth could they have been? I wanted Lucy to come this afternoon more than ever. Perhaps I could convince her to tell me how she received the wounds on her neck. I had believed they were self-inflicted—a common prelude to a suicide attempt. But now I had serious doubts.

I left the dining house and made my way into Berkeley Square. Standing before a statue of semi-draped nymph carrying a large vase by her side, I forced from my conscious thoughts the memory of Hannah's mutilated body lying under the statue in Cavendish Square and considered instead the benign figure before me as my lovely Mina, with a vase filled with water to refresh and sooth my agitated spirits. How I desired to have her comfort me now and for the rest of my life. I again determined that I wouldn't squander whatever chance I had to make her my own. And yet, given all that had recently occurred in my life, I couldn't have found a more inconvenient time to fall in love.

IN MIND OF THE VAMPIRE

I walked until I stood in front of 50 Berkeley Square—the one place in the city The Dasher vowed never to go because of its reputation for being haunted. Legend collaborated with more recent accounts to paint a chilling portrait of the structure—where George Canning, our former Prime Minister, once resided. Even he reported hearing peculiar noises and experiencing strange phenomena while living there. But Canning's claims were nothing compared to other tales of mystery. Supposedly the attic of the house remains haunted by the spirit of a young woman who took her own life by throwing herself from the top floor window. The Dasher insisted that anyone who catches the spirit's eye will immediately die of fright. Other accounts spoke of a young man locked in the attic until he slowly went mad and died, and two others were said to have perished after spending a night in the upper room. Another poor man survived his visit but left the house paralyzed with fear to the point that he was never again able to speak.

Memory of still another report—that of a maid having gone mad and dying in an asylum after spending the night in the attic of 50 Berkeley Square—brought to mind Amelia Reeves and Joseph Styles. Pulling out my watch and noting the time, I turned from the residence and began my way back to my office, but I hadn't made it to the other side of the Square when I recalled one further detail about the spirit said to inhabit the attic. Some have said that it takes the appearance of a brown mist.

. . . . . .

I opened the door to my office at twenty minutes after four. I expected Lucy—if she was to come—in half hour or so. Would she also be accompanied by Mr. Kincaid or would she come alone, as she seemed to have done yesterday? She had staggered me previously with her chilling voice and behavior—and that word *Nosferatu*. I did my best to prepare myself for whatever she might say or do. Refusing to be as affected as I was the last time we met, I knew I must remain in control of this session, because it might be the best chance to save Lucy from herself and inevitable death. And I had to know about those fresh puncture wounds on her neck.

"Dr. Hemmings, sir." The Dasher walked in nonchalantly as usual, which I never minded in the least. I cherished our special bond—where familiarity was welcome and not merely tolerated.

"Yes, Dasher?" Had I been in better spirits I would have teased him about

182

having just been to 50 Berkeley Square and then watched the terror creep across his face before assuring him that the spirit in the attic was merely a legend. Yet today I felt I could hardly make that case to him or to anyone else—in spite of my general ridicule of ghosts and superstitions.

"You asked me to find out about that unfortunate woman's burial."

I had completely forgotten about the request. "Indeed. What did you learn?"

"They plan on burying her tomorrow. The medical men kept her longer than they at first thought they would. Something about the nature of her wounds interested them."

"And did you get a response to my offer to pay for a private burial?"

"I did—not more than ten minutes ago. Mr. Kincaid said he would hold the body until he gets more information from you about what kind of burial you're requesting. He seemed to know you and said you were a fine gentleman."

"Mr. Kincaid?"

"Yes. Elderly gent with gray hair and beard. You do know him, don't you, sir?"

"I've only just met him." A custodian of the dead accompanying Mina to my office earlier today? It seemed so improper and more than that—repulsive.

"Then you must have made a good impression on him."

"Thank you, Dasher. Here's for your pains."

"Don't hurt a bit when those coins drop into my hand, Dr. Hemmings." He grinned expecting me to smile at his witticism, but I was unable. "You need me to do anything else for you this evening?"

"No, I don't believe so, Dasher. I'll be heading to Dr. Maybrick's asylum after I see my next patient."

"Want me to travel out to with you tonight? I could inform the people that keep me. They'd let me go with you."

"No, my boy. But thank you for offering."

"Very well, then. I'll see you when the sun next rises."

Strangely, The Dasher looked at me as though he wanted some assurance that such would be the case. I realized he was probably worried about my journey to and from Putney at night—especially with the wolf still unaccounted for.

"You will indeed, Dasher. Now off with you."

IN MIND OF THE VAMPIRE

I went to the front door and watched him tear down the street. He was so full of energy—so full of life. The Dasher was a welcome antidote to much I had been dwelling on of late. I looked at the sky. The late early November afternoon was delightfully cool--the air not yet suffocated by the blackened smoke from every working fireplace in the city. Now able to smile, I could imagine no sweeter scene than sitting outside of a modest home in the country, with Mina as my wife and the Dasher as my adopted son. We would then go inside and listen to Mina play soothing music on the piano. When she was finished I would kiss both her lovely hands and thank her for bringing such melody and harmony into my life.

184

CHAPTER 27

It was now half past five, and Lucy had not come. Understanding that she was in no state to give a thought to punctuality, I had waited much longer than I would have ordinarily. Having jotted down the questions I wished to ask and the topics I wished to pursue with her, I had spent the past thirty minutes sketching a country house—one I had never before seen and had only taken shape in my imagination moments before I reached for paper and pencil. Much to my surprise, my skill for scenic depiction had not deserted me in all these years. I easily drew the house in what many have called the "Eastlake" style, with porch posts, balustrades, pendants, and perforated gables. When I finished depicting the front of the modest two-story dwelling, I began a second sketch—of the rear of the house, complete with garden. I spared little detail, even adding a stone bridge across a small pond which led to an oval area enclosed with high hedges. In the middle of the oval area I drew a facsimile of the statue I had earlier stood before in Berkeley Square. I looked at the sketch of the garden and felt it required one further addition— the figure of Mina on the stone bridge, elevated above the plane of the statue. I sketched her outline but then stopped. I decided to finish the small likeness of Mina in my rooms, rather than here in the office. Now accepting that Lucy wouldn't be coming, I placed in a folio volume the two sheets on which I had sketched the front and rear of the house and made ready to leave.

Unsure of how cold the weather might have turned or whether it was raining, I went to the front door instead of looking out the window, owing to the darkness that had just descended on the city. If the conditions were satisfactory, I would leave behind my heavier coat and scarf. Momentarily staring at Charles's desk, knowing how much I would miss his company in the days ahead, I opened the door.

The thick fog had totally obscured my view of the street. I thrust my arm forward and my hand literally disappeared from sight. Could I even grope my way back to my lodgings in these conditions? Regarding the wolf, the animal's senses would no doubt allow him to find me in the heavy fog, but I would have no chance of seeing him before he was upon me. I would have to stay in the office and hope the conditions would soon improve so that I could leave. And how would I get someone to drive me out to Putney and to Maybrick's asylum if conditions remained the same for several hours? I took two steps forward from the door and found myself completely enveloped by the fog.

I didn't see the body until it fell against my chest. I dropped my head and looked into a tangled mass of dark hair. The figure let out a soft moan.

"May I come in, Dr. Hemmings?"

It was Lucy. I feared she was injured, for I detected the unmistakable odor of blood.

"Lucy, what has happened? Are you hurt? She made no movement to enter, but remained pressed against me in the leaden fog. "You should not have come on a night such as this."

"You expected me to come, and I am here. May I enter?"

I tried to step away from her and permit her passage, but she wouldn't change her position, her head and body still pressed against my chest.

"Can you help me in, Dr. Hemmings?"

"Of course, Lucy." I placed my arms around her and literally maneuvered her lifeless body through the door. I feared her health had so deteriorated that she could barely move forward on her own. But then how did she make it to the doorstep?

"Please take me inside to the sofa."

Because I had already extinguished the gaslights in my inner office, only the light from the outer office provided guidance to the sofa. I sat her down and grabbed the matchbox on my desk and re-lighted the two lamps. What I saw frightened me. Lucy's skin was even paler than it had been yesterday. Her cheeks were sunken and she seemed barely able to prevent her head from tumbling toward her shoulder. Yet her lips were lush red and her eyes were brilliantly alive. I was alarmed to see that she wore nothing but a nightgown, which bore traces of blood at the neckline. Her feet were bare and remarkably free of any dirt.

"Lucy, how were you able to come here? Who brought you? Was it Mr. Taltson?"

"No, he is too ill. He and his wife." Her voice was soft but steady.

"Mr. Kincaid then?" For a moment I thought how Kincaid might have stared at Lucy, sizing up the next body he would commit to burial.

"Who?" She seemed genuinely unaware of such a person.

"Then who brought you, Lucy?"

"I was brought by the mist."

I shook my head to clear the thought of the other strange mists I had recently seen as well as the legend of 50 Berkeley Square, but to no avail. I held up my hand in a gesture of "excuse me for a moment," and I stepped out of my office, went to the front door, and jerked it open. As I feared, the sky was completely clear, my vision of the street now unimpeded.

I felt my strength ebb quickly, forcing me to brace myself against the inside of the doorway. So much had happened of late of a mysterious and horrifying nature that I could no longer trust my intellect to supply a rational explanation. I turned and looked at the opened door to the inner office and beheld Lucy on the sofa waiting for me. With all my heart, I wished at this moment to return to my rooms and leave her sitting there.

"Dr. Hemmings?"

I reached in my coat pocket and felt the list of questions and topics I had written down earlier. I would keep our discussion on these matters and not allow anything to divert me from learning all I could about her past life and recent traumatic experiences.

"Dr. Hemmings?"

"Coming, Lucy."

As I stepped into the inner office I saw that she was sitting with her body pressed against the rear of the sofa, both her bare feet firmly on the floor, and her hands placed down open-palmed on her knees. I thought it best not to press her further on how she arrived, but I would warn her that she needed someone to accompany her back to the Taltsons.

"Lucy, you may have heard about the wolf that attacked and killed a young woman last night." She gave no response. "Since it is dark and the wolf unaccounted for, you must have an escort after you leave here. If no one is coming to collect you, I will see you home myself."

"The wolf will not harm me, Dr. Hemmings."

"You don't know that, Lucy."

"I do know that, Dr. Hemmings. The wolf is a child."

"A child?"

"A child of the night."

I took her meaning as poetic or metaphoric. "Yes, you might say that, Lucy. Still—"

"He will not harm me."

Again, I chose not to argue with her. Freud had also warned me of the damage caused by a therapist who debates with his patients. "You are not there to educate or to preach, Hemmings. You are there to listen." Because I knew how frequently I had already violated this principal, I was determined to allow her as much freedom as possible in her discussion with me.

"Lucy, I am glad you have come. I thought that first we might talk about how you characterize your relationship with Mina. Both before you arrived in London and right now."

"It is the same."

"The same?"

"We are now and have always been rivals."

"Why do you say that?"

"She may win. I am in great fear of it."

"Lucy, you are special in ways Mina cannot be. You are both beautiful young women."

She displayed a wicked smile. "You find us equally beautiful, Dr. Hemmings? You appreciate our beauty equally? Mine as much as hers?"

I would not allow her to pry into my private feelings. "Mina cares for you, Lucy. Whatever breach has separated you both, it can surely be overcome."

"Only one can be chosen." Lucy looked away from me with disgust.

I changed the subject. "Lucy, I am very much interested in your family history—your history."

"I have no history. All is now."

I took a moment to check my impatience at these terse and contrary replies and interruptions.

"Very well, Lucy. Can you—"

"I want. Forever I have wanted."

"What have you wanted, Lucy?"

Her head dropped to her breast. She began speaking, but I couldn't make out the words. Once more they sounded foreign. I came to her.

"What are you saying, Lucy?"

She raised her head and captured my eyes with her own dark gaze. Her lips slightly parted. She slid her hands from her knees and placed them on the sofa with her palms up and her fingers widely spread.

"Have you come to beg for a kiss, Dr. Hemmings?"

"Dear God, no. I only approached to see if you were all right." I took a step back from the sofa.

"It would be an unforgiveable violation—in so many ways." She smiled triumphantly— without showing her teeth, as usual.

My professional demeanor was cracking. I moved back to my chair and groped for something to regain control of the session.

"Tell me about Whitby, Lucy. Did you like living there?"

She emitted a childlike sigh. "This is only the second time I have ever been away from Whitby."

"Have you missed being there this fall?"She remained silent. "What part of Whitby have you thought of most of most since you've been in London?"

"The view of the ruins of Whitby Abbey. The abbey is so beautiful. So full of romantic bits. And the harbor—and the church yard. I would walk out by myself and feel everything that I truly am."

"You walked by yourself in the mornings or afternoons?"

"Never. Then Mina was with me, and it was all a different place. Only later, when I was alone, could I feel all of its beauty . . . and power."

"What else did you feel there, Lucy?"

"The longing. The time. The untold."

I looked at my desk and saw the volume of Shakespeare I had brought in with me so that I could read further into *Hamlet*, as Freud advised. A quotation came to me, and something compelled me to articulate it. 'There are more things in heaven and earth, Horatio, / Than are dreamt of in your philosophy.'"

Lucy took a labored breath that made me fear she was in respiratory distress. "I didn't care for *Hamlet* when Mina read parts to me. So much deep thought, but I found not enough passion to enthrall me. But now I understand a line that I gave little thought to when Mina first read it to me."

"A line you re-read yourself?"

"No. A line that was whispered to me only recently."

"May I ask which one?"

She lifted her head and I saw that her eyes were closed. "To sleep, to sleep . . . perchance to dream."

In my notebook I jotted down the line from Hamlet's famous "To be or not to be" soliloquy. Later I would ponder the line's possible connection to

Lucy's past or present history. "Lucy will you tell me who whispered those words to you?"

She shook her head so violently from side to side that I was certain she would harm herself.

"Lucy, please stop that." I stood and stepped toward her. "Stop that!" She obeyed and dropped her head to her breast. I couldn't tell if she was beginning to weep or laugh. "Lucy?"

"I won't betray. Other have already suffered and will soon suffer horribly for doing so. I will not."

I returned to my chair and decided to shift the conversation back to her impressions of Whitby. The tone in my voice was desperate. "Lucy, please tell me more about how you loved being by the sea in Whitby." Her pleasant expression gave me assurance that she could carry on.

"Have you fully known the dark side of twilight, Dr. Hemmings? How I wished it could be endless—all the lovely and horrible imaginings. When the trees sang and wept as they did in the land of my mother's birth."

"And where exactly was that, Lucy?"

"Beyond the forest. Past the trees. Among the rocks and stones. I feared being alone. A young girl. I wasn't ready, he said. It would happen later—in England. At Whitby I again feared being alone and I set forth. I thought I heard a voice. I looked and saw a dark figure on the beach. It called me, and I went. It calls me still. Even in my dreams when I did not set forth, I heard the sound of lapping waves and the gentle and then violent rush of water. I sensed the darkness and the need. The red eyes. The wind. I go. And I do not want to be free."

I was utterly mesmerized by her words. She spoke now as though she were alone, out near the sea with the wind billowing her nightgown and raven hair. I closed my eyes and visualized her arms reaching out, beckoning the dark figure to come to her. Suddenly to my horror her face became Mina's. Startled by the image, I opened my eyes and found Lucy standing in front of my chair.

"I soon must go, Dr. Hemmings."

As I expected, the session would end prematurely. "Yes, yes. I will see you home Lucy." I tried to rise, but she closed the distance between us.

"You cannot. My home is beyond whatever place you might imagine."

Her lips were now of a plum color. She lifted the upper one to expose part of her gums, which were deep red. Her hypnotic eyes held me fast in the chair.

"The blood is the life. The blood is the life."

"Lucy, what do you . . .?" I didn't finish my thought as my eyes dropped to her bare feet. The veins in each foot were pronounced and blue.

"I must go, Dr. Hemmings." She walked back to the sofa but did not sit.

I had little control of my quivering voice. "I will see you back to the Taltson's."

"I am not going there."

"Then where are you going, Lucy?"

"To Highgate."

"Highgate Cemetery?"

She merely smiled, once more with her mouth closed. I was certain she was speaking of what she believed was her impending death.

"Lucy, we will make you well. First you must get stronger. You need fresh blood." Her reaction to these words was dynamic. Her body swelled with a flash of health. Her breath was deep yet vigorous, and the color returned to her cheeks. Her eyes opened widely, and her fingers on both hands spread open. Although frightened by this latest alteration of her appearance, I was at least encouraged that she would finally agree to a transfusion, even though at present she hardly seemed to need one. "Lucy, we can go now to a physician friend and he can transfuse blood into you tonight."

"No!" Her face wrenched in pain, and she shaped the outstretched fingers on both hands into a semi-claw, which she lifted and turned toward each side of her face.

I expected her to rip at her cheeks, but she remained stationary. "Lucy, very well. No transfusion. But please, you must at least eat something hearty and get more rest. Come. Let us return to the Taltson's."

She dropped her hands passively to her sides. "No, Dr. Hemmings, I am going to Highgate."

"Lucy, you must stop thinking of death."

She replied in a voice of chilling calm. "I am not thinking of death, but of the un-dead. It is my time now. I must go. He calls to me. I must obey his summons." She stopped as though she was waiting to hear something. Finally, she sighed. "And still God has not said a word."

CHAPTER 28

Shaken, I rose from my chair to look outside for a hansom cab to drive the both of us to the Taltsons. But when I opened the front door, I found that the heavy mist which earlier seemed to usher Lucy into my office had returned. I rushed back into the inner office and saw that Lucy was gone. I darted past the sofa to the narrow hallway that led to the rear door, which was now open. The fog had gathered there was well. As was the case with the front door, none of the mist had drifted into any part of my office. When I returned to the front door, I saw—as I mournfully expected— that the fog was gone. I slowly retraced my steps to the rear entrance only to verify what I was certain I would find there. The air was clear—the stars and moon visible in the sky. I knew I would never see Lucy again.

I collapsed into my desk chair and tried to convince myself that the sudden appearance and reappearance of the fog and everything I had seen and heard had a rational explanation—one grounded in science. I reached into my desk for the bundle of letters I had received from Freud since my return to England some seventeen months earlier. I opened one after another seeking his wisdom. How I wished I could speak to him about Lucy Westenra and receive his immediate impressions. I still hadn't sent him the letter I had begun about her. I would finish it tomorrow and send it off, but I knew anything he would say in response would come too late to assist her.

My Austrian friend noted in one letter that the conscious mind was similar to a fountain playing in the sun and then falling back into the massive subterranean pool of the subconscious from which it had risen. At this moment I had no confidence that I could ever plumb the depths of a mind as unique and terrifying as Lucy's—and for the first time seriously doubted my fitness for the work I had chosen. Could I ever understand the complexities of the human mind well enough to assist or rescue anyone? I remembered the lesson my father taught me about faith. When one sinks into doubt, he will soon be lost in despair.

I opened another letter in which Freud had written that the goal of psychology is not to eliminate complexity but rather to get the patient's mind in accord with it. Yet how could this apply to such an acutely disturbed mind as Lucy Westenra's, especially when she spoke in so many contradictions? She implied that God had called her and that she wished to obey his summons, but then she quoted the Browning poem Mina had introduced me to—"And yet God has not said a word."

I searched for the one letter in which Freud mentioned the sexuality of young girls. Soon I found it. "We know so much less about the sexual habits, experiences, and thoughts of young girls than we do young boys." He added that we need not feel either guilty or frustrated knowing so little about the subject, for the sexual life of adult women has always been a kind of "dark continent" for the analyst. By Lucy's own admission, she had active fantasies, if not actual experiences, of something highly sexual when at Whitby, in her mother's homeland, and here in London. I believed she wished to tell me clearly what they were, but she hid them beneath her unexpected and dramatic outbursts and changes of demeanor and the self-harm she inflicted at least through her refusal to eat well and receive proper medical attention.

I waited another half hour in my office, in the futile hope she would return. As I debated whether to stay longer, I discovered the note from Edward Maybrick that The Dasher had earlier delivered. I needed to go immediately to Putney. Locking the office behind me, I headed down to the street to find a cab to take me to Maybrick's asylum. The first two I flagged refused to leave the immediate confines of Oxford and Regent Streets, owing to the assumption that the wolf had headed west in the direction of Hyde Park and South Kensington, both of which we would pass to make the cross-over the Thames to Putney. Fortunately, a third driver was more fatalistic about the whole thing and agreed to transport me. The night was still clear and crisp. There was no wind. The moon cast just enough light to provide partial illumination of all we would pass. Had it been for any other reason, I think a night's ride of this distance would have soothed my mind and relaxed every muscle in my body. But both mind and body were still reeling from the effects of Lucy's visit—as well as the assumption that something unpleasant was waiting for me at Maybrick's asylum. Still, how blissful would be a ride out on an evening like this with Mina at my side.

Heading southwest, we finally approached Putney Bridge, the only one in all of Britain with a church on both ends of the span. As we rode past All Saints on the north end, I detected a cloud of hovering in front of the church's tower but nowhere else. I wondered if it was a hallucination of some kind, inspired by the mysterious fog and mist that had appeared in the front and rear of my office building. I almost asked the driver if he saw it, but I didn't want to hear him answer in the affirmative. As we began the 700 foot journey across the stone bridge, I wrestled with the temptation to stick out my head and look behind me. Half-way across, my curiosity won out. I glanced back and saw nothing but what was visible in the clear night. As we neared the end of the bridge I gazed at St. Mary's Church on the south side of the Thames. I was relieved that I saw no mist or approaching fog. But when we were parallel with the church, I looked out once more and saw an unmistakable figure of the fugitive wolf sitting placidly on the church grounds. Tonight I would demand that Amelia tell me if she was specifically warning me about this wolf. It sickened me to think that the beast still had the taste of Hannah's blood and flesh in its mouth.

The driver gave no indication that he had seen the animal. Twice I glanced back before we reached the gates of the asylum, and both times I saw the wolf running slightly behind at a distance but at the same speed of the moving cab. When I alighted at the front entrance, the beast had disappeared. I commanded the driver to dismount quickly from the cab and wait inside until I was ready to return.

I found my friend Maybrick standing in his office, staring out the window into the night sky. I cleared my throat to signal my arrival.

"I've come, Edward."

Maybrick turned and my spirits sank. The misery evident on his face told me that Joseph Styles was dead. "Julian, please sit." His voice sounded haunted.

As if moving in his sleep, Maybrick poured me a brandy. I saw that his glass had contained the same amount, but surely it wasn't his first one.

"Edward, what happened? Is it Joseph?"

He resumed his place by the window. "No. Amelia Reeves."

"Amelia?"

"Dead."

"Dear God. I am deeply sorry for the poor woman—and for you—but she couldn't be helped. You must see that, Edward." He said nothing. "How did she die?" I hoped for Edward's sake that her heart had simply given out and that it wasn't a suicide. "Edward?"

"Murdered."

The next thought terrified me. "Please don't say it was Styles."

"He opened her throat with a cut piece of glass." Maybrick sagged in front of the window. I leaped from my seat and caught him before he slid to the floor. I placed him in his chair and brought the brandy to his lips, which he drank greedily.

"When did this happen, Edward?"

"Sometime during the night. We don't know when. The crime was discovered at 3:00 a.m."

"I don't understand. How did Styles get access to her room?"

"Julian, no one knows. For some reason I thought it best to remain here for the night instead of going home. But I was still awake when the attendant informed me that he was going to look in on Amelia. Could I have known something was going to happen? If so, I was unable to prevent it. But you must see that I was helpless to protect her. You must believe me when I say that." The man was overwrought. I doubted he had been able to sleep at all since the discovery of the murder.

"Edward, of course you couldn't have prevented it." I offered the words out of friendship. In truth, I had no idea if something might have been done to prevent Amelia's death or if something was in fact done to allow Styles to make his way into the woman's section and then into Amelia's room. It was utterly perverse, but I ached with curiosity to learn more. "Edward, can you tell me what happened next?"

"I had accompanied the night attendant to check on Amelia, and when we opened the door we came upon Styles sitting on the floor holding the piece of glass. His hands and forearms and much of his face were covered in blood. I then saw Amelia's body lying several feet away. In all my years working in public and private asylums, I had never seen a sight as grotesque as this one. She lay in her own blood, her throat savagely ripped apart, her hands frozen in a claw-like manner—her eyes wide open yet without a trace of fear in them. They seemed almost peaceful. I looked with horror at Styles, but he said nothing other than "I should like to go back to my room."

"And where is he now?"

"Still in his room. He is restrained. You see, Julian, I hoped he would tell us how he managed to enter her room, but he won't speak to us. He wants to talk only with you."

"My God—he's still here? You haven't informed the police?"

"I had to find out how and why he had done it. My only chance was to have you come out tonight and speak with him."

It was of no use to tell him that the "why" might take a very long time to discover—if ever at all. I steeled myself by downing my brandy. "Very well. Take me to him."

Maybrick shook his head. "I want you to go first to Amelia's room. There is something there you must see."

When we entered, I noticed that the initial washing of the room hadn't obliterated all the blood on the floor. It was evident where Amelia had fallen and died. I assumed Maybrick wished for me to see the spot, but I was mistaken.

He pointed to a small table that wasn't in the room the last time I visited Amelia. "Julian, we brought this table in after we took her body away. Here is the piece of glass Styles used to slash her throat. He was holding it in his hand when we discovered him in the room. Or have I said that already? Forgive me. But I don't believe I told you that Amelia had a cut on her left hand— where the index finger meets the palm."

"A defensive wound, then?"

"No."

"How can you know that, Edward?"

"By this."

He handed me a thin piece of wood approximately five to six inches wide and 10 to 12 inches in length. On it were three words written in blood. The first two were "of" and "beware." Each of the eight letters was lined through separately on the diagonal—again with blood. Under that phrase was "UNDERSTAND"—all in capital letters, although the terminal "D" was partially smeared.

Amelia had asked me to "understand" the four peculiar phrases she handed me upon my first visit to her, and I had concluded, although not firmly, that she was warning me about women. I easily saw that transposing "of" and "beware" supported that view, but why was each letter crossed out?

"Julian, she evidently wanted you to receive this."

"We can't know for certain, Edward. She may have written this for herself, or for you or for one of the attendants."

"Julian, turn over the piece of wood."

When I did I saw that she had also written in blood. "For Dr. H."

Maybrick pointed to the mattress on which she slept, which was now leaned up against the wall. "When we moved it away from the pool of blood, we found a slit into which she had evidently hidden the piece of wood."

"Was that where you found it after the murder?"

"No. It was placed against the far wall there. She evidently wanted it found and knew it would be. But how could she have known she was going to die? The wound on her left hand, from where she took the blood to write her message, was fresh and couldn't have been made too long before her death. I imagine she tore through her skin with her fingernail. The blood on the tip of her right index finger showed that she used the digit to write the words. Can you tell me what these three words mean?"

"I can only say that she was attempting to warn me—about what I'm still unsure."

Maybrick nodded wearily. "Take it with you, Julian. And if you come up with a full meaning, please let me know."

"I will. Tell me. What are the burial arrangements for Amelia?"

"Her family up in Holywell has been notified and we expect to hear from them by tomorrow afternoon."

"If for some reason they don't wish to claim the body, I will see to it that she is given a decent burial." Now two of the women who had warned me were dead, with Lucy perhaps having already joined them. But I had no time to grieve for any of them. Joseph Styles was waiting to speak with me.

CHAPTER 29

When we entered the male section of the asylum, all sounded peaceful. Not a single soul muttered, wept, or cursed his God, his family, or his fate. And yet fully restrained in one of the rooms sat a profoundly disturbed man who had somehow, without detection, left his room and entered that of Amelia Reeves. A man I had treated and for whom I had felt some affection. It was my idea to have him enter Maybrick's asylum, trusting his stay wouldn't be long and hoping I would be able to treat him successfully in the weeks ahead. I had never believed his claims to have murdered women in the streets of London. I had continued to check with the Metro force and Scotland Yard to be sure my instincts were correct. Was Styles merely telling me through his exaggerated accounts and violent dreams that he would indeed kill a woman if he wasn't stopped? Could I have been naïve enough in my new profession to have missed something so obvious? But I had reached a point where I feared for his as well as for others' safety and accordingly brought him out to Putney. How tragically ironic, then, that he only killed when he was "safely" situated in Maybrick's asylum? I couldn't be blamed for that—or could I?

Yet these self-centered thoughts evaporated at the moment we reached the door of Joseph's room.

"Please come in, Dr. Hemmings."

He obviously heard our approaching footsteps and was apparently confident I would come to see him. Maybrick unlocked the door, and he, one of the more muscular attendants, and I stepped inside the room. Styles sat on the floor, resting his back on the far wall. He was tightly secured in a straightjacket. Regardless of what he had done, I couldn't help pitying him.

"Joseph, why?"

"I should like to speak with you about all that, Dr. Hemmings. But only to you."

Maybrick of course insisted that he couldn't allow me to be alone with

Styles. I assured him I would immediately call for help should Styles make any attempt to harm me.

"Please, Edward. He is fully restrained. It will be all right." I then whispered, "This may be the only way to learn how he got into her room. You want to know that, don't you?"

Maybrick nodded and instructed his attendant to check the jacket for any loosening. It was tightly secured.

"I'll be right outside the door, Julian."

Styles began shaking his head violently from side to side, reminding me of how Lucy did the same earlier in the evening. He spoke as he continued his frenzied movements.

"I will not speak to Dr. Hemmings unless you are down the hall and away from the door."

His request was exactly that of Amelia Reeves when she wished to speak with me.

"Edward, do as he asks. I'll be fine. I promise I will call for you as loudly as possible if anything happens."

It took Maybrick several seconds before he acceded to my request. After he and the attendant left, Styles requested that I open the door and check to see if Maybrick had indeed walked to the end of the hallway. I did as Styles asked, and saw that Maybrick and the attendant were standing a good fifty feet away. I signaled Maybrick that all was well and returned inside the room.

"And how have you been, Dr. Hemmings?" There was eerie serenity in his voice.

"Joseph will you tell me why you killed Amelia Reeves?"

"I had been well-practiced in my dreams and my thoughts. It was exactly as I dreamt or imagined it, Dr. Hemmings. Yet how odd. I did not kill a pretty one after all—but I believe that this one was once pretty. I am sure of it."

"But why did you do it, Joseph?"

"Betrayal is the worst of sins, Dr. Hemmings. Did not Judas deserve his rope and his place in the last circle of Dante's hell?"

"You killed Amelia Reeves because she was guilty of betrayal?"

"I have always admired you because in spite of your learned vocabulary and advanced studies you still have the ability to understand the simplest words and the simplest concepts."

I accepted that I wouldn't have enough time to probe into his fanciful and violent imaginings, but I wanted some answer as to why, in his mind, Amelia was guilty of betrayal.

"Joseph, what did Amelia do to betray you?"

"Me? Nothing. I didn't know her at all. Her sins were against another far greater than the two of us. I was merely the deliverer of a just retribution. You see, she tried to educate you with her cleverness against his will. She shared with you words she should have kept locked within her soul."

I was aghast that he thought of himself as an avenging angel, doing the bidding of God. "What did you know of her, Joseph?"

"I learned of her travels beyond the forest. I learned of her meeting with him. I learned of the wolf. I learned of what he said to her afterwards. I learned of his promise to her. I learned of her promise to him, which she did not keep. I learned how she thought to obey her promise while betraying it at the same time. And I learned what is the most deserving of all punishments." He took a deep breath, one made most difficult by his restraints. "You thought you could know everything by opening the minds of others. But now you see that I know things you do not."

He had brought me to the point where I was about to shout at him to stop. I looked at my hands, my wrists and my forearms. They were vibrating noticeably. "Joseph, you are dominated by your dreams—your wild imaginings—your fears."

"An interesting diagnosis, Dr. Hemmings." He continued to speak to me as an equal, not as a deranged perpetrator of a gruesome crime. "Sad that soon your doctor's vocabulary will be painfully obsolete. All your learned words will wither, leaving you only the lifeless strands of basic utterances."

"Joseph, will you tell me *how* you came to be in Amelia's room?" Styles had so unnerved me that I struggled to maintain even the slightest sense of composure.

"If I may speak to you as a colleague, dear Julian. You have limited yourself by accepting the wisdom of that learned man from Vienna. You will come to find that he is not the true wizard. He is not your Merlin."

He must have heard more of my office conversations with Charles than I had believed. "Joseph, as a token of our friendship, will you tell me what I want to know?"

"It is better I tell you what you *need* to know, my friend. You should not have sought Merlin. It is rather the young Arthur who truly fascinates you. Yet, you must not pull out the sword and wave it high above your head. No, with all your strength you must stick it *in—deeply* in. Can you do it? Or has your Merlin, with all his incantations, so confused you that you know not who you really are and where you ought to be? Can you let it go on? Don't be a physician, dear Julian. Be a thing. Be a naked being with no logic."

I stood over him, utterly subdued by his speech. I, not he, was the one helplessly restrained. "Please, Joseph, please."

"How wrongly you have assumed almost everything. Did you really think to reason through this nightmare? How many times do you have to read the passage? 'There *are* more things in heaven and earth, my dear Hemmings, than are dreamt of in your philosophy.' It has always been and will always be so."

What had touched this man's mind to allow him such maturity of expression? Had he deliberately played a role when he came to my office? How could I have missed discovering such signs of his intelligence?

He smiled and continued. "You wonder how I have been given the power of speech. It is recent gift, one which I must return the moment you step out of this room. Perhaps even before then."

"A gift? Given by whom?"

"I will die but not because I have betrayed. I have served, and my duties are about to come to an end. Now that I have seen, I cannot live in a world given to those who will accept only what they can prove or replicate. And do you truly think that you may study the human mind and unveil its deepest secrets? It is too vast and forbidding a place for you, my friend. You will get lost there. You will be unable to return the way you came."

My legs would no longer support me. I sank to my knees in front of this man whose body was restrained, though his mind soared far beyond my understanding. "Joseph, please tell me what I have asked you. I will see to it that you will be kept here." In truth, I knew not what kind of influence I could have to keep him at Maybrick's asylum. Given his crime, it was likely he would be taken to a horrid place—if in fact he wasn't put to death. I went on. "I renew my promise not to abandon you."

"I release you of your promise. Besides, it is I who have abandoned you."

"Joseph, please believe me. Together we will get to the bottom of your troubles."

He smiled benignly. "Oh, my friend. To get to the bottom of anything all one has to do is fall. Blessed are the weak for they shall *not* inherit this earth. They will die and never be free. But those who hunger and thirst shall be satisfied. They will. You cannot stop them, because you will soon be one of them."

"But, Joseph, there is God. There is Christ." I had no choice but to fall back on orthodoxy.

"Didn't Christ battle the demon, intending to emerge victorious?" He paused to ponder his remark. "Apparently, he did not."

"Joseph . . ." I could say no more. I was now mute.

"We must welcome the coming, Dr. Hemmings. You have been baptized but not confirmed. Will you let it happen? Will you walk unaided to the altar? Will you touch the sun as it sinks?"

He stared at me for several moments before I saw a tear forming in the corner of both of his eyes. His face altered once again. Now he appeared as he had always looked when he came to see me. Frightened, confused, anxious, helpless.

"Dr. Hemmings, I mourn, but no one comforts me. No one. I so fear that my words will not be believed. I cannot die not being believed."

Beginning to panic, he started fighting his restraints. I fell back while on my knees, but quickly jumped up and reached for the door. As I did, I looked back at Styles. He was weeping.

"I will never see your kind face again. I would drink to your health, Dr. Hemmings, but they won't give me a cup. Not even a simple cup."

"Goodbye, Joseph."

"Wait, please wait. You have been my only friend, and I am grateful to you. I must tell you . . . I must tell you even though he will punish me for it."

"Tell me what, Joseph?"

"You have been his challenge. It has been you because he sees you as an emblem of those who believe they can control the effects of fear and passion through cold logic and understanding. Don't you see? You remained safe from passion while you gave yourself to knowing all you could about the mind. He has played games with you, Dr. Hemmings. You cannot hope to win. Go away. Please, I beg you, go far away. You must!" Styles opened his mouth to scream, but no sound escaped his lips.

I opened the door and moved quickly down the hallway to where Maybrick and the attendant were still standing. Looking at my face, Maybrick grabbed my shoulders and sent the attendant to deal with Styles.

I remained nearly an hour in Maybrick's office, drinking more brandy, hoping I would become intoxicated enough to lessen my pain and restore confidence in my sense of reason, which had been further stripped from me by the chilling and devastating words of Joseph Styles. When I felt calmed enough to begin the journey back to my residence, Maybrick placed in my hand the blood inscribed piece of wood found in Amelia's room and instructed one of his staff to place a bottle of brandy in the hansom cab, in case I needed more drink on the way back. Maybrick was about to escort me out to the cab, when one of the attendants burst into the office.

"Dr. Maybrick, I . . . I . . ." The man wore an expression of disbelief.

"What is it, Guthrie?"

"It's Styles. I don't know how it could have happened. It's impossible, really."

Maybrick was completely unsettled. "Damn it, man. What happened?"

"He's dead, Dr. Maybrick. He's dead."

Maybrick looked at me. "His heart."

I knew it wasn't that. I just knew.

"No sir," Guthrie interjected. "He's cut his throat—all the way across."

"Was he not restrained?"

"No, Dr. Maybrick. The jacket was lying next to him on the floor. I don't know how he could have gotten out of it. And . . . and . . ."

"And what?" Maybrick was uncharacteristically impatient with the man.

"He used a cut piece of glass to do himself in with."

"My God." Maybrick sank into his chair. "Was it . . .?

"It must have been, Dr. Maybrick. The piece of glass is missing from the table in Amelia Reeves' room."

Maybrick put his hands to his temples. "Julian, good night to you. I need to begin a formal investigation of the staff and other patients to see who could have betrayed us all and done this. If it takes all night, I'll discover the truth and I will send word to you when I do."

"Dr. Maybrick?"

"What is it, Guthrie."

"One more thing, sir."

"Go ahead, man. Go ahead."

"One of the attendants said he saw a cloud of mist coming from under

IN MIND OF THE VAMPIRE

Styles' door, which then floated away and escaped through the open window at the end of the hall."

Maybrick expelled a bitter laugh. "And it looks as though I have also to investigate the possibility of intoxication on part of the staff."

He wearily smiled at me. I couldn't smile back.

CHAPTER 30

On the journey back I refused to look outside the cab. I paid the driver his fee and without casting a glance at anything on the street made my way inside my rooms gripping Maybrick's bottle of brandy. My body ached for rest and sleep, but my mind wouldn't permit it. I hung up my heavy coat, and removed the slab of wood from one of the pockets and placed the bottle in the drawer of my desk. The brandy I had consumed at Maybrick's asylum had only wearied me further, and I would take no more. Feeling no other effects of the alcohol, I set about making a reasoned attempt to understand what Amelia had written in her own blood. I again wrote out the four phrases she had given me at our first meeting and compared them to the words "of beware" with a diagonal line drawn through each letter on the piece of wood. Obviously, her "UNDERSTAND" wasn't part of any clue; it was merely an instruction. The word "beware" wasn't in any of the four original phrases, and "of" was only in one of them—"anemia brew of." I drew a diagonal line through the word, leaving me with "anemia brew." I became agitated at the prospect of spending hours trying to decipher a possible connection between the phrases and her final message to me. I continued to resist the fact that a good night's sleep would be necessary if I hoped to translate Amelia's message—that is, if it was decipherable at all. I wrote her name next to "anemia brew." On first glance I thought that her name was embedded in the phrase—leaving me with the strong possibility that Amelia was merely warning me to beware of her. Five of the six letters in "Amelia" were in the phrase, but there was no "l." That was enough. I took the phases and piece of wood and placed them on a side table. If sufficiently rested, I would give it another go tomorrow.

I cast my eyes around the room for something that would occupy me long enough to divert and fatigue my mind so that I would be able to sleep. I noticed on my shelves Freud's *Studies in Hysteria,* a book he published two years ago with Josef Breuer. But I was at present too physically exhausted to wrestle with the German text. Regardless, tonight my friend Freud couldn't help me. My confidence in my chosen profession had been battered by my experiences and by the deaths of Hannah, Amelia, and Joseph. I had never felt so alone and miserable as I did at this moment. Without wishing it, I felt a compelling need to confront my past.

I retrieved from the wardrobe the two paintings I had done at the ages of fourteen and thirty-one. I took them to my desk and un-wrapped the earliest one, now for the first time forcing myself to examine it minutely. My body tensed, and a palpable feeling of nostalgia swept over me. The face of the prostitute on Greenfield Street still revealed the sensual and unpitying expression that had inhabited my imagination for almost twenty years. I had always been afraid to behold this face so directly. Staring at it now, I thought nothing of its value as a portrait, but rather I felt the clashing sensations of longing and fury welling inside me—emotions I endured upon first seeing her, but now experiencing with a deeper intensity. How much had this face shaped my life? For all these years, I had refused to consider the effect of that day beyond its immediate aftermath—the ruining of my special relationship with my father and my eventual abandonment of the one talent that had marked me as a prodigy. Could that moment have done more to affect me than my father's rejection? I couldn't imagine how this woman, with such a young and alluring face, had allowed herself to be purchased for sexual favors. I could see in Hannah's visage a young woman who might have had little choice. For a woman in need of money on which to live and to feed an infant or child, the options were still limited, even as we approached the new century. But this woman on Greenfield Street in early 1878 seemed so much in control of herself and her situation when I came upon her. There was no embarrassment or disgust in her features, even though her breasts were exposed and she was engaging in a graphic and unsanctioned carnal act. Was I afraid of her or of a female like her—that is, one who defied societal and moral expectations and refused to be controlled by guilt or by God?

My stomach further tightened as I imagined Lucy Westenra's face as the one I saw when I was fourteen. I had no desire to paint or sketch a portrait of Lucy because I knew it would be similar to the one I was contemplating at present. Lucy was as beautiful and no doubt she had the capability of being equally pitiless. I wondered how the memory of Lucy might affect me from this point on. I didn't wish her dead, of course. I wanted her to recover and live a serene and normal life—but I feared seeing her again. I wasn't sure I could bear another visit to my office, given the traumatic results of our previous two meeting. Yet my instincts told me she was no more. I closed my eyes and immediately appeared the image of Lucy standing near the edge of the sea, with her wavy hair and nightgown blowing freely in the wind. And the back of her hand touching the wolf I had just seen in Putney.

I removed the portrait of the prostitute Greenfield Street from my desk and un-wrapped the one I had painted of Yvette Auger just over two years ago but had not studied since. The face was angelic, with her blue eyes expressing comfort and innocence. Her mouth, as depicted on the canvas, invited a kiss, and I felt my head lower before I caught myself. The hair of spun gold, the eyebrows of even lighter blonde, the cheeks blooming with a color I didn't observe when she was lying on my table. How devastating was her loss. I had never operated on any patient—male or female—I wanted so desperately to save. It wasn't that she was only barely past twenty, for I had confidently cut into younger flesh than hers on several occasions. I had also seen my share of children and young women in the deceased state. I always lamented their loss at such an early age, but never had I experienced the fear I sensed after Yvette raised up and kissed me. My heart told me then I couldn't save her, no matter what I professed at the time. I knew I would fail this lovely young woman who depended so much upon me.

For weeks afterward, I would imagine and even dream of her waiting for me in the street, a smile of appreciation still on her face. We would walk arm in arm in the fading afternoon light, my eyes looking only at her and never toward the side streets or alley ways. I sensed in these dreams and daytime reveries that Yvette was cleansing as well as soothing my soul. Nothing Charles Yates or any of my medical colleagues could say convinced me that I had done all I could for her—that her cause was hopeless. Yet I realized on the night I painted her that I couldn't continue as a surgeon. Because her family took the body back to France for burial, I had no way to visit her grave, as I would have done every day until I had adequately conveyed my sorrow at my failure and my promise never to forget her. Painting her portrait was all that was left to me.

I took both portraits and returned them to the wardrobe. I removed the recently begun portrait of Mina—and understood that I had to finish it. I needed some kind of intimacy with her, and recreating her face with my art was all I could do to satisfy this compelling need. But I would begin anew on canvas—the surface of more permanence. Removing from the wardrobe the bare canvas I had kept, I walked quickly to my desk and pulled open one of the bottom drawers, where I kept my paints, which I had purchased—and for some reason still kept—over two years earlier when I decided to paint Yvette.

As I began recreating on canvas what I had already drawn of Mina's face, I heard tapping on my window. At first I was startled, but I calmed when I realized that it was only the rain. Soon, however, the drops hit the panes with more force. I walked to the window and saw the rain pelting down, but seemingly more horizontally than vertically, almost as it had done when I was in Cavendish Square. How appropriate that the weather perfectly reflected the state of my scourged spirits.

I worked on Mina's face for the next hour, depicting her hair—free from the chignon—with meticulous strokes of the brush. With relative ease, I formed her nose, cheeks, and chin. But what of the shape of her mouth? How to present my darling Mina? Should she be inviting me with her comforting smile or tantalizing me with a more enigmatic expression, perhaps with a slight touch of aloofness? I chose the latter, even though I censured myself for doing so. Was I selfishly and improperly indulging a secret and most pleasurable thought at a time such as this? I wondered how she would judge my choice. Would she frown or laugh—or try to simulate the exact expression I set on canvas?

I was then left with the eyes. I hesitated. I had to portray them accurately, especially if I was never to see her again. Yet what expression would comfort, inspire, and warm me for the rest of my life? Suddenly I experienced a sickening feeling. What if I couldn't do justice to her eyes? Would I be spending the coming years painting many portraits of her, seeking the sublime effort but never achieving anything near such perfection? I had enough artistic sense to understand that I should sleep and wait until morning to complete the portrait, but I couldn't shut my eyes for hours leaving hers vacant—even though I was physically and emotionally spent. The last thing I wished to see before falling asleep was the fully realized face of the woman I loved. I did close my eyes, but only to concentrate more fully on the image I most wished to depict.

There was a light knock at my door.

I was tempted to leave it unanswered. I dreaded that it might be Lucy.

A second soft knock.

As quietly as possible, I placed the portrait against the wall with the rear of the canvas facing outward. I stepped to the door and opened it, but at first saw no one. Then into my line of sight stepped my darling Mina.

"Mina, what are you doing here?" I immediately regretted my words. She might take them to mean that I was annoyed by her presence. I quickly recovered. "Dear Mina, it is such a joy to see you. Won't you come in?"

She didn't move, and I noticed that she had come with no apparent chaperone. Perhaps she had a message to deliver and would only do so without stepping into my rooms. She wore no bonnet. Her hair, in its flawless chignon, was wet, as was the large coat she wore. Her lovely face revealed pain and sadness, and I knew that she was about to inform me of Lucy's demise.

"I wish to come in, Julian."

Although she had come in grief, I felt a rush of exhilaration knowing that soon I would be able to comfort her. "Yes, yes. Of course. Please do, Mina." I stepped back so that she could move inside.

"I feel a bit faint." She began to sag. I stepped out and caught her in my arms. "Here, let me."

I helped her into the room and thought of my similarly assisting Lucy into the office several hours earlier.

"Mina, I'll begin a fire to warm you."

"You are so very thoughtful, Julian."

I smiled at the dual meaning of her compliment. Tonight I wished *not* to think or to analyze but only to allow my impassioned feelings their expression. "Mina, please remove your coat; it's saturated with the rain." Turning away from her, I knelt and placed some paper and small pieces of wood under the larger split pieces resting on the andirons. I lit the paper and used the bellows judiciously, starting the fire in quick order. "In a moment I want you to stand next to the fire and dry yourself. Can I fix you some tea?" I heard no reply but only her measured breathing. I was still astonished that she was here—alone with me in my rooms.

"'The rain set early in tonight, / The sullen wind was soon awake.'" Her voice sounded removed, as though the verse had come to her mind when she was alone contemplating the stars.

I adjusted the wood lying on the andirons and wished to hear more of whatever poem she was quoting. "Please go on, Mina."

"'When glided in Porphyria; straight / She shut the cold out and the storm.'"

She was quoting the Browning poem. For the first time I felt she might truly love me and that tonight I would know a bliss I had never experienced but had always fervently desired. She briefly paused and went on.

"'She rose, and from her form / Withdrew the dripping cloak and shawl, / . . . and let the damp hair fall.'"

Still on my knees in front of the fireplace, I turned my head and beheld her standing in her nightdress, her coat now fallen to the floor at her feet, and her beautiful dark hair unloosened and draped over her shoulders, covering both sides of her neck.

"Mina . . ." I could say nothing else.

She held out her hand to me, and I rose and took it. Leading me to the sofa, she released my hand and sat. I noticed that her feet were bare.

"Please, sit with me."

I hesitated, terrified that I would act on my passion for her. There was little I could do to suppress the urge to embrace her and rest my head against her soft body. She again held out her hand.

"Do you care for me, Julian?"

I took her sweet hand and sat with her. "Dearest Mina, I care for you more than I can ever express—more than anything in my life."

"My love, you look as though you are lost in a dream."

"I am. This cannot be real." I saw in her eyes the image I wished to immortalize in my portrait.

"But you believe that dreams are reality, do you not?"

I couldn't be sure if she was teasing me by alluding to the work of Freud. "Yes, they surely can be, as my mentor has taught me," I said with a smile.

"And do you dream of others?"

"Others?"

She took my hand and pressed it to her lips. "Do you dream of other women?"

I answered truthfully, even though by doing so I risked insulting her. "Yes, I have. Two others. But may I explain?"

"You need dream of them no longer. I can give you freedom from those dreams. Is that what you want?"

My desire for her was forcing my caution into retreat. Soon it would be completely overrun. "Yes, Mina. I want my dreams to be of you only."

She sighed, "For so long my guardian angel reason stood over and protected me. But his presence came to depress me—more as each day

210

passed. In the past several days, since I have known you, I have refused his assistance, telling him "No" many times—in whispers, which I wished for you to hear. But because I have turned my thoughts away from my guardian angel and toward another, I have been permitted to dream. I am where I perhaps have always wanted to be—a place from which I know I do not wish to return. Like you, my Julian, I have never known my passions until now. I cannot turn away from them. Don't you see? Now you and I have come to the same place in the same dream."

I was enthralled by her words. She leaned toward me and placed her face against mine. I felt her wet hair caress me.

"One small kiss to forget all your pain, Julian." And now her warm lips were pressed against mine.

She broke the kiss, not I. She smiled without opening her mouth and stood up from the sofa. I saw the flames from the fireplace across the room framing her body in the white nightdress. Mina seemed paler than I had ever seen her. She began a melodic movement of her head—up and down, but on a diagonal not vertical course.

"Honey sweet. Touch. Love." Once more she seemed to be in a place far removed. The crackling of the blaze added an arresting complement to her voice. Yet her words were so reminiscent of another.

"Mina, are you quoting Lucy?"

Mina stared at me with eyes that flashed anger. "Lucy is gone."

I feared asking if she had died or had merely disappeared. "Yes, of course, Mina."

A residue of her momentary fury remained as she looked toward the rain-pelted window. "I tried to frighten that young boy when we left your office. I feared I would harm him if I became like Lucy, and I wanted him to stay away from me. Tell me. Is he safe?"

"He is well, Mina." I couldn't completely understand her meaning, but at least I had an explanation for why she looked at The Dasher the way she did.

Mina's eyes lost their fire and again she held out her hand. I rose from the sofa and pressed her hand to my lips, keeping it there while she continued to speak.

"My Julian, you have always been so lonely. You have had no one to comfort you. Now you have found the one you have been waiting for. You have touched my mouth with yours. You long for me. Come, my arms are hungry for you. Come and you will rest with me always—free from all memory."

I tried to embrace her, but she put out her open palm checking my movement.

"What is this?" She was looking at the side table, on which I had placed the slab of wood and the small piece of paper on which Amelia had written the four phrases.

"It is nothing, Mina. Merely the expressions of a tragically disturbed mind."

She picked up the two items. She stared at the bloody printing on the wood—her eyes expanding—and again she began to swoon. I rushed to her side and placed my hands under her forearms to steady her. She took such a deep breath that she emitted a sound I had heard several times before when I was a surgeon—that of one dying and gasping for what would be the last intake of air. I was so startled that my hands dropped from her arms, causing her body to fall against mine. I caressed her tightly and heard her murmur inarticulate words or sounds before she finally whispered my name.

"Mina, are you all right?"

"I am. It was the sight of the blood that . . ."

She didn't finish her thought, and I began to fear for her health. She seemed even paler, and her breathing appeared more labored. I held her closer. Her hair was still damp. I took my fingers and attempted to comb some of the moisture out of the raven strands, but she lurched back from my touch.

"Dearest Mina, please forgive me. I only wished to remove some of the wetness from your hair."

She took the hair on the left side of her head and pulled it forward, dropping her chin as if to pin it to the side of her face.

"Mina, please let me take the wood and paper from you."

"No!" Her flash of defiance quickly dissipated to an expression of pain and then resignation. "I must read what is written here, Julian. I must do it for your sake."

With seeming reluctance, she walked to the desk and placed both the narrow plank of wood and the paper next to each other. She ran her finger over each letter on the wood. "Julian, please give me that brush."

In my haste to hide the portrait, I had no time to remove the paints and brushes from the large desk. I handed her the one with which I had painted her black tresses. She pressed down the sheet of paper on which I had written

Amelia's peculiar phrases and crossed out with the still blackened brush every "o" in the four phrases. She then did the same with every "f"—and then with every "b." She was crossing out one-by-one the letters in the "of beware" that Amelia had crossed out on the wood. And as Amelia had done, Mina crossed out each letter with a diagonal stroke of the narrow brush.

"Now Julian, write down the letters of each phrase that have not been crossed out."

I took a pencil and a piece of paper and found that in "a baron wife me" the four letters "a-n-i-m" remained. In "bare waif omen" "a-i-m-n" were left. Then "m-n-a-i" from "bowman faerie." And "n-m-i-a" from "anemia brew of."

Mina touched my hand. "Now do you understand of whom you should beware?"

I easily transposed the letters. "m-i-n-a." I was horrified, but the complete meaning of Amelia's puzzle was still beyond me. Could Amelia have simply been warning me that I would fall deeply into love with Mina and that by doing so I would risk everything should the relationship end unhappily? Or was she telling me that my newly chosen profession would suffer as a result of my passion for Mina? That I could comprehend, for at this moment I cared for nothing other than being with Mina, no matter what I might have to sacrifice.

"Julian, now that you understand. Do you still come to me willingly? Freely?"

"Yes, my darling Mina—willingly, freely."

"Bring me what you have painted."

She pointed to the canvas lying against the wall. She must have sensed that it was of her, fully confident that she was on my mind continually. I felt proud of what I had painted, exactly as I did many years earlier when I showed my latest sketch to my then doting father.

"I have not completed it. I have yet to finish the eyes."

"You have."

"No, my dearest. I still need to choose the expression in them that best conveys—"

"They have been expressed already."

"I know that is true, but your beauty offers the artist so many possibilities."

"You have already chosen, Julian." She held out her hands to receive the portrait, which I turned around so that she could see herself. My eyes drank in every bit of her loveliness. The fire crackled and the rain continued to pelt the windows. And for the first time I knew what heaven would be like.

"Here, Julian. You see?"

Mina placed the portrait on the desk. Everything within me ceased. The eyes were completed. The expression in them both frightened and invited me. In my earlier state of fatigue, had I simply been oblivious to the fact that I had finished them? No, that couldn't be. I was certain I had left them undone. But before I could express my confusion, Mina came to me.

"Kiss me now."

All I knew at this moment was the moistness of her lips on mine. Nothing else existed. I then felt her lips press against mine more ardently. I tried to respond in kind, but she broke the kiss. I felt as though she had broken my heart.

"Julian, let me take you far away. Beyond the forest. Forever."

She once more pressed her lips against mine in a kiss even more passionate than the one before. "You will always be with me, Julian, and my love will always be with you." Her hands caressed the sides of my neck. Mine brushed her still damp hair away from the side of her face. She uttered no protest but still kissed. My hands wished to do what hers were doing to me, and I dropped them to the side of her neck. The palm of my right hand ran across two welts side-by-side. As I touched them with my fingers, I felt the moistness of something that had recently trickled from them. A feeling that matched the moistness of her ardent kiss, which she had not yet broken. Blood. Her blood.

She slowly removed her mouth from mine and whispered into my ear.

"And still God has not said a word."

She had healed me and opened my soul. All I was, all I desired, all I hoped for was now fast in my arms. She gently sighed, as her open mouth slid down the side of my neck.

In a moment I was lost in ecstasy.

THE END

www.ingramcontent.com/pod-product-compliance
Lightning Source LLC
Chambersburg PA
CBHW010447100726
47904CB00008B/2507